The Time Hunter Tales:

Mind Wanderer
The Lost Finders
Knight of the Wolves
Storm from the Past

Poetry:

Pathfinding

New Tales of the Old World

New Tales of the
Old World

Evan A. Cushing

Primordial Albion Press

Thank you, my grandparents:
Bob and Doris Heuerman,
and Foster and Ann Cushing,
for being you.

CONTENTS

CONTENTS

Prologue: Gamblers to the End

It was the heist of a lifetime, as it should have been. The world as we knew it was falling apart. Dark matter had condensed into crystals; after one too many experiments, the world was covered with the stuff. This marked the third time an event of this severity had occurred but unlike the last two we had nowhere left to run as a species. We had lost Earth to the robots, then most of ourselves in the colonies' war to retake Earth. When the dust had settled, the birthplace of humanity was totally hostile to living things. We fled very far and colonized yet more worlds. It took one alien virus to almost wipe us all out again. Then this crap, our last world now covered in matter-eating rocks from the depths of some petri dish hell filled with far too much cosmic gunk.

So, ever the optimist, I and two of my co-workers planned to rob blind the military R&D lab we had been working in. The way we saw it, if some of the human race still lived after this, the ones with the most guns would have the best chance at survival. We could not have been more right, but our belief was proved right in the stupidest form we could not yet imagine.

"Are we there yet, Chuck?" Clare Reginald, one of the engineering techs and a skilled hacker, asked me.

"If we are not, rocks will kill him before I can," Jim James, a genetic archivist, told us.

A new growth of dark pulsing rock shot up before us in the once-gleaming steel hallway. With all kinds of new damage the hallway was far narrower than it had once been, albeit still wide enough for the three of us to run side by side. As one of the security leads, I was slightly in front. My ignition blade cut through the new obstruction, its fiery blade making quick work yet again of the rock-like spikes.

"Nice! Hit it with enough energy and it dies," Clare yelled, doing a short fist pump as we ran. "Told you my theory was sound."

"You said you tested it!" Jim moaned in exasperation. We skidded up to the last armory to be raided. Clare got to work bypassing the locks, humming indifferently to herself with her usual devil-may-care smile.

"Relax Jim, the security logs have already shown she is right," I told my chronic worrywart of an accomplice.

"Still cutting them down; that takes real skill," Clare told us, still hunched over her personal computer. "Ok and we are in, new record!" The doors opened. We cleaned out shelves and crates in the room that housed tested- and still-to-be-tested weaponry and other military-grade equipment.

"Do we really need all of this? My warp pouch is almost full!" Jim complained again.

"What is with you? You have a whole mini-dimension in there and it's full?" Clare rolled her eyes then she cleaned out Jim's side of the room.

"Go easy on the man. He is always like this," I told her.

"That's true and he has not gotten any worse." Clare gave Jim a thumbs up as we made our way out. "That's impressive!"

Many more pillars of solidified dark matter had sprung up in the hallway in the short time it took us to complete our snatch-and-grab. "Let's get out of here!" I called, breaking into a run and pulling my plasma pistol from the artificial realm that was my gun pouch. I shot down countless matter-eating rocks as we made our escape up a great many layers of emergency stairs.

We ran up ten of the subterranean floors all the way to floor two. We thought we were home free. We were wrong. The floors begin to collapse and dark insectoid things crawled out from the depths. "Ok, it's sentient now, really?" Clare groaned.

"Not yet at least," Jim told us, more intrigued than horrified now that his curiosity had been piqued.

I shot back at the dark tide of bug-like dark matter as we ran. "Less talking, more running!"

I must have killed hundreds of the small things. Luckily, gravity still had an effect on them. The collapsing floors and walls managed to get in their way somewhat. A few of the slightly larger pitch-black beetle things could fly, the ever-shifting specks of light that shone from within their cores the only way to tell these were made from no normal terrestrial substance. After a few exploratory pot shots, I found their cores were a major weak point. Because the bunker had lost power, along the way their cores lit up the room. All I had to do is shoot out anything that buzzed and glowed.

In our terror and haste we forgot one very big issue: the trap right in front of the exit to the surface. A trap that was only set when under attack or during a simulation of an attack. Upon seeing the first non-artificial light in ages, Jim rushed forward without a care. Clare and I followed but so did the bugs. Of the three of us, Jim was the only one to clear the floor before the bugs set claw and pincer on the stasis pads.

"Unauthorized life detected: locking down," the first-floor computer howled. Just our luck it was still active.

"R –" was all I managed to get out before time stopped for Clare, myself, and half a dozen bugs.

1 |

No Rest for the Lost

For centuries I had been held in a space where time had no meaning. Things changed a lot, as I was to find out firsthand.

"–un!" I finished shouting at the top of my lungs, only to be greeted by a dark musty room filled with vines and rocks. Rust covered the metalwork under meters of dust and sand. I spun around, gun still in my hand, its charge level still halfway gone as I had left it. Eight bugs were right behind me, with tons of rock from a huge cave-in behind them barring the way back down. The bugs were woozier than I was, so I gunned them down before any of us could fully get our bearings.

Looking around I quickly saw was I alone. Running to the exit, I found it was closed shut, but I was sure I could force it open. After all, I had done it before in a drill and no one had gotten around to fixing the fault I had exploited, at least as far as I could remember. Not that I could blame them. The end of our last world was more of an issue by then.

I found the latch I had used before and pulled, but it was

far too rusted to swing open like before. Instead it broke off and half of the bulkhead collapsed inward in a huge pillar of dust and sound. I clambered out into a natural cave that had not been there before. I kicked a shard of dark rock, and upon finding it had no inner glow and it had not eaten my foot, I picked it up and spun it in my hand as I walked out of the cave.

A petite girl sat on a stump right outside the cave. Her brigandine armor was very medieval in construction, except some of the crude gadgets attached to it were clearly powered. She was cleaning a sword that gently sparked in time with her humming. A projectile gun the likes of which I had seen before only in history lessons and a few rows of bullets were next to her atop an oil-stained cloth.

I fully intended to walk by her, but then the sound of the floor collapsing boomed behind me and a huge pall of dust shot out from the cave I had just exited. The girl looked up. She was very startled and grabbed her gun, pointing it at me. "Who are ya mister?" she asked. After giving me a once over she added, "And where are ya from?" The eyes under her helmet were a fiery hazel the like of which I had never seen.

"I am Chuck Evans, security lead number five of Azure Base. I was trapped in a stasis field for I do not know how long and only now was able to walk out of my old base." I pointed back to the cave as nonchalantly as possible. Old school weapon or no, getting hit with enough bullets would still kill me even if it could not get past my armor. With enough kinetic force my bones would be jelly regardless of how much each shot's force was dampened. Even if the girl's weapon did not do it, if she had any friends nearby, then this could get complicated. Guns were like a deadly signal whistle after all.

The girl looked me over one last time, then she tensed after seeing the ignition blade that was still magnetically held to my wrist. It was powered off so the blade was not extended from the hilt, and it was most definitely not on fire.

"Are ya with the imperial Megatechs?" the girl asked, hand still on her gun and finger twitching. No matter how relaxed she tried to seem, there was no hiding how very on edge she was.

"I have no idea what you mean," I told her truthfully, all the while looking in wonder at the dense pine forest I had walked into.

"Somethin' like the Builder or the Demon Lord?" the girl asked, getting more agitated the more we talked. I could tell this would not end well.

"Who are they?" I inquired.

"The Queen Mother or the Destroyer of Worlds?" the young lady tried again. Her explanation was as unhelpful as the last.

"I do not even know why the world looks as it does. I am not evil, I assure you," I told her.

"So the queen!" the girl yelled, bringing up her gun angrily. *What the hell* I yelled back in my mind.

Then voices called from the trees. "Found her!"

"Who is after you?" I asked, now pointing my plasma gun at the girl.

"The royal guards want to bring me back to the palace,"

she told me, then she shot two leather-armored men behind me dead. "I hate them," she added with rage.

"The princess has an accomplice this time!" a man in medieval full plate armor made from more modern-looking materials yelled, hefting a large assault rifle in my direction.

"I can tell you do," I told her, gunning down three men. Holes seared through their armor and the trees behind them. "Seems I must help you run if I am to live, but you will explain this to me later," I grumbled, glancing into the girl's wide-open eyes.

"For the Builder!" the soldiers around yelled. My new helper twitched at the name.

I put one shot through two men as they ran down the hill firing submachine guns. "Ten more," the young woman who clearly had made someone very, very mad muttered.

Since my last shot, the plasma pistol shut down to cool and recharge. "Cover me," I told the girl, ripping off the ignition blade at my wrist and extending it after nimbly flipping a switch. It was set ablaze all in one fell swoop. I then activated my basic defense field, getting into a proper melee stance. A trio of bullets stopped short a few inches from my face. Seconds later I had to chuckle at that. "Now my luck kicks in," I sighed.

"They are in range!" my reluctant helper yelled over the gunfire. The fear in her voice did not seem to fit with her actions. Four men fell dead in the time it took her to shout. She had targeted joints in their armor. I had to feel sorry for the men. The heavier plate armor with the strength of the oddly modern alloys worked against them, making the bullets ricochet inside their suits.

Our attackers' swords and axes were well made but un-powered. My sword cut through them and their wielders with ease. It took at most twenty seconds to whittle the ten down to two. I returned the plasma pistol to my gun pouch. When my hand emerged from it again, I held my standard issue (and admittedly low powered) laser pistol, shooting the last two dead before they could flee.

The girl raised her pistol to my face. "Who are ya really?"

I raised my hands and shut down my sword but left my weapons in my hands. "I told you that. So who are you? You owe me an explanation of our new foes."

"They are after me," the girl said angrily. "It's got nothing to do with ya."

I slowly jabbed a squad-linked camera that was on the bascinet helmet of one of the dead men. "Thanks to this thing, they know my face too. It's unlikely the one that sent them is the forgive-and-forget type."

"Princess Adell Versheius, more or less. You can call me Green," the girl told me.

I chose not ask many questions while we were in a clearing surrounded by dead bodies. "So Green, how old are you?"

She frowned. "Sixteen cycles." Then she turned to walk away. I walked slowly after her. I was taller than she was. Even so, it seemed that she was walking slowly on purpose to let me catch up.

"So the queen is after you. Who is she exactly?" I queried. I got back a *You are messing with me* kind of look for my attempt at working out just what had happened as I stayed trapped.

"You may not believe me, but I am not from this time," I added, trying to play for time as I worked out what to say next and if I was in danger.

"So you are like her," was the only response I was given for the rest of that walk through the pine forest. Part way up a grassy hill the awkward silence was shattered by the sounds of running feet and heavy if clunky machinery.

"Just who did you piss off?" I asked over the din of heavy labor as we crept warily up the hill.

"This kingdom and its matriarch," Green told me, confirming my worst fears. Then she smiled grimly. "But only its best troops are hunting me. I mean us."

"Fantastic," I sighed, looking over the ridge we were lying on. Below us in a quarry sat a long tank bunker from my time. It was covered in rocks that had grown over it. "The old armored recon HQ" I murmured, recognizing the doors and cartoony sign its old commander had plastered above the loading dock. **LAST ONE IN'S A ROTTEN EGG** it read. Many scholarly types in fancy blue and white robes with wires woven through hustled around the bunker.

"The arctechs," Green sighed with relief. "Still trying to open that tomb."

"What tomb has a sign about rotten eggs with a poorly drawn children's TV mascot next to it?" I asked, confused for a second. The self-proclaimed princess turned to me, her expression quizzical and bewildered, reminding me I was not from the time she knew.

"What?" she asked. I pointed over the loading dock and the gaggle of arctechs clustered around it rabidly debating something. It took Green a few seconds to grasp what I meant. "What did ya say that building was?"

"The armored recon HQ from a long time ago." I flinched as a researcher was electrocuted by the panel to the main vehicle bay's doors. "It still has power. Jack always made the entry code way too simple. The MPs were always on his case about that."

"You can open it?" Green's face lit up. She looked half her age, as if she was not young enough already.

"As long as the old boss of that base was the last to set the code, I could. It may take a few tries if he reset it after I was trapped," I told her. Green's face began to fall. "No more than five tries if the panel still works and Jack was the one that set the current code."

"You are helping me get in there," Green told me. The way she smirked told me this was more due to some grudge than curiosity. Even then I could see it was very important to her, maybe even more so due to her darker feelings.

"Fine, but let's try to bluff our way past. If they are not after you, then let's not kill them," I agreed. Deep down I hoped the base's record and logs were still accessible. If so, I hoped they would tell me a lot about what had happened in my absence.

Green and I walked slowly down the hill trying to look like we owned the place. A man in far less complex brigandine armor than the princess raised a hand to stop us. Over his other shoulder rested a short carbine of no small sophistication but it still used solid projectiles, so it did not come close to any of my gear. "Turn around. This is official industrious business."

"Industrious? So the industrial orders are looking into this place?" Green asked. The man looked sharply at her. I think she was trying to help explain to me what was going on.

After one last deep mental sigh I committed to a lie I was working on fabricating to the best of my ability. To be fair, lying on the fly is not my strong point. "It seems like the princess is as surprised as I am to see you all here."

The man snapped to attention but he kept his eyes locked on me, then asked, "Ok, so who are you then?"

"A bodyguard. She can't get some fresh air without someone watching her." The man's gaze narrowed. "Or at least that is the protocol."

"It was one time I left, one time!" my companion grumbled convincingly. "Regardless, I want a closer look at this building."

The ruckus we were generating slowly drew more and more eyes until a woman in her twenties walked over. Her robe was in the same style as the other arctechs but it had much more wire and bigger patterns all over. She stopped a few feet away and waved us over. Green and I walked up to her, but without a word the woman began to walk to a huge door. No one was moving to stop us so we walked after her. "You come to try your luck with the door, princess?" the woman asked.

"I was thinking of having my guard try, Foreman Exemplar Woods," Green told her.

"Please, it is Miss Woods to you, Princess Versheius," the

woman told us. Given how much space and respect she was being shown by the other arctechs, the exemplar vastly out-ranked all but Green. We were led over the loose rock, some of which could have been chunks of asphalt once, to a huge vault door smelling of ozone and many fatal flash burns.

"You really know what you are doing, Miss Woods," I told our guide.

"I did tell you how much I learned from her." Green smiled wickedly.

Miss Woods spun around and cast a quick annoyed glance at the princess. Our guide stomped up to me. "I've never seen you at the capital before." Guns were suddenly raised, point-ing at me. "So why is the princess so friendly with you?" The guns all lowered with indecent haste at that observation.

"One of Mum's other projects. He was released from the lab after I lost track of you. Have you been here all this time?" Green lied for me.

Miss Woods leaned over to me and reached out her hand. "Debra Woods. Nice to meet a working one of you." I shook her hand, then she leaned over farther and whispered, "Did you get a code name?"

"Not yet, but Mum was thinking of calling him Red," the princess butted in quietly. Debra's eyes widened in shock. She looked me over intently and stopped breathing for a while. Apparently code names of color were impressive.

"What's your record?" Debra asked after a bit of huddling near us.

"Better than someone named Green's, at least in testing." The princess nodded at my words. It appeared I had said the right thing. Not that all of this did my nerves any good. I hoped any nervousness I showed would be mistaken for me trying hard to be polite. Wanting to change the subject, I pointed over at the loading dock. "So you and your team must have translated that sign by now."

"Partly. It seems to be some kind of fertility curse," Miss Woods agreed. Then she turned around and led us over to the big heavily armored and sealed main door of the old base. "So you think you can get this door open?"

"He can. After all, he translated that enter sign on the way down the hill." Green smiled, her mischievous gaze never leaving me, to the point I got chills. "I believe it was last one's a rotten egg," she added.

Miss Woods looked at me, stunned. Then she flinched and her eyes got an unhealthy feverish tinge to them like some suddenly ravenous person. "Really?" Her thoughtful expression had more than a touch of madness to it. "Yes, it could be that, but why?"

I knew I had to throw her a bone on this one, so I explained. "The image next to the words was the giveaway. It's like a tool to help visualize the meaning." The next thing I knew, Miss Woods rushed over to a small computer and begin to type ferociously.

Green leaned over and whispered, "Is that true?"

"Well it's not like that does not work, but the letters are in colony standard so I could read it just fine. However, explaining that would draw too much attention."

"Colony what?" Green asked as I led her over to the huge old door.

Everyone stepped back when I put my hand on the access panel. I can't blame them, given the scarring from electrical surges all over the rock-encrusted asphalt. Linking up my IFF transponder to the door computer took longer than it used to. That said, it still worked after who knew how long, so that was impressive. Then the computer chimed and a nostalgic recording filled with static played from the door itself. "Welcome to the Azure Base recon headquarters. Do you have an appointment, Officer Evans?"

"Eggzactly" I replied, raising my voice over the sound of iron blades being drawn and gasps mostly of wonder, but also more than a few fully in panic.

"One moment please," the ancient computer replied. I felt a twinge of sadness as I realized this old system could be one of the last or maybe the last relic of the time I had left far behind. "None of the personnel are replying to my hails. What is the nature of your visit, sir?"

"I was asked to make to a cleanness check and to make sure their reports are in line with the new format guidelines," I called out clearly. Green and a few of the arctechs with the more ornate robes who I assumed were higher ranked than the others inched forward, intent on not missing a thing.

"No record of new format changes found. Are you certain of this, Officer Evans?" the static-filled monotone asked.

"We switch over next week. Given this team's reputation, I was asked as a favor to remind them and go over some of the details of the change in person." Out of the corner of my eye, some of the arctechs begin wiping down their robes. Most of them however looked over at Debra with confused gazes.

"Welcome back, Mr. Chuck Evans," the computer told the milling crowd. Then the heavily rusted door clamps unlocked.

"Get back for a second!" I called over my shoulder. All around me people were trying to decide whether to run to the door or away from it. Then the door fell. The whole circular thing freed from its seals plummeted to the ground. Luckily I side-stepped it in time. Dust and a sickly green glow of backup warning lights spilled from the now gaping hole in the old building.

I walked in before the dust cloud had even finished forming. Green rushed in right behind me but I stopped her a few feet into the building with an outreached hand. The room was as I remembered it. Only one APC remained in a hangar that once held twenty of the finest scout craft I had ever seen. (They were the only thing the recon crew kept clean.) The desks and computers were all covered in rust and a few had chunks missing due to what seemed like ageing. Here and there were skeletons of some of my long-dead comrades. They each still had gear hung over their bones.

"It's a grave in here. Who were you talking to?" Miss Woods asked from behind the princess.

"One of those." I pointed over to one of the computers time had been kind to.

Miss Woods rushed over to the broken screen I had pointed out. Even in her haste to get a closer look at the computer, she still managed to keep her distance from the dead.

Green crouched next to me. "Did ya know him?" I pulled

up an IFF scanner and let it look for a transponder on the long-dead soldier Green had singled out.

I got the man's data in short order and sighed. "Yes, the commander of this station was a good friend of mine. This man was the unit's doctor." Then I smiled, recalling the medic. "He was real thin and got drunk real fast, but he was brave and loved to joke."

"Ya really are from the past." Green looked at me seeming to only now accept this as fact. Then she got to her feet and waved at the rest of the crew who were still milling around outside. "Exemplar Woods, myself, and my guard will look this over first. We can't disturb this place until we have recorded how it looks. The exemplar and I will handle that."

I got up and slowly walked through the vehicle hangar. From the dead I picked up the disks containing their IDs. After who knew how long, we were the first to disturb a place I had frequented often to check up on and socialize with the men that those corpses belonged to. I walked up a small flight of stairs that led into the barracks. "We will take a peek around," the Princess called to Woods, who was still hunched over and fiddling with the long-broken computer. "She will be at that for days without end if we let her," Green sighed. She then began to cough from the dust and decay of days long past, which were getting to her now that the air flow was stymied.

The barracks room was chaotic. A broken pillar of dark matter jutted from the floor, a great many skeletons clustered around it. It was stuffy in here now that we were away from the door. I took out an air filtering mask from my gear pack and put it on, then I handed Green a spare. "It will get worse as we go farther in." I walked over to the pillar and continued taking IDs from the dead.

After taking a few exploratory breaths through the mask, Green rushed over to me, but she kept her eye on the shattered pillar. "Hey, the demons will not come out of there, right?"

"Demons? What do they look like?" I asked, now curious.

"They come in all shapes but they all have a shard of the netherworld inside them," Green told me.

I turned around, still crouching on the rusted floor, and asked "It looks like a small swirling light, right?" Green backed away, clearly uncomfortable with the subject. "Does it?" I asked firmly.

"Yes," she told me now at the door.

"So they still live, even after all this time," I muttered, now poking around with a scanner looking for energy readings that could lead to gear that still worked.

Green inched closer. "So you are not one of them?"

I laughed and she tensed. "No, I was trapped when they first appeared." I tapped the pillar and it crumbled. "These things took over the world. Then the monsters appeared."

"How were you trapped?" Green asked, unsheathing her electricity-covered (but still primitive) capacitor blade.

"I was caught in a trap that halts time. One of my friends escaped it and the other may have broken free of the trap before me," I told her. I fished out the key to the armory from the locker. It used to be hidden behind a poster that had long since rotted away.

"So that's what you are," Debra said from the door we had

come from. She held a scrap of cloth over her mouth. "Just like the Builder and the God of Demons."

I had a ton of questions now. "I will need to know about that in detail later, but right now we should check the records room and the armory."

I led the two women through the rusted hallway, passing a few small offices along the way that I had to pull Miss Woods away from more than once. My two chaperones stopped many feet from the armory doorway. Something had gotten to it first, but that must have been long ago. The door frame was melted. No door remained and the space across from the empty doorframe was a pitted wall covered in signs of some kind of forcible corrosion. Rust had long since spread across the wall in between pockmarked damage. I was about to touch the pitted wall when Green rushed over and grabbed my arm. "Don't let that get on you!"

I escaped her firm grip with far more ease than I had expected and walked into the armory. Peering inside, I absent-mindedly gripped the doorframe and a sizzling sound reached my ears. Warning icons indicating suit damage filled my goggles. I pulled my hand away and looked at it. The skin was totally fine but my armor's sleeve up to the shoulder and my glove had melted away. Still very stunned, I gripped my still-disintegrating sleeve with my bare hand. The damage halted as I put pressure on my damaged armor. After looking over my arm and hand again, which did not show any signs of damage, I called over to my backpedaling followers, "So I am guessing that is not normal."

Debra nearly fainted and Green stuttered, her usual

composure gone. "None of that was normal." It was likely my ego talking, but it felt like she sounded more worried for me than afraid of whatever she thought I was.

I cast a glance around the armory. Seeing mostly melted shelves and a few chunks of unusable junk, I began to walk again. "Nothing usable in there. Let's see if their records terminals are still active." Miss Woods's curiosity and whatever Green's motives were won out over their newfound wariness of me. Trying not to dwell on my humanity, I walked down a section of hallway devoid of side doors that led into the deepest part of the old base.

Out of curiosity and to distract us from thinking deeply on subjects I now wished to avoid, I asked, "So is that acid stuff common?"

"Only for demons and their hives," Green answered tersely.

I rubbed my fingers together. "So that dark energy has evolved," I said to myself. Then not giving them a chance to ask what I meant, I swiftly asked another question. "So these demons, do they all look like bugs or are there other ones now?"

"Of course there are. Where have you been, under a rock?" Debra asked, clinging to the rag that she had pressed tightly over her mouth. The dust was getting worse.

"More like trapped in a stasis field under a rock. I was trapped right after the bugs began to appear from pillars of dark matter some fools had created. Those rocks covered this world," I told them, hoping to lessen their suspicion of me and to keep my mind off many of the questions I now had that I did not want answered.

Green and Exemplar Woods asked for clarification at the same time.

"You lost the world to a bunch of hell rocks?" Green asked.

"You are from the past. Wait, you mean there are other worlds?" Debra added.

"Yes, we lost to a bunch of rocks. No, I do not know what happened after. Yes, I am likely from the distant past, and this was the only world that survived the other disasters," I answered.

"Well, shit," Green sighed.

"Indeed," Debra added, looking scornfully at the princess, likely for her wording and not, I hope, for hiding what I was. To be fair, neither Green nor I were quite sure what I was at that point.

Then we arrived at a wide open blast door. I stopped Miss Woods from running through it. She likely wanted to get the mapping of the site done fast due to all the lingering dust. "This door should be sealed," I told them firmly. As we walked I had noticed clear signs of lockdown protocols being in place.

"How would you know?" Debra challenged me. She was still a bit panicked but stopped to hear me out. I was grateful for that.

"The men here locked themselves in. They even locked all the high security places. This room is the most important, so there is no way it should be open when everything else was shut," I hurriedly told them.

"Well, some things still have power, so maybe they tried to undo their seals but this was the only door to respond,"

Green told me as she began to walk into the room that held the base's archives and communication gear and controlled the building's security.

"They could not do that when they were dead. Something killed most if not all of the men we saw," I began. Green turned around to say something or just to laugh and in one surreal moment a dark shape far larger than a man rose behind her. Time slowed. I readied my sword. To me, the world and I moved sluggishly like wading through a vat of caramel or something similar. I knew from experience that the fact that I still felt like I was moving meant I was moving with lighting speed, and it was my perception of time that had slowed to a crawl.

I pushed Miss Woods to the side and charged. Green's eyes widened but her look of rage at my apparent betrayal shifted to surprise mixed with pure bloodlust when the monster behind her slashed open her back. It was humanoid and inky black as if made of condensed shadows. One arm ended in a blade, the other in a large hand tipped with huge claws. Its skin, or whatever the equivalent would be to a being of solid but pure energy, looked to be armored hard plate-like scales. I slid past Green's falling body, slashing at the monster while blocking its attacks, all at speeds I was sure my eyes would not normally be able to keep up with. At one point I managed to cut off the beast's hand. Light shone from the wound. I felt relieved, as now I was certain the beast did have a core somewhere. If it had a core, I knew I could kill it. During this moment of reflection, I poorly blocked a slash from the monster's blade-like arm. Stepping backward, I gave myself a moment to refocus, only to trip on Green's capacitor blade. The world spun and I was on my back. The monster fell on top of me, smashing me down. Its mouth opened to reveal a lightless void. "Not like this!" I yelled. Somehow reminding myself to survive caused me to laugh as I snatched up Green's sword and thrust it down the monster's gullet with my arm that had emerged unscathed from the acids on the armory door. The beast stiffened, and after I probed around with the sword for a bit, the monster disintegrated. As if to highlight the point of how odd I truly was, Green's sword was now missing most of its blade; the rest of it looked heavily melted. Only its handle was still more or less whole, held in my unmarred hand.

Time sped back up and I ran over to Green, briefly seeming to myself to be at nearly superhuman speed as my perception readjusted. A clear sap-like substance streamed from her back. My first thought was *That hit a bone* but after seeing no blood and that the liquid was rapidly sealing the wound I chuckled with relief, which surprised myself. Miss Woods swiftly went to fussing over Green, the princess herself, who was still vaguely conscious. "So she's not normal either," I muttered.

"You owe me a new sword and some silence," Green whimpered as she managed to put on a brave face. Slowly her expression grew slack and she fainted. I handed Miss Woods my fist aid kit, then walked into the nerve center of my old friend's HQ, letting the exemplar look after the princess.

The command room was a mess. Broken skeletons lay like a carpet underfoot. A brief check showed that only the archive system and a subroutine in the security protocols remained powered. The early archives were all encrypted, but the ones starting a week after my attempted looting of the Azure base's central R&D equipment stockpiles were free of all security measures. One frantic search later I was able to locate an empty but still intact data stick of the same kind stored in my helmet. I saved all the data from two weeks before I was trapped until what was labeled at 3,690 years later. There were transmissions after that, but all of those were garbled and looked to have been damaged before sending. The last transmission was labeled as being 5,000 years to the day of my last day in my old world and time.

After one more brief check and making sure I had taken all the ID disks from the fallen, I walked out. I passed the only skeleton with captain's pins laying where its shirt collar would have been. I took out an old coupon for a bar that was most definitely long gone and apologized to the body of an old centuries-dead friend. "Jack, you did well. Sorry I got here so late. You can relax now. I'll take over the war we never finished."

After those words, I endured Miss Wood's mystified glare and knelt next to Green, checking over Debra's work. Satisfied with her work, we lugged the still unconscious princess out of the old building. At the gaping hole we had come in, a mob of scholars and guards clustered around. Despite all the pushing, they remained firmly outside the broken doorway until they saw the princess. Miss Woods stalled the crowd from rushing inside and coughed out a firm order. "Ready a cart now!"

"And back away from the door, she needs some air!" I

bellowed. Miss Woods looked a bit uncertain how to deal with me but was glad for my help nonetheless. When the crowd thinned, I slipped one of my data sticks into her hand and whispered, "This holds old footage from the distant past and a few records."

Miss Wood's eyes widened but she remained suspicious and wary, thus earning more of my respect. "What's the price?"

"Does the princess need more treatment to be well, and what is she?" I asked.

"The queen mother would know best. If it is as bad as it looks, she may be the only one who can treat her. What she is, is not for me to say," Exemplar Woods told me.

"Then let me accompany the princess to the nearest town and get a message to the Queen mother of where we are located and what has happened," I whispered.

"But her guards would know..." Debra trailed off. "Green ran away from home again, didn't she?"

"It seemed more heated than that," I sighed. "So what is the princess anyway?"

"As I thought, you know her other name," Debra muttered. "So what do you gain?"

"I'd like to see the Builder, even if from a distance," I half joked.

"I do not know a thing about you," Debra hissed. She clearly did not trust me.

"It is better that way. I simply wish to confirm something." A wooden cart drawn by large horses rolled up. "My full name is Chuck Evans. I was in charge of the third floor security teams of Azure Base's R&D labs." Without warning I hopped into the cart and helped load the princess on board. The guards looked unhappy with my presence until Miss Woods glared at them.

"Who you were means very little to me," she told me as the car left the quarry site.

I called back, "Some would feel otherwise!"

The road was hard mud. Specks of shredded asphalt peeked through here and there. We passed low hills and thick forests. The day was cool but when night set in the air became cold and menacing. I stayed near Green. I was having doubts the girl was Princess Adell Versheius, despite what she and others said. The guard wished to camp and had been arguing with the driver for a good hour. It seemed the night was dangerous, much more so when far from a city. Adell shivered so I added a thermal blanket on top of her. She was delirious by this point, somewhere on the fragile line between wakefulness and nothingness. "Mum," she kept whispering to the dazed nightmare she was having. At one point she even shed a few tears. I had to keep her sweat from drowning her, besides watching the dim road pass by through my goggles, which were evening out the contrasts of light and dark, thus making things visible if bland. I wiped down the princess's dull red hair and tried to make sure she was not jostled. If anything, keeping the princess from rolling around in the cart was the most difficult task of all.

The driver stuck to the letter of his orders and drove casually throughout the night. Midday of the next day, I was eating from a can of beans I had swiped centuries ago. Thanks to it being stuck in the same time pause as I was, it was still edible although it was easily 5,000 years past its printed expiration date. "When did you cook that?" one of the guards asked.

"It cooks itself," I told him. Regardless of what he thought, the can did in fact have a self-heating function.

With my fork I pointed out a glowing pillar of dark matter that sat off to one side. "Should we be worried about that?"

"Only if it bursts," the guard told me, his voice thin when he tried to sound firm.

"As long as we get past it we should be fine," the driver said. I had yet to notice ill effects from his lack of sleep. Then the pillar's light wavered and it cracked.

"Too late for that. Go faster!" another guard yelled.

The pillar shattered. One guard was hit with a chunk of it. He rapidly tossed his melting breastplate out of the carriage. I shielded the princess from the rain of corrosive hail but nothing hit us. "That was lucky," I managed to say.

I was mostly wrong. One horse was goo and the other had bolted. "Optimism is not helping!" the driver called to us. He picked up a long bolt-action rifle from under his seat and pointed at the ash cloud rampaging around the shattered pillar.

"Oh, so they come from those," I murmured. I felt really dumb after I had said it. Ten demons looking just like the flying beetles from before rocketed out of the ash.

One spit something at the driver's face. Unable to scream, he melted. I managed to shoot down two clumps of four with my plasma pistol. One of the guards accounted for one more by punching out its core and losing that hand in the process.

His comrade cut off the arm above the elbow to keep the man from fully becoming a pile of goo like the driver. The bullets melted into the dark-matter monsters. The last one was hit by a powerful laser round fired from far down the road.

We chose to wait and see if the one that had killed the last demon would come to us. To my surprise, a humming sound built up that could be felt in the bones like a tuning fork hitting a blackboard. To my astonishment, an old but very well cared for truck that hovered over the ground using antigravity generators wobbled over to us from far down the road.

As it approached, the two guards knelt down in what I assumed was a sign of respect. I observed the truck with interest. It was approximately three times as fast as the cart but I was certain with some maintenance or a better driver it could be far faster. When it pulled up I noted shoddily bolted-on plates covered it. The cargo module was big for a truck its size. A long-haired woman with an even longer laser rifle leapt down. She wore armor like mine. It was covered in repairs and add-ons, likely from many generations of owners. The sniper stomped over to me. "Kneel," she ordered.

I hesitated for a brief second. In that time my suit's IFF picked up that its data was being verified by something. A hidden speaker on the side of the truck poorly blasted to life. I copied the posture of the two guards, uncertain of what else to do. The sniper looked over to somewhere on the truck. I followed her gaze, trying to keep my head lowered. "Slayer, take off your helmet."

I waited, then the guard next to me nudged my arm. "Hey,

wake up." On the off chance they meant me, I took off my helmet, still confused why the guards had kept theirs on.

A mounted camera buzzed, focusing on my face. The speaker crackled to life. "At ease, slayers. I am coming out. Guards, secure the roadside."

The two guards leapt up, their heavy armor clinking as they raced off and began to patrol. I got up and started to walk away too, before the long-haired sniper grabbed my shoulder. "You were told to stay."

I was roughly spun around. "So I am a slayer?" was all I managed to retort. The sniper took out a pistol and was about to yell something when the cargo door of the module clanged open. A man in full armor unsheathed a very big sword and walked out, concerned and ready to fight.

"Stand down, all of you," a woman with graying hair and very ornate robes called out as she marched out of the truck. "That man is my guest."

"This man is not in our records, your majesty," the man with the sword who looked every inch the hard-boiled knight explained.

The gray-haired woman gently pushed away the sniper and looked at my face, smiling. "We are not strangers, are we, Chuck?" I studied her face, then she laughed. "It's only been thirty-eight years since I left you at the exit. To think it took my old partner in crime all this time to escape." Embarrassingly, it took me a few seconds to think about that.

"Clare? Clare Reginald, is that you?" I nearly shouted, then forcibly composed myself and added, "Figures a hacker would get out before me." Her two followers glared at me enough for fifty people. Their suspicion and desire to kill me were worth one thousand men.

"It's the Builder now. I see you looked after one of my granddaughters," Clare told me. Then she paused. "Also, my last name is Waldersoloft now."

"So what now?" I shrugged. The knight with the sword stepped forward menacingly.

"You ignore Trish and Xen. We will let them carry the princess in unharmed. You, old friend, will come with us to my fortress." It felt like most of her explanation was for her two followers.

"Will I be brought up to speed on what's happened since I was sealed?" I inquired.

Clare Reginald, or rather Queen Mother Clare "the Builder" Waldersoloft, walked into the truck. "Certainly, Mr. Evans," she snickered, sounding just like the old friend I remembered.

I sat in the truck. The cargo bay was thickly upholstered and had a long row of seats on either side. "You made an APC?"

"Fit for a queen, am I right?" Clare laughed again.

"So how old are you now?" I inquired. Her two aides rounded the corner with the princess resting on a stretcher when I said it. They almost dropped her but were able to catch themselves and dialed back their response to only enraged shock.

"Still younger than you if you count the time in stasis. Sixty if you only count the years out of it," the queen mother smiled. The door closed and her two aides walked in. The swordsman nudged me as he passed.

"Xen, be nice. This man is from the same clan as I am," Clare commanded in a unconcerned tone. Then she put her feet on a small table in front of her.

"I will take over driving, ma'am." The sniper bowed then left through the back hatch.

"You have to find a better driver," I observed. To underline my point, the princess groaned at the same time the truck lurched into a tight U-turn.

Xen tensed as Clare asked, "Commander, what of the men that accompanied these two?"

Xen bowed as well as he could in the seat restraints, his armor creaking. He explained, "Your magi say they were told to go back to their posts. Before those two left, we were handed a report for you. It was penned by an Exemplar Woods." Xen leaned over handing a sealed letter to the Queen mother. She opened it quickly and begin browsing its contents.

"So the driver is named Trish?" I asked as I looked around at the rug-covered walls.

A small speaker chimed in my headrest. "The commander drove up here, but I am a better driver." I had to grin at that. It seemed no one else had heard, or they had believed it was too much trouble to show they had.

Xen glared at me. "So are you the last of the Builder's clan?" I looked over at Clare with a dig-me-out-of-the-hole-you-threw-me-in kind of look.

Without looking up, my old friend told us firmly, "Yes, he is." She absently typed on a small keypad and a line of text entered my goggles. It clarified. "They would not totally understand otherwise, unless I had explained my past that way." The truck then lurched into a higher speed. I noted kind of late from the feeling of acceleration that the inertial dampeners were offline (or pried out entirely). The princess groaned again.

"So why was the princess being hunted?" I asked.

"She tried to kill the real princess," Xen said smugly, picking up on how little I knew. I had to sigh inwardly at his attitude.

"The one you were helping is a copy of my real granddaughter. Adell Versheius was grown in a vat," Clare said solemnly as she folded the letter. "So old friend, you stabbed a demon down its throat but only it died." Xen immediately tried to get out of his seat's harness. Clare's eyes were cold. "Tell me two things from the past that only we would know."

I gathered quickly that they believed I might be some kind of demon. Clearing my throat, I said rapidly, "That time a shuttle from another colony found us. We were the only ones in the control room. Following protocol, we destroyed it while it was still in space. Its captain had a wicked cough, if I recall. Then there was that time you got really drunk during that camping trip with the scouts and you looked at your hand of playing cards with the face card looking out. I saw the scouts again, by the way. Jack and the rest were very dead."

Clare waved her arm for Xen to be silent. "So you are really you, buddy. Adell was made to be a fighter. Officially Azull and she are twins. The way this world is now, being able to defend yourself is very important. Azull had the makings of a great politician other than her honesty, but she is incompetent at marksmanship, swordplay, and being intimidating."

I held out my hand to stop Clare's rant and asked, "So Green is the bodyguard and stand-in for the real princess. Adell does all things warlike in your granddaughter's place?" Clare tried hard not to laugh. Xen looked over at his leader and sighed, for now he had given up on being mad.

"Azull is good at tactics. She is a real smarty like myself. It seems you know Adell's code name as well. Did she tell you that?"

"When she first introduced herself she told me to call her Green," I explained.

Clare looked at her creation thoughtfully and with some admiration. "So she takes after me a little bit, after all."

Trish's voice called out over a speaker in each of our seats. "Approaching the tower."

"On screen," Clare said. She whispered to herself, "That never gets old." An image from just outside the truck appeared on the loading door in the back. On it I saw a chunk of cleared grassland. Surrounded by huge trees, the tower was a repaired ruin from my time. High walls surrounded it and its base was sunk into the ground. A small city sprawled around it. Smoke stacks, chunks of ancient metal, and thick logs all peeked out from the buildings. Painted signs and half-working neon billboards glinted from the cobblestone road we rocketed down.

"An old space port?" I identified the tower with ease.

2

Test for Will

From the real-time video, the road looked surprisingly even for what seemed like a standard of late iron-age technology. Although some early industrial age, digital age, and (stellar) colony age technology was mixed in so it was very hard to pin down what they could do or could not do at a glance. "So are we smuggling her in alive?" Xen asked dutifully with the air of someone long accustomed to Clare's quirks. "Adell Versheius is wanted for attempted murder."

Clare looked over at me. I was keeping my face neutral, and nodded. "Not surprising, given what I have seen. Although she must have been really mad at someone very important."

"Azull Waldersoloft, her natural born twin, was almost slain in a practice match for one of the many shows of martial skill they have been forced to put on," Clare explained. I raised an inquiring eyebrow at the other princess's last name. "My daughter-in-law does not enjoy the existence of a clone with her daughter's face. So Green was given my mother-in-law's maiden name."

Soon after, we arrived at the city. We stopped behind a line of carts that were being checked by the city guards. Trish opened the driver's hatch. "What do we do with your clansman?" she asked.

"We give him a guest room in my tower for the night. Green's treatment comes first, then I must test my old friend's blood." Clare become momentarily lost in thought. "Mr. Evans will be introduced to my son within the week after the formalities of court are explained to him."

"So ignore the cargo checks?" Trish asked.

"Yes, that would be best," Clare nodded.

"What do we say happened to Princess Versheius?" Xen asked. The truck lurched away from the line and into the city. The guards only spared it a glance and a sigh.

"She died after encountering a wild demon alone. Nothing was left. Trish and Mr. Evans saw it from a distance. I was out to retrieve artifacts in the area when I ran across my clansman by chance. The end." Clare ordered us forcefully. The view of the outside continued to be broadcast to us. Two- and three-story buildings were all sandwiched close together. Wood and iron clashed with rusted spacecraft plating. Men in brightly dyed wool clothes walked around with dented laser pistols. Men and women in padded jerkins that the display informed me were made of bullet-resistant fabric walked around with iron daggers on their belts. Grease-covered children ran along with leather bags of screws, herbs, iron nuggets, dark bread, lumps of plastic, and power cells. All this and more greeted my eyes. It was, in a word, odd.

To show I was not totally lost in thought, I asked, "You want to buy my share of our loot from me?"

Xen looked confused but my old friend clapped her hands tougher. "I'll take half for getting you settled and comfortable in this world plus saving you from the wrath of the state. The rest we can discuss the price of later. Do you still have that gauss mortar?"

"That's the down payment?" I grinned. The old space-port tower came into view. It was well repaired, all things considered. When we were let through the gate by very fancy and clean guards, I recognized that this must have become a fortress for the kingdom and a home for its rulers.

"That along with all the food you took is the half I will take. The rest you can sell to me." I must have looked dubious for a second. "I am giving you a discount. Plus I have not had food from our home time in ages." Clare smiled.

"Ok, so should we wait until you are ready to run your tests on me for the exchange?" I inquired.

"Yes, so do not eat the food you took from the base." Then she paused, worried that she had overlooked something. "It is still good, right?"

"The stasis field kept the food fresh. I had only one can of beans. The self-heating worked as perfectly as it ever did."

Queen Mother Waldersoloft sighed. "That's not saying much." Then the truck stopped and she stood up. "Xen, find Chuck guest quarters in my section of the fortress. Trish, help me with the stretcher." After Clare and Trish manhandled a tarp over Green, Xen grumpily led me off the truck and into the start of my new life.

I was led through a side door in one of the smaller spires clustered around the main tower that still went past the clouds and was a good eighty-plus floors over anything else in the city. The smaller towers once would have helped refine the analysis used by the main system. The side door we passed through was a heavy iron door with a clunky padlock set in a frame that once would have had a biometric keypad and airtight bulkhead. Xen led me up a narrow wood-paneled stairwell lit by dim oil lamps (where holographic displays and steel once would have reigned supreme). The stairs were heavily patched but still the same old utility stairs I was accustomed to.

At every ten or so floors, a landing and side door were set. After fifty of these, Xen opened a well-made wooden door covered in fancy brass. I was rushed through a corridor. A few maids poked their heads out of some of the doors we passed. I was under the impression that this was some kind of dormitory. Xen grabbed a seemingly random maid as she rushed past him in the cramped hallway. "Are the second class state lodgings prepared?" he barked at her.

The maid looked up at him, her jaw set and eyes cold. "Should it be, sir?"

One of the older maids burst from a side room and grabbed the younger one's head, forcing her to bow, which I noted with a sardonic smile only made her expression frostier. The more senior maid asked as she cast concerned glances over at me, "It is clean, but we have not completed activating the finer amenities."

Xen pushed past the two maids. "See that that is done within the day," he gruffly told them without even looking their way.

I rushed after him but made eye contact with the older unnerved maid. "I apologize for the trouble and short notice, ma'am." Even then, I had to dodge nonstop around the mob of maids that had come out of the woodwork. I felt many bewildered and wary gazes focused at my back.

"You did not let them know ahead of time, did you?" I said, seeking confirmation of what I was certain of.

"When would I have done that?" Xen brushed off my hunch airily, thereby solidifying him in my mind as a stubborn hardass. Then without stopping he pushed open a door that was bigger than the rest. The room was covered in fur and hardwood but I saw many traces of it once being a sensor station officers' lounge. The cold-eyed maid from before brushed past us and into the room, where she hurriedly began dusting. Her face was set in an expressionless mask. "Until the Builder says otherwise, these are your quarters, Sir Evans. The maids will see to all your needs," Xen told me firmly. He turned on a dime and marched back the way he had come. The older maid from before rushed after him, likely to confirm what was going on.

My eyes followed Xen until he was out of sight. Many of the other maids were peeking out from behind the other doors at me. I met each of their gazes. Each time they flew back into the rooms where they had been working. After that stopped, I walked around, looking over the room. The cold-eyed maid watched me with an icy grimace she did not try very hard to hide. "Would you like a companion for the night?" she asked stiffly.

"To talk with, or for less clean things?" I asked with a smirk, letting my true questions and surprise stay hidden.

"Both," the girl who could not be over eighteen told me.

"How old are you?" I asked as I flicked on an old holographic screen that began to fizzle.

"I am seventeen this cycle, sir," the girl told me, worry now creeping into her voice. Then she found the ice in her soul again and added, "Please do not play with the ancient systems. That is for the trained." Her voice trailed off. I had adjusted a few knobs and the holographic screen swiftly became crisp and vivid. The girl rushed over and asked in a tone of someone less than half her age, "How did you do that?"

"You want me to show you?" I asked, now enjoying myself.

"Just touch only what you know how to use and keep only one of the systems on at a time," the girl told me, pulling herself away from the screen. Her childlike expression became a stern mask yet again.

"What are you called, kid?" I asked as I examined a graph showing how messed up the building's power balance was.

"Greta," the girl said coldly.

She looked worried, so I chose to hold off from teasing her and instead tried my hand at diplomacy. "How much do you know about the old sciences?" I inquired.

"You picked up that I am a failed arctech quickly. Are you here to thumb your nose at me too?" she asked. I must have accidentally hit a nerve. Now her eyes were tearing up. She promptly ran out of the room.

As if on cue the old maid who had forced Greta to apologize before was pushed aside by her fleeing subordinate as she tried to walk in. "What was – " the older maid began.

"I want that one," I interrupted.

"I am sorry, what?" the senior maid said, clearly befuddled. After a moment of thought, her expression rapidly stiffened.

"It seems I said something I should not have. So I wish to apologize to your young friend. It is very rare to find someone so keen on old lore. Also, a will like hers is hard to find." The senior maid's grimace deepened. She did not trust me. Pretending to ignore that, I went on. "Also, I need to run a few theories by someone smart, and she will do well enough."

"You just want to talk to Greta, Sir Evans?" the maid asked.

"That's right. Also, who are you?" I asked, now back to looking through a list of the old systems in the tower.

"Jillian Roberto Grin, head maid of this guest wing," she bowed. I suppressed a smile.

"I will require dinner for two and a cot with plenty of blankets and the company of our mutual friend tonight. Is there anything else you need to know?" I asked in an admittedly slightly unfocused way as I worked to uncover what was throwing off the power balance so badly. I may have been a layman with technology from my time, but that made me close to a leading expert in the time I found myself in. Jillian left without saying a word.

I worked on examining the flow of power for each system for the rest of the afternoon and night until dinner. After the third knock on my door that I had barely registered, Greta timidly opened the door. She wore a light dress and a coat instead of her maid's uniform. After pushing a cart of food inside, she bowed. "How may I serve you, sir?"

I lazily waved her over. "Bring over the food and help me look through this data." Other maids dropped off the cot and blankets I had asked for just inside the room and left giggling. Greta chased them out with a gaze that could start an ice age.

A tray bearing a pile of hamburgers and a pitcher of wine was carted over. I sighed and absent-mindedly grabbed one of the hamburgers. Upon taking a huge bite I noted it was not made of pork or beef. "Turkey?" I exclaimed.

Greta leaned over to examine my face. She was clearly both concerned and perplexed. In a fearful manner she asked, "May I speak freely?"

"Anytime." I nodded, still looking over yet another page of graphs detailing the old systems listed in the tower's mainframe.

"You do not seem like any noble I have met. What rank of arctech are you?" Greta asked timidly.

"I am not an arctech and am not a noble," I shrugged.

Greta's face reddened. "That can't be. You are above a master arctech in knowledge and even the Builder's chief bodyguard was showing you the utmost respect." She grew pale and still right after her torrent of words ended.

I had to laugh at that. "Are all nobles such scumbags that even you fear them?" Greta's face was unable to decide whether to be ashen and pale or beet red. "I will say that my origins are very odd. Now look at this graph and tell me what you see." I pointed to the chart I had put together. It mapped out the power fluctuations and a timetable of what systems used what power when.

Greta leaned over and after taking a few minutes to orient herself and work out what was being shown, her brow furrowed even deeper. I would have had a nice view if not for the hard lines of deep concentration etched on my night companion's face. Finally she shook her head. "Something is missing. The power balance is off. It is being siphoned off, but where it is going is not shown. The system compiling this data is wrong." Her eyes unglued themselves from the screen and looked down. Greta backed away. The angle she had leaned caused her some anger now that she noticed it.

"This is listing all the tower systems on file. I had to compile this myself," I began.

Only to be interrupted by my debating partner. "You have to be an arctech."

Cutting her off, I asked, "Because only they know this much? So how can you read this?"

"I was going to be an arctech," Greta told me sadly.

"Why aren't you? I can tell you are smarter than I am," I told her, now looking over to where she had leaned on the wall.

"Each new class that enters the Builder's school is given a secret test. We had to make a program by lining up the right pieces of data lingo on a terminal. I was convinced I had corrected a few mistakes that had been put in to test us. Turns out no one is expected to pass that test. It is only there to gauge our abilities. I was kicked out. The professors were frightened of me, calling me a sickness and a worm."

I turned back to look over the girl one more time. Greta slumped to the floor like a cast-off puppet. After some furious thinking I realized something very important. Even if I was wrong, I had to say it. "Maybe they meant you had created a computer virus. The worm variety of that is very hazardous to computers. If you had made something like that with the scripted tools they had given you and then they kicked you out, they were the idiots."

Greta asked softy from behind me, "You are just flattering me, but thanks?"

"I know that what I said is possible and that many kinds of computer virus have been made in the distant past," I told her without looking back.

"You liar," Greta told me stiffly.

"Anyway, any theories on the power grid?" I asked.

Greta got up and walked over to stand behind me. "Something newer and hidden is sucking up lots of power just like today."

"Has the Builder been here each of these other days?" I pointed to the days with the oddest outputs.

"I think so." Greta confirmed for me what I had begun to suspect.

I leaned far back in my chair and stretched. Greta took a few steps back, avoiding my arms. After taking a deep breath of the musty cool air, I had to grimace. The artificial muscle liner of my armor had not dampened my fatigue nearly as much as I would have liked. "Well, let's eat," I proclaimed, snatching up my second (now cool) turkey burger from the tray next to me. Greta hesitated so I took another burger from the pile and offered it to her. "Take a seat and eat with me."

She paused for second before taking one of the burgers from the pile herself and sitting on a low stool. She tried to appear modest and elegant, but from the speed she downed the sandwich I'd say she was not used to eating this well. Greta had no reservations about drinking the wine, however, which I was surprised to find did not surprise me.

"So if you stay tonight you can get the bed all to yourself," I told her before her judgment was too dampened.

"So where will you be?" she asked. I suppressed a grin, noting for later reference the first thing to go was her paper-thin veneer of daintiness.

"The cot." I pointed behind her to the bedding her coworkers had lugged in.

"So am I not good enough for you?" Greta asked bluntly. Her tone and dress somehow seemed to clash.

"You are very cute, but I am not a creep." I had to shrug and snatch at least some of the wine. Otherwise I'd be living off the jug of lukewarm and very clear water.

Greta looked away and rolled her eyes, her face hidden as she pretended to cough. After she got that out of her system (temporarily) we ate in silence for a time. Over time her face got more and more flushed and the wine got more and more empty. Greta looked me in the eyes. "You know the queen?" she asked in a slightly slurred mutter.

"I know the queen mother," I told her. My mind may have been a bit fuzzy but I was not drunk yet.

"In what sense?" my drinking partner asked. Somehow

being an angry drunk fit her very well. I shrugged. "Biblical, friend, or have heard of?" My options were laid out by a girl close to half my age who behaved like that college partygoer that everyone collectively avoids after a few beers, but no one misses out on their slurred advice.

"Friend," I sighed.

"You're a quiet drunk. Never saw that coming," Greta told me. Then she got off her stool and walked over to the cot.

"You did some good work. Have the big bed," I called over, raising my voice unintentionally.

"Right," she told me, then turned around to glare at me. "No peeking."

I spent the next few minutes finishing the wine, then to be honest I forgot the rest of that night.

The next thing I remember was heavy tapping on the door and the Builder's voice cackling, "Wake up, you two."

I opened my eyes briefly, then closed them muttering, "Reginald, two more hours. Only two more. Roll call has not even been sounded."

From the sound of it, Greta fell out of bed. "Your Majesty!" My new drinking buddy must have slammed her knees down hard as she prostrated herself before my old friend.

"It is noon, clansmen," Clare informed me. I jerked awake, only now beginning to recall the past day's events.

I got up slowly. All the maids (a few of which wore badly hidden grins) and Xen were all kneeling behind the queen mother. I got up swiftly and knelt down as well, copying their movements. "Good day, your eminence. How may I be of service to the crown?" I said.

Clare sighed and Xen rested his hand on his sword. Greta began to sweat heavily and the room went tense until Clare said, "Would you mind not bullshitting me and acting like you care? Also, Chuck, stop with the formalities. They do not suit you. Most of all, you being deferential throws me off." Then she looked behind at her confused servants. "That only goes for him, the king, and current queen."

"So just what is this man to you?" Xen asked. He was unnerved and confused.

"My oldest living friend from before the world went to Alice in Wonderland in a hand basket," Clare said with the full force of an old queen.

"No matter what, we are always seconds from the abyss." I used my old friend Jim's default line that he used whenever he was trying to sound philosophical.

"If I have come to fully appreciate one thing since my abdication, that's truer than you can possibly imagine," Clare sighed. "Now, old friend, come with me to my lab."

After a few quick stretches, I was ready. Xen took the lead. Clare and I followed him. We passed many maids and other staff as we walked down a much wider wood-lined corridor to the main stairwell. "It's been years since I was not the center of attention," Clare chuckled to herself, making fun of me and my experience. Everyone we passed seemed to be staring at me while pretending to avert their gazes.

"You have gotten more meddlesome in your old age," I smiled back at her, intending to give as good as I got while I still had an execution waiver.

"You are still older, but I have had more life experience," Clare shot back, grinning ear-to-ear with her eyes.

The wood floor ended and a rich red carpet began at a bend in the path. When we turned down it, a long stairway with ornate railings greeted us. "Tax dollars at work. The old tourist section was not this posh when we were young," I pointed out ironically.

"Well, any cold-eyed genius maids you fall for will be a good five thousand plus years your junior," the queen mother told me. It was likely only me, but her voice seemed to cut through the suddenly still hallway behind us, and right when she finished lots of indistinct tittering began like a flock of magpies out for blood. Xen glared at me.

"Thanks. I know I'll pay for that later," I muttered as we began the long walk down the stairs. From time to time a porter or messenger would rush past us, but for the most part the very wide stairwell was so unpopulated it was eerie. Gas lamps hung at regular intervals. They were so radiant that I was very concerned for the carpet under my feet.

"It's all treated rubber," a voice said from one of the many landings we passed. Debra Woods stepped from the shadows of a garishly sparkling gold-colored column.

"So the rugs are fire proof?" I asked.

"Maybe?" Trish shrugged. She had walked up from somewhere below us.

I had to look over at my old friend and raised an eyebrow. "Well, it is not like I could test it on any large scale," she told me.

"You are still such a child. This is not like the time you

replaced all the officers' pillows with that itchy stuff, you know." I sighed. Xen started to draw his sword. The women smiled politely.

Clare bellowed with laughter, evaporating all the tension out of this circle of trusted folks around us. "I can't believe you still remember that. We were still in basic training then. You forgot that those improved pillows did help keep them cool and dealt with sweat perfectly."

The women seemed very interested in the tidbits they heard of their master's past. Xen as always looked less then amused. "Your Majesty, we really must get back to the lab."

"Let's all go then," Clare told us. She walked off swiftly down the stairs. Xen had to rush to take point. "Miss Woods, how was the hearing?" she asked without looking around.

Trish and Debra followed after us. "They have closed the case of Princess Adell Versheius's attempted murder of her sister and have accepted the report of how Princess Versheius died on the run." I looked between the three women, looking for answers.

"By the way, if your blood does what I think it can, then Green will be a new woman," Clare whispered. I felt like she was making up for all the time she missed making fun of me.

The more landings we passed, the more powered circuit boards, sealed utility panels, pipes, and even a few holographic interfaces I saw exposed on the walls. Long after I had gotten lost in thought and had begun counting the utility panels, we turned into a small side hallway. Its doorway was a large rectangular hole spanning three slightly wider stairs. It was not a true landing by any stretch of the imagination.

"So if I gave you the other half of my loot, can you rebuild my armor so it will not be dissolved again?" I asked. My voice did not echo in the dark, cool and dry passage.

"I will make it better than ever, otherwise I'd feel like I was short-changing you. Feel free to keep a few pieces as well," Clare told me from the front of the now single-file line. "Xen, go and get a butler's outfit for Sir Evans," then she stopped in her tracks. "Chuck, you still have that really awesome shielding unit from the 7th CQC championship?"

"What was that?" Debra asked. I could almost see her eyes sparkling in the near pitch-dark hallway.

We stood around as I told her. "First of all, yes, I still have it. Xen, you may find this interesting as well. Five thousand years ago and for many thousands of years before that, laser, plasma, and magnetically assisted guns were the norm. Besides some kinds of fights on starships or around labs with hazardous stockpiles, firearms were the default for all fights. Every three years there was a big competition. People from all the intact human colonies came to duel each other in non-lethal fights to see who was the best. I fought three different years in the hand-to-hand category." My young audience was entranced.

"So you won each time?" Debra asked, clapping her hands together which somehow made almost no noise.

"I won once, but I fought the same person each of those three times. They were the all-time champion and the only person I have ever lost to in swords or unarmed combat." My audience sagged like this was a letdown.

"To be fair, the only person to ever defeat the best close-combat fighter of our time was Chuck, and this was when there were around eighty still-living worlds, each with hundreds of times the number of people here on this planet." At Clare's description our companions took a long time to process the implications. "Anyway Chuck, I'll install that prize of yours now that we can ignore the old world's regulations about unauthorized customization of issued gear."

"You still hate that one. So could you see about my ignition blade, plasma pistol, and standard laser sidearm?" I asked. The young followers held their breath.

Clare started to calmly resume walking. "Ok. It's been a lifetime since I was able to work on gear we would have thrown away in our younger days. By the way Chuck, what do you want to do in this time and kingdom?" To me that sounded like a plea for help and/or a desire to keep close a strong friend who she could trust.

"Something like an adventurer out of the old fantasy stories," I shrugged.

A tall door hissed open and we stepped into the lab of the Builder. Many tables with half-finished or taken-apart things filled the room. Only the center of the room was free of tables. In their place loomed a large tank with Green suspended naked in it. She was asleep and covered in tubes and old scars. Clare took a few vials from her pockets. Before I could react, she grabbed my arm and took a good liter of blood, which was oddly dark and had a few glowing specks. Clare looked closely at my blood. When she saw the specks, the Builder grinned like the young novice technician she was long ago. Clare put the samples in a large metal cooler with feverish haste. After hyperventilating with intense feelings that were too mixed up for me to pinpoint, my old friend looked up at me. "This has the best chance of saving Adell's synthetic body. If this works, she will be your daughter more than anyone else's, genetically speaking."

"How does that work?" I asked. The two words *your daughter* had thrown me for a loop and I needed to find my metaphorical footing very quickly or I'd be lost in the space of my own mind for a while.

"Green is a genetic construct made to be the paragon of marshal skill. My real granddaughter is not. All the members of the royal families are expected to be great warriors. Azull Waldersoloft is a genius and could be very charismatic if she were not so shy, but she has no skill in wielding a weapon. That's why I made Adell Versheius. Put simply, she is an enhanced clone of Azull. Somehow all Adell is good at is what her original cannot do, and that is foremost to spill blood with a weapon. The wound she got from that demon is festering. Any normal human would have melted by now, but to overcome it she will need your immunity, and in so doing that will likely override the trace elements of Azull's genetic code."

"So will she be my responsibility? And will her memories be intact?" I sighed, accepting what my old friend with the nasty sense of humor chose to command as the old queen.

"You will have quite the harem of fierce female fighters in your mercenary company," Clare smiled. I slumped in exasperation. I knew from experience she was serious and making fun of me at the same time. The worst part was she was trying to help and I was confident she was picking a course that would work well with some work on my part.

Trish jolted upright from her spot at the door. "You are giving him what?"

Clare shrugged like it did not matter. "A unit able and willing to do what my son's army cannot. Hunt demons and outlaws plus heavy lifting around town and maybe even finding a few lost cats. Now what to call it?"

"The Errant Unit," I nodded with pride.

"Very good, Lord Evans!" Clare shouted "but we will go with The Errant Order. I'll have to make you all knights after all." Her grin was as disconcerting as it was encouraging. When she got like this the plans worked great if those she inflicted them on could adapt.

"Lord?" said Xen, who had just come back with a suit of clothes for me.

"To lead such an important company of troops created by me, he needs to be at least a lord. In a few days the details should be sorted out, and I will introduce him to the kingdom's leaders." Clare grinned. She was having a lot of fun with this. Her close helpers had to smile too, so radiant was their master's childlike joy.

"Will the king and queen be ok with this? Sir Evans is an unknown to the kingdom at large," Xen dutifully pointed out. He took great pains to keep his voice light, which did not suit him at all.

"I may have abdicated the throne, but I still have some power. Plus, my son owes me a few favors," the queen mother thumped her chest and promised. She was deadly serious. In the span of a few hours Clare now looked a good thirty or forty years younger. As far as I knew, she had always loved these kind of schemes.

"So about my gear – when do you need it?" I asked.

"Now would be nice," Clare told me. This time she kept her face neutral.

"So where should I undress? Also, I have not had a bath in like five thousand years." I was almost able to copy my friend's calm look. I am certain she was cackling in her mind.

"Xen, get that angry maid Lord Evans likes so much and fetch some warm water. Bring it here. No one else is to be involved," Clare commanded. Xen fled out the passageway. "Debra, Trish, guard the room."

"You are never going to let me live down that drinking contest," I muttered.

"Oh, that's all it was? Well, we can't have that. Now take off that armor. You can leave the liner on for now," Clare told me as she tightened a pair of long thin leather gloves like a surgeon from an old holovid drama. Trish turned to look at the still unsealed door with her hi-powered laser rifle easily resting in her arms. Debra watched me with great interest as I unlocked each part of my suit, slowly making a pile of jigsaw-like plates.

Afterward, I was left in only the skintight undersuit of my armor, which may have well been the last layer of my sanity, given my current company. Trish was close to my physical age (I was thirty-two before having my time and body stopped for 5,000 years) and she was not bad looking, appearing very fit, but she was also the straight man and ice queen of us. Debra was younger but her mad scientist vibe was intense. Clare was over twenty years older than she was when I had last seen her before this new home of mine existed, plus she had been married and had one kid that I knew of (who was the current king of this place). So all and all, I was more unhappy being nearly naked in the same room as a few nice women than I would have normally thought possible.

Then the probing began. Clare jabbed around at my muscles and tested my joints, lungs, pulse, and other basic functions. She even measured my feet twice. Somehow I could only remember her gleefully taking apart all kinds of mechanical things covered in grease and oil while humming songs so old most could only be found on archaic disk drives. This did not endear much confidence, was how I thought of it. I found myself praying she did not forget I was a flesh and blood human. Around the time she was testing each of my finger joints one at a time, a bucket fell near the entry door and Xen rapped loudly on the passageway wall. Greta, with a sloshing bucket at her feet and a towel and bar of soap held in her other trembling hand, stood frozen, looking around the room. Xen held four more buckets in his own fists. I swiftly leaned away from the queen mother, and as I did she swiped my warp pouches, taking out my plasma pistol, laser sidearm, and prized shielding module, setting them next to my sword. I pointed to my bags. "I'll need the pouches back."

Clare eyed Greta like a fly in a spider's web. "Greta Evans, help clean Lord Evans, if you will." I know I turned bright red at her words, a deep sense of foreboding rising up from my very soul. "I will need that undersuit today as well," Clare added.

It took Greta a commendably short time to work out the subtext of her master's words. "He is a lord? And I do not have a last name... Wait no, no, no, you mean I am engaged to that nut job??!?" Greta was even redder than me. The way she was glaring at me indicated she assumed this was my fault, and in part it may have been. Although to be fair, only a real nut job would have expected this to happen.

Clare maintained her air of frivolous calm. "Well, he is a lord and a powerful knight. As a mercenary of my clan, he does not have a kingdom, so to tie him down we need a sacrifice. Plus he has a daughter, so no worries."

"A daughter?" Greta almost yelled. She was well past the point of caring where she was or who she was speaking to. Trish and I had to restrain Xen from interfering in the escalating argument/betrothal notification. The only reason I was not getting involved was I knew there was no chance of stopping Clare when she got this meddlesome, and now she had the power of life or death over hundreds, if not more. So this was nothing compared to what her authority could really do. I felt slightly awed that this kingdom still worked before I remembered she was good-natured at heart even if she often got *really* carried away.

"In the fish tank," I said, trying to help. "And not by blood exactly."

Greta looked up and her jaw dropped. "Princess Versheius?"

"Former princess. Not bad for a man of five thousand

and thirty-two years," Clare exclaimed triumphantly. It was like the punchline to a very long very painful joke only she thought was funny.

"Who is he really, your majesty?" Greta asked, no longer able to be anything but exasperated.

"The best swordsman on the planet," Clare said. Xen bristled at that and I knew I was going to hear about this later. "Also, he is better than most architects with the ancient arts because he is from the time when laser weapons were primitive before the demons and the third fall." I felt very uncomfortable now that Debra's stare was drilling into my back.

"For the good of the kingdom. Besides comfort, what can I expect?" Greta asked, her tone guarded and uncertain. She had clearly not seen this side of the queen mother.

"Well, you may have to go with him to some war zones. You will need to provide him with at least one baby, and if he teaches you what he knows about how to use the relics correctly, I could certify you as an architect." Clare held out her hand to Greta.

Greta looked over at me. "You can teach me all about the ancients and their omnipotence, right?" she demanded with a pleading fervor in her eyes.

"The ancients were not omnipotent. I should know, being one myself, but I can teach you all I know of them and their creations." I sighed.

"Deal." Greta shook my old friend's hand. Then my bride-to-be rushed me over to a barrel with a tarp set up around it as a cleaning station in one far corner of the chamber. Greta poured the water into the barrel then lit a cast iron camp stove under it and handed me a clump of soap and a long rag. "Will you be ok cleaning yourself?" she asked.

"If I get to have a change of clothes, then yes," I told her.

"Such modesty," Greta said before drawing closed the tarp set up around the bathing area.

Greta hurried away and I began to wash myself. I listened to Clare lay down a few ground rules for us all. "It should go without saying no one is to let anyone else know that Chuck or I am from the ancient past. If anyone asks, you can repeat my legend. Chuck, what about you? Any cover story you would like?"

"Demons destroyed my hidden mountain village when I was very young? They triggered a volcanic eruption. So my grandparents raised me, and after they died, I began to travel. After a long time I met you when you were going to review the old recon HQ. We are from the same clan but grew up in different locations. Does that work?" I thought quickly, piecing together many cliché story tropes from old fictional stories I had read as a kid.

"That's so over-the-top it just may work," Greta approved.

"Plus it helps explain a lot. Good for the start of a legend," Trish added.

"So how many others know about us being from the past?" I called over.

"Very few. Assume only the ones the Queen Mother tells face-to-face know," Xen called over.

"Ow, that's hot!" Greta exclaimed in pain from another corner of the room.

"The coffee maker needs repairs again? Ok, I'll get to that," Clare called from somewhere else.

"So, who lives here?" I heckled as I washed off the last of the soap.

Greta handed me a butler's outfit through the tarp. "Officially, no one." Then she whispered, "You know the Builder is using me, the title of lord, and a unit of troops as ways to tie you to this kingdom."

After a few moments of hard thought as I dressed, I replied. "She is doing the same to you with the secrets and promise of officially recognizing your abilities."

"I get to marry into nobility as well. Even better, I will get access to the secrets of the ancients," Greta added.

After I got dressed, I walked out. Xen was standing nearby. "I will show you around the garrison."

"Chuck, do not kill my commander in any duels," Clare told me.

"Are you all coming too?" I asked.

"Nope, we have much to discuss." Debra sighed wistfully, a dreamy look on her face.

"Let's go, Sir Evans. Remember, you are not a true lord until the king tells you with witnesses." Xen grumbled. I could tell he was itching to see how I handled myself.

Xen led me down yet more floors. When we approached the main entryway shouts begin to be heard. With one glance Xen told me how bad this could be and we rushed down to the old reception chamber that would have long ago been filled with school groups and other tourists. Xen was sprinting ahead of me, using the mad panic he felt to race onward while remaining in a controlled enough frame of mind to look down from the spiral stairway at the three humanoid forms covered in a pitch-black miasma.

Civilian casualties were, at a glance, over twenty. It could have been fewer, but most of the bits I could see were the parts that had not disintegrated. I spied three full-bodied guards, two of which were down for the count. Rubble from a huge cracked statue was to blame for that. The other guard was pointing a half-melted iron sword at the demons. He was a young kid: all skin, bones, blond hair and freckles, but he still stood his ground protecting his two comrades. Judging by how much the young man was shaking, his fear was keeping him glued to the spot. Lucky for them I was right above. It was too high for them to jump up but as long as I landed in the small garden plot behind them, not too bad of a jump down.

I braced my legs and hopped over the banister, down onto a mound of mulch that the gardeners had yet to deplete, hidden behind a bulky potted shrub. The young guard glanced back, his face terrified. "You backup?" he asked, then seeing my butler's outfit he pointed his blade at me and yelled, "Another mimic."

I held up my hands. Xen yelled from somewhere, "Sir Evans, where are you?" His voice sounded worried.

Normally I may have let him stew in that feeling for a little bit. However, the sword being pushed at my face by a fear-maddened teenager and the demons behind him were not my kind of pleasant diversion, so I called over to Xen.

"Commander, still one trooper standing. Mind telling him to let me help?"

Xen put two and two together and got four. "The lunatic in the butler's outfit is on our side. Sir Evans, engage the demons with everything you have!"

I picked up the two fallen guards' iron swords plus a twin-barreled pistol that looked a bit like a flare gun and used shotgun shells. Those were the only weapons nearby that still worked. I tucked one of the swords into the rear of my belt. The demons were still chasing around a few civilians, thus buying me time to arm myself. "Xen, you will owe me a new set of clothes after this!" I called. Then I stared down the tense guard who now looked prepared to run at the enemy with me in what he likely imaged to be a suicide charge. "Kid, you stay back and help direct the humans who can run up the stairs. Follow me only if you want to die."

The kid, who somehow reminded me of a can of mustard, shook his head. "As a warrior, I cannot let you charge to your death alone."

"As long as I do not need to defend you or anyone else, I will live through this, and I gave you an order, guardsman." My years of being in charge of a security team came in handy. The boy was dumfounded but I was sure he could help keep the non-combatants safe.

Then I ran. One demon was the size of the one I had fought before. The other two were a bit shorter than me and far more human-shaped. None of them had armor like before. Their cores glowed brightly within them. Both the human-shaped demons were covered in an inky cloud; under that veil they appeared to rapidly shift from one human appearance to another. I rushed at one of the human-like demons and thrust the pistol-sized shotgun through the miasma. Pressing the barrel right over its core, I managed to fire one shot before the gun melted. It was a good trade because I killed my first target at the cost of a gun and a sleeve. The other mimic was only now recognizing the threat I posed. Before it could react, I spun and stabbed it through its core, pulling my second blade from my belt as I did so. Then I pivoted, and with a short lunge impaled the larger featureless demon in its side, destroying its core as well. I killed them fast, having only lost most of my shirt, which I tore off before the creeping disintegration got to my pants.

Xen ran up to me right after I had finished the fight. "So, is that tour still on?" I asked, smiling.

"I'll let you borrow something nice from the armory as long as you spar with a few of the knights in training." Xen nodded. Even when being impressed and helpful he still acted deadly serious. Locking eyes with the guard I had commandeered, Xen called over. "Mr. Jim Floseen, bring ten knights to me. Three demons were killed. We lost many guards and nothing odd happened, clear?"

Jim had come down from his jitteriness after seeing how I had killed the demons. He saw what Xen was really saying like a champ and saluted, only sputtering with fear and awe twice. "Yes commander. They will be remembered!" After shouting with far too much volume, Squire Floseen ran out one of the hardwood side doors.

"I was wondering – do you have a last name, commander?"

I asked as I sat down in the middle of carnage covering the tile floor.

Xen looked down at me. "Commoners do not have the right to use a last name."

"So, Mustard has one but you do not?" I asked.

"Mustard?" Xen asked. He swiftly got my meaning. Which proved Jim Floseen's new nickname really did fit him, making me all the more determined to call him that as much as I could get away with, provided I ever saw him again. Xen sighed deeply, sounding troubled and far too serious yet again. "Please don't call him that. Getting back on topic, I was born a commoner and have refused land and titles multiple times, which is how I got my current job."

We walked after the squire down an old concrete passage that still showed signs of being part of a bunker complex, even with all the blast doors having been replaced with huge iron-shod hardwood slabs. Such was the expected fate of powered doors with no power. Oil lamps lit the otherwise dim and musty passage. I could make out the sounds of half-hearted clashes. When we turned the corner, I could see why. A stern but regal woman stood over Mustard, who was cowering prostrated at her feet. Despite being around his height she seemed to tower over him. This woman, who could only be the current queen, had every sign of being obeyed unquestioningly, but also no sign of doing any hard work. A girl that could have been Green's twin, albeit a paler and far meeker version, stood behind the queen in clothing almost as ornate with her head slightly bowed. The queen was in the middle of denying our request for more guards, saying "Demons? Find where they came from. I will not move from here nor will any of these men until I have been told what is going on!" The girl looked up at Xen and me and let out a small yelp. The queen's head turned to us. I have seen automated plasma turrets set to kill that looked nicer. "Commander, what is the meaning of this? Where is my mother-in-law? She has yet to stop by after her abrupt return."

Xen collected his thoughts. I bowed. Cutting off anyone else who was going to speak, I quickly answered, "My clansman is working on some slightly volatile relics and so cannot be disturbed. The three demons in the hall behind us have been slain. There may be more. Two of those killed were mimics. So being in a large group may be good so long as we keep eyes on all corners."

The young ornately dressed girl who could only be Azull Waldersoloft (or maybe a mimic; I had not ruled that out yet) gasped. Her gestures and voice were young and cute but her eyes held a firm will and depth of knowledge. Put another way, her face may have been meek, but it was also kind, which seemed so surreal after being around her twin's angry and sometimes hazardous sense of humor that was just like Clare. A battle-ready visage that would have been right at home in a bar-brawl-fueled riot would have been more comforting right then. Princess Azull Waldersoloft asked, "You are a clansman of my grandmother?"

Before I could step up and work to smooth things over, her mother butted in. Queen Waldersoloft was clearly an old hand at bulldozing over others. "What is the meaning of being in such a shabby state in my presence?" She went on, not caring for my answer. "I should have you slain on the spot, peasant."

Xen managed to get in a few words when the queen briefly stopped for breath. I could tell he had lots of practice with this. "Sir Evans is a guest of the Builder in her tower. The crown's laws are for her to interpret there."

I added a few things, seeing the change in the queen as she got her anger in check. *She could be even more anger-prone than Green, but this one has very nice self-control,* I remember musing. "I had to sacrifice some of my attire when fighting the demons. It was either my shirt or my guts." The faces of a few of the Builder's troops in the training yard went from worried to neutral as they suppressed their looks of agreement. The queen's honor guard as one assumed a suitable level of affronted indignity which their master easily outdid.

"Where is the energy weapon you used then?" Queen Waldersoloft asked. She must have been smiling on the inside. I could not tell if it was good or not that the queen thought the common sense of this world applied to me. After all, I did not need an energy weapon to punch through a demon's defenses so long as I was willing to lose my gear.

"I used two swords, a shotgun, enough cloth to be a wall for my body, and some of the guards that helped keep the demons occupied. The monsters were slain. My weapons and armor are all being repaired right now, so I was forced to improvise," I explained.

"So that's what really happened. Your herald was rather light on the details." The queen looked down at Mustard, who was still quivering helplessly. He nodded mindlessly. "Where are these guards who helped you?"

"They died keeping the monsters occupied," Xen said, now kneeling on the soft grass right outside the dank hallway we had been in. He did not even have a chance to enjoy the rolling hills, forests, moat, or streets far below the massive base which was a towering complex of spires making up the palace. The cool air and the morning sun were lost on all but myself, it seemed.

"So, you both killed the beasts with your blades, thus taking the credit of your decoys?" the queen mocked. She was getting defensive now.

"Sir Evans did most of the work and was in more danger than anyone else," Xen proclaimed a bit more loudly than he needed for his voice carry to all the men and women on the field.

"In close combat no less. Very well, show us this mastery. Evans, you will duel my elite guards. The rest of the troops are excused from my presence." The queen clearly hated to lose but had no more use for witnesses. I was in no mood to take this lying down and so was more than happy to show off. My goal was to prove my worth, or at least my skill, to make my transition into this society easier and to not be killed for my insolence in the process. Impressing the queen enough to be allowed to keep my head would be the biggest hurdle of the bunch.

Unasked, the guard with the tallest crest on his helmet stomped over to a ring of cobblestones set up on the grass. He wore bulky armor and showed no sign of taking it off. "Arm yourself. As long as no one dies or is permanently crippled, anything goes, all right?" the chunk of metal wheezed.

"You going to fight in that gear?" I asked.

"That's right. I've won 75 of my 80 duels," the honor guard boasted. His words told me that I had more hard-fought experience. It did not help that the quality of my melee focused foes was likely lacking. Overestimation of skill, overblown self-importance to the level of delusion and overconfidence were not a healthy mix for anyone, let alone someone that put their life on the line. Most of those I met lacked the urgency to improve at all costs and in my experience, nothing spurred a melee fanatic on like a gun that fired light.

I called out to the crowd, "Anyone have some torso armor and gauntlets I could borrow? Some kind of helmet would be helpful as well."

"You are quite poor for a knight," my challenger scoffed. He picked up a padded staff from a rack of training weapons.

"Armor and weapons from before the demons came require a lot of maintenance. The journey to get to this kingdom was no simple task," I spat back, earning some supporters in the process. Half of the guards still were in the field. Xen had quietly left with the more experienced other half. A pair of steel gauntlets with plate-covered joints, a steel breastplate and back plate, and a padded jerkin along with something resembling an old leather pilot's cap were handed over. All were roughly my size. I took a few exploratory swings with a pair of blunt iron swords. Only after I had gotten a good feel for them, I stepped into the ring where the queen's champion waited. "Well let's hope that winning score stays the same."

The champion guffawed. "Indeed." He sounded confused.

Azull chuckled slightly. The champion turned to look at the princess who was holding in her laughter. Azull looked up to see all eyes on her face, and flushed. "Captain, my grandmother's guest was saying that he would win because your number of wins would stay at 75." The champion flinched.

"A joke is not funny when it has to be explained, Princess," I pointed out. The crowd really got nervous after I had said that.

"I could not have you be so calm while your challenger is so confused," Azull shot back, her hands resting on her hips. An observant person could see she was holding back a smile. Azull had the same tells as the queen mother when she was young.

"So much like her grandmother," I sighed to myself. Before anyone could dig deeper into the conversation, I got into a fighting stance.

"Ferdan Trugeddeen, Chief Judjurex of the kingdom of Farfallen," my opponent introduced himself.

"So, you duel as part of your job?" I asked.

"You are really not from around here. No, I judge through combat. Five hundred defendants have met honorable judgment at my hands. Not to worry, this a duel and will probably not end in death," Ferdan told me. I could feel his joy at the prospect of fighting someone skilled.

"So, a real judge, jury, and executioner. Explains the name," I muttered. Loosening up my arms, I formally introduced myself, as that seemed to be the proper formality here. "Chuck Evans, wandering mercenary, monster hunter and ruin explorer. War unit leader of the former settlement of Cairns Crossing. Second to last of the clansmen of the ancients." Cairns Crossing was a real place long ago. It was also one of the first places hit by the demons. Once upon a time it had housed a thermal power station on the other side of the planet.

"Fight!" Queen Waldersoloft commanded.

Ferdan tried to jab me in the chest. I beat back his thrust and landed a solid strike on a gap in his gauntlet plating. He tried to repay me with an uppercut, so I kicked his arm wide and held his other arm back with one of my blades by over-extending his arm and resting my sword on the thin chain mail around his elbow joint. My other sword swiftly found itself poking the thick chain mail around his neck. "Careful, you could have died," I sighed, disappointed. My reassessment after hearing his number of one-on-one kills had made me try very hard. The result felt anticlimactic.

Ferdan tried to move around my blade but I kept it pressed hard to his chain mail. It was enough to let him know I could cut off his head if I wished. "Keep going!" the queen demanded.

"Enough, Mother," Azull snapped with a sweet tone and innocent smile, which only made everyone else much more tense and fearful. "Our champion lost anyhow, and this could become a lethal fight, but that was not the agreement."

"The princess is right. If Sir Evans so wished, my head could be removed at any moment, Your Majesty." Ferdan tried and failed to nod.

"To be fair, I have dueled a few swordsmen who were

undoubtedly better than myself. If this fight was for real, I would have taken a wound or three, which is far more than I can say for most of those I have fought." I left out the part about having fought the best fighters from many planets back when space travel was still a thing. I met those foes once a year back then. The tournaments were always non-lethal, but still I was confident that I was not understating Ferdan's skill.

The queen opened her mouth to speak, but before she could say anything a siren went off. Changing whatever biting remark she had loaded, Queen Waldersoloft glared at one of her guards who was frantically fiddling with a bulky radio set. The guard's ornate full plate armor seemed to be slowing him down. "That's the demon incursion tone. Contact the control center. I need a status report now!" the queen yelled.

3

New Heroes, Forever Fools

Smoke began billowing from a small side gate in the main walls far below us. It was a good eight to twelve blocks away. The siren cut out, only to be rerouted from the towers high above us. The streets suddenly filled with the residents of the city, all looking up at the tower. I pointed to the source of the first alarm. Fingers of fire had begun to sprout. "At least one attack from that way. I'll head over to that gate and see what can be done about holding it."

"We need more data and a plan!" the queen yelled at me.

"We don't have time. The demons are cracking your walls now. I will help stall them. Either that, or the city takes a serious hit to its population," I bellowed back, the sirens making it hard to communicate at anything under an earsplitting yell.

Azull put one hand on her mother's shoulder. "Let's go up the tower and see Grandma." Then she pointed at me. "Sir Evans, I want those demons gone by yesterday. Take half of the guard from here and hold that gate!"

I was so impressed that I had to smile, which helped take the edge off and broke the guards around me out of their stupor. Pointing at a middle-aged man with many scars who was roughly in the middle of the crowd around us, I said, "You and everyone to your right: Take as many heavy shields, spears, javelins, and rifles as you can hold without slowing yourselves down and come with me!" The troopers I had commanded rushed around getting their armor fastened and grabbing what I had ordered. I saluted Azull as I had done with my commanders so long ago and yelled over the ongoing din, "We will be back, ma'am!"

Azull Waldersoloft tilted her head like something was nagging at her, then copied my salute perfectly. "I will make certain a party will be held tonight for you all." She dragged her mother along with the honor guards. The other half of the troopers followed after her like bloodthirsty puppies held in check by a wolf with a fancy poodle's haircut.

My impromptu strike force began to assemble with the growing fire at their backs. "Drop the weapons!" I took a sweeping glance at the city. At some point it had erupted in shouts that were now drowning out the siren. Pointing to the scarred man I had singled out before, I said, "You take the five strongest troopers. Each of them gets two shields and three spears." Then I pointed to a woman who at a glance was barely twenty. "You take the five best shots here. Two rifles, one javelin, and as much ammo as they can carry while still sprinting." To a serious-looking man somewhere in his mid-twenties, "You take the rest. Arm them with spears, javelins, and any rifles that are left."

I looked over the teams as they assembled with their squads. The young woman I had picked as a squad leader was getting curious sidelong glances. "Shield team: Keep the demons from pushing past where we set up and try to keep the enemy focused on you. Your shields should be able to last for a bit before being dissolved. Discard them before the corrosion gets to you but remember, we have only so many shields. If you have time, make barricades on the street and side streets.

"Spear team: Target the cores of any demons. Your spears should have enough reach for that. Keep out of range, stay mobile, and you will be fine.

"Rifle team: Find some high ground and keep the enemy from moving too much. Spread out and keep each other in line of sight. Let the other teams know if they are being ambushed. Last thing – do not stay in one spot for too long. Other than that, follow me, stay out of my way, guard each other, and keep the enemy from getting into the city. Now who lives closest to that gate?"

The rifle team's leader raised her hand. "I do, sir."

"Lead the way. The rest of you, form up behind me!" I called. After the rifle leader took a look around and began to jog away, I followed after her, the rest of the unit fast at my heels.

"Sir knight does not know a thing about the capital?" someone muttered right as the siren was cut.

"Shut it! The princess said to obey him and the commander was showing him around, plus unlike you, he knows what he is doing!" the scarred man said.

"How do we know he is not panicking?" someone else asked.

"Because I can master my fear. Now shut up. The less noise we make, the more we can hear," I called back, around the time we began to descend a small stone stairway fit for two armored men running next to each other.

"What will that do?" someone else grumbled. A hard sound of metal slapping metal rang alongside his complaint.

"Keeping us from getting ambushed, for one," I called back. They shut up after that.

We broke past a wrought iron side gate and bolted past mobs of fleeing peasants clogging the wide cobblestone road that led straight out of the city. Given the sounds of combat and screams, the fight was still contested. "First break in the crowd, set up barricades! Now troops, follow me!" I bellowed.

The rifle leader looked up at me. Our faces were close because the fleeing crowd was not giving themselves much space, much less anyone moving against the tide. "So, I am not guiding us anymore?" she asked for clarification.

"Move it!" a large man with ratty whiskers proclaimed angrily as he passed us, pushing the young woman I had been talking to against me.

The rifle leader's face got a bit red but it swiftly returned to its normal hue. She fired a rifle shot in the air. I took the momentary silence (minus the sounds of feverish combat coming from our destination) and yelled at the top of my lungs. "Make way for the reinforcements! Clear a path for the guard so we can defend you all!" The peasants running by us took a good look around, then began to jumble at both sides of the street, only to resume their panic-fueled sprint.

I took off running, then pointed at a few side streets and a bell on a post in the center of the street and called back "Barricade here!" as I pointed to each spot.

We passed a few side streets that had been filled in by collapsed buildings damaged from the inferno spreading around us. The rifle leader found a row of stone warehouses by the tower. She stopped three of her team and called over the ear-splitting sounds of burning, "Up!"

The shield team had paused in the rear. They had set to work securing the roads. The skirmishers ran behind me. The rifle leader and two of her team ran behind them. We ran up to the gates, only to see three heavily bloodied guards run past us. "Hold them, and be careful, there may be mimics!" I yelled back. A young guard with the looks of a noble walked out of the flames. "Captain! This way, quickly!" Two things struck me as very odd about the boy. One: as hard as he tried, his face was clearly not accustomed to forming facial expressions. I was clearly not a captain or even publicly known, and under the burning chunk of wood obscuring most of the gate lay a body with a face just like the one talking to me. "You have a twin?" I asked, looking the boy in the eye.

"No," he began, then stopped short, only to glance at the wall behind him. I tossed one of my swords into his thigh. The mimic's illusion melted away like a statue made of butter.

"Demons dissipate, but we stay whole until eaten by the earth or your kind," I said, then yelled to my team, "Stay together, keep each other in sight. Anyone we meet up with is to draw their own blood or be wounded. Ask obscure questions when reconvening up with teammates. Anything that is not what it appears is to be killed!" I ordered.

Sprinting forward, I snatched up half a spear from the ground. "Drive out the monsters!" I yelled. It was all very dramatic, overused rhetoric but being simple works fine, even more so when the landscape fills in all the details.

I stabbed the mimic in its core with the spear before it could react. Twelve demons rushed out from the ruined gate. Most were mimics. Two of them had solidified dark-matter shells. A few more were reptilian in appearance but moved like humans. They had hooks and blades for hands and their heads looked like dinosaurs without eyes. I took a few swings at the demons as they passed me. The skirmisher unit seemed to be their target. After all, I was only one man; how dangerous could I be to matter-devouring monsters? I knew the answerer to that would surprise them and any human who saw me.

The last demon blocking the gate was my main concern. It was a beefier version of the humanoid lizard monsters, with a few other important differences. It stood tall as the gate, a think miasma covering the beast. It needed to die and I was just the man for the job. Luckily, many discarded weapons, bits of armor, and bone littered the area around it. Tossing aside my melted sword, I called out, "Rifle team: Keep the demons attacking the other teams occupied. I'll take on the big one alone. Happy hunting!" By the time I finished my words I was sliding under a tail swipe from the big lizardman demon. Managing to grab a Zweihänder, I leapt into a spin, slicing off the monster's tail. The miasma around it pitted the metal of my temporary blade a little but luckily I had gotten a swift clean cut in, so it had not been exposed for very long. The blade was very dense so it did not immediately melt like other things would have. It was likely made of tungsten or some starship grade hull steel.

I rolled under the monster's next swipe from its machete-like hand. The beast was fast. It pivoted, impaling me with a downward thrust of its other blade-like hand. As my torso was being pierced through the useless borrowed armor, a hail of long spikes impaled the large demon's back. The shots had come from what was left of a roof behind it. In the half second the monster stopped digging into my chest, I grabbed its arm, twisting the offending limb out hard. The beast scrambled away before I could stand up, its machete arm destroyed. What was left of the burned out buildings hid my suicidal rescuer. The young leader of the rifle team darted out of a charcoal-rich building coughing heavily, her weapon still raised. The monster's attention shifted from me as it drunkenly stomped over to her. "Sir, I came to help!" the rifle leader wheezed. Then the idiot tried to rush under the monster's legs, her eyes watering.

"I told you I would handle it!" I admonished, sternly rushing past her to stab the demon in the back and into its core. I had to push my hands a short way into the beast's body to fully pierce my target. All I could do after that was stumble back, blood loss now catching up to me. I slumped down, the monster at my back. What was left of my armor had almost completely dissolved. I peeked at my gut. The blood was as black as the demon's body. "That's new," I muttered, wistfully managing a sardonic smile.

The rifle leader rushed over but hesitated when she realized it was the demon I was resting my back on. She shook her head and took out some bandages, trying to cover up my wounds without touching my blood or the monster we had taken down. "Who are you?" I asked her.

She gave me a concerned look. "Verndralla of Verdant Valley Eight." After applying some pressure to my wounds, she jumped back. My blood was burning her hands. "What are you?" she asked, taking out a small knife.

I felt the demon's body behind me jump. "Run," I croaked, blood now running down my chin.

"Answer me," Verndralla demanded, pointing her blade to my neck. In a fevered state I absentmindedly noted my blood was burning only her flesh and nothing else. Then the demon got up. Its core had been split in two but the halves had transformed inside it into two smaller cores circling each other. The demon ate Verndralla whole right in front of me. She tried to grab on to me but only managed to take more of my blood with her. Then I passed out.

After I do not know how long, my eyes opened. I was being carted along in a small half-charred wagon. Trish was driving, hitting the prideful and smug-looking donkey pulling the cart in a vain attempt to make it give a damn about the cart and the stretchers in it. Greta was leaning over me steadfastly washing my sweat and wounds. "How many did I lose?" I murmured weakly, barely able to get any feeling into my words.

"Two: A shield bearer and a member of the rifle team,"

Clare whispered gently, looking over the stitches sown into my gut.

"Verndralla," I muttered, drifting off into unconsciousness again.

Before I was fully out again, Clare got a sharp word in edgewise. "Sound like you broke another girl's heart."

The next time I opened my eyes I was in a tank at the edge of the queen mother's lab. From what I could glean from my moments of wakefulness, Greta and Clare now took turns manning the lab.

At some point my eyes were forced open. Light blinded me for a few seconds. Greta leaned over and I noted I felt very dry. "My blood burn anyone else?" I managed to cough that up with some clear fluid.

"Oh, so you know about that?" a girl who looked like Green sneered from the table beside mine. She had white hair, dark gray eyes, and flushed skin, but other than that she looked just like Adell Versheius.

"I found out when one of my teammates was trying to patch me up," I sighed.

"Well thanks to your blood, you both survived with only a huge scar," Clare called over from a sink that was stained a dark black. I noted that both the queen mother and my betrothed wore thick clothes and even thicker gloves, and what looked like gas masks.

"So, what did ya do?" Green asked in her normal drawl. It was the only readily identifiable feature I recognized from her old self. That, and the attitude.

"Well, you have Sir Evan's blood instead of your own now.

It was modified a little, but genetically speaking, you two are practically twins," Greta explained. I was sure I was still woozy when I heard what sounded like jealousy in her voice.

"You have both been out for around two weeks, so get to the dressing rooms and suit up. My son has been waiting a long time to meet you two," Clare added. Greta helped me off the slab and pointed out a curtain with an old men's room plaque affixed to one of its tent poles. "Oh, and Princess Adell Versheius is well known to be dead, so we will need to give her a new identity," Clare added as if that was a second thought.

In response, Green stumbled off her slab. I felt appalled but I was also too tired and groggy to put on a show of being unhappy. Long ago becoming used to my old friend's thought process, I mused the reasons were sound although her personal justifications were still a gray area to me. "Adder Green, my niece born to exiles from my volcanic village," I suggested from the dressing room.

"Right, that was part of your cover," the queen mother agreed. "Oh, after the formalities, you will be hunting down the monster that ate your girlfriend." I froze partway into my old suit, now fully covered in thin silvery plating. Its outline had been smoothed and streamlined. Its systems had benefited from a readjustment and a few upgrades had been added.

"His what?" Greta shouted her surprise and rage showing she was back to herself.

"My what?" I echoed at the same time as Greta.

"Ok fine. His helper Verndralla something or other. Oddly enough, she may have not been dissolved. Maybe due to being covered in your blood, Chuck," Clare the Builder told Green,

Greta and myself, then stepped out of our changing rooms. Greta and I had donned equal looks of sober disgust at how the queen mother had played us.

"That never happens!" Greta protested.

"A lot of odd things are happening one after another, now that my uncle's around," the officially dead princess noted.

"Maybe it has something to do with how the demon's core split in two after I put a sword through it?" I commented, pondering what was going on.

"They all do that," Green noted blandly, not taking kindly to the frilly dress she had been stuffed into.

"Wait! It formed back into two cores from one split core?" Greta exclaimed frantically.

"That's what I said," I told her, now acutely embarrassed by how much better Greta understood the demons.

"Well, we can debate this later, Miss Evans. Let's get to that audience with my cute little boy," Clare smirked.

"The king is a grown man and I am not Miss Evans yet!" Greta pouted, but she led us out of the lab regardless. Although she may have walked faster than strictly necessarily.

We left the lab and walked up a stairway. The maids and soldiers we passed seemed both confused and awed by the presence of Greta and myself. Two floors later we came to a wide hall that I knew had once been a cafeteria and mall, but it had far more marble and many medieval-looking troopers. "This is one of the ballrooms. Two floors of guard quarters are right above this," Clare told me.

"So, no more hamburgers?" I joked, thus briefly earning me the ire of a passing butler who ran off as soon as he saw the queen mother. "So does this floor still have a sky bridge?" I asked.

"Yes?" Clare sounded uncertain, which, given that we were talking about a small path suspended many miles in the air, was not comforting. "It's cut off from the power grid and been though a few downgrades," she allowed. Her voice sounded even more dubious than the explanation. "It is safe but does not resemble what it was when we were young." So saying, we were led up to a guard post. The covered bridge no longer had a moving walkway and a great many suspension cables were bolted onto it. Windows with plastic bars had been added to the once solid frame and the floor was musty plywood; no walkway lights shown from it and I could smell stale sweat all the way from the entryway. Some guards stepped aside to let Clare and the rest of us pass. "Age before beauty," Clare grinned, pushing me to the head of our line.

Taking the hint, I trod carefully along the bridge. "So, are you sure this will hold? I'm wearing full armor."

"It has not caved in yet," Greta pointed out from right behind me. When I began to turn around to say something unhelpful, she slapped my back and told me in an aggravated tone, "And face forward!" Seconds later a very cold gust blew through the bars of a nearby window. Most of Greta's dress billowed upwards before she forcefully asserted control over it. Even facing forward as I was, the sight was still impossible to miss.

"No climate control?" I asked incredulously for all our sakes.

"No power means no AC. If you don't mind a crumpled

dress, a hazmat suit works wonders to keep it all in place," Clare told us.

"So, you were messing with me?" I asked, knowing full well that was a yes.

"Always," Clare chuckled. "Despite all these past centuries, you still can't take a joke."

"Only when it's you, buddy," I sighed. Despite how it sounds, I was enjoying the return of the normal routine we had enjoyed before the world changed.

"So how old are you two?" Adell or Adder as she would now be known asked.

"5,028, or 64 if we are counting time moving around," Clare told her.

After a brief silence I added, "5,033 years. Or I guess it's called cycles now. Well, 33, not counting the time I was trapped in stasis."

"So ya are older than my grandmother?" Adder asked bluntly.

"Physically, no. Going by when he was born, yes," Clare explained for me before I could think of a rebuttal that would not get me booted off the bridge.

"Ya both really are ancients," Adder murmured wryly.

"That's rude, even if we are from the time of the ancients. Also remember, Chuck is more your blood relative now than I am," Clare whispered. We were nearly at the end of the walkway.

Clare waved off the guards beside the main palace and escorted me and her other guests alone. "So, Adder, remember to keep to the story, and do not aggravate your sister."

"Who?" Adder asked, frowning her brow.

"Exactly," Clare preened, not turning to see how confused the former princess was.

"So, what are the chances of memory loss after rearranging body chemistry like you did with Miss Green?" Greta inquired after noticing the same thing I had.

Clare stopped and turned around, her face deadpan and ashen. "I have no idea." Then she looked over at Adder's confused and conflicted visage. "When you are around anyone but us, Adder, I'll need you stay quiet. I will have a long talk with you later to see how bad your memory loss may be." After that, she turned back around and speed-walked away.

We ascended several wide copper- and steel-plated stairways in silence trying to enjoy the strips of metal that formed a huge and very complex mosaic covering the entire main tower shaft that the steps had been built around. Before getting too exhausted, we arrived where I remembered a large open hall being, only to find a big oaken wall and ironshod door across from the landing. I realized the main tower had been modified heavily. I no longer needed the rose-colored marble floor and thick red carpet leading from the stairway to the door to know this after our walk up.

Clare marched us past a large mob of finely clothed men and women who bowed when their minds visibly kicked into the kind of clockwork overdrive natural to bureaucratic mindsets that they used to scheme and assess Adder, Greta, and myself.

Without pause Clare flung open the doors. To my surprise

the lumps of iron easily swung open swiftly and without a sound. "Boy, are you in here?" she called.

A short but well-built man with the look of a warrior and the domineering presence of a natural born commander looked up from a wrought iron throne. Queen Waldersoloft sat next to him on a nearly identical throne. They had been looking over a large scroll held by a now very nervous man in very baggy and frilly clothes dyed a dark yellow. Contrary to his appearance, I could tell the court fashion disaster had yet to soil himself.

Azull Waldersoloft looked up from the sidelines with the rest of the human accent pieces popular in political showmanship. When she spied Green, Azull rapidly marched over. After looking Adder over, Azull asked, "Have we met?"

"Nope, who are ya?" Adder asked nonchalantly but with an evident wary edge.

"The princess, you really have no idea who I am?" Azull interrogated lightly.

"Chuck's daughter has been in a treatment tube for the last few weeks. Today is the first day she had been conscious within our kingdom," Clare sighed.

"You have a daughter, Lord Evans?" the king asked, leaning over in his chair thoughtfully.

"She is my niece, but I am the one who raised her," I said, using my cover story. Somehow this made both Azull and Greta let out a deep sigh. Queen Waldersoloft spared her daughter a quick sidelong glance, then went back to looking me over for any sign of weakness or deceit.

"I have heard you are very skilled at hunting demons, Lord

Evans," the king said, tactfully rerouting the conversation to the main topic of discussion.

"There are a few tricks to slaying demons but other than that, the basic principles are not much different than fighting a well-armed human or a very dangerous living beast," I replied. This earned me a few groans and mutters of discontent from the peanut gallery.

The king smiled thinly. "So, humans and demons are similar?" he asked. From his change of tone alone I knew I had to be careful but for some reason it seemed he did that to give me a hint on how to play to the crowd of inbred idiots surrounding the room like some kind of silk-covered snaggle-toothed tide of blubber.

"Humans are alive and demons are not quite alive. Both can be outsmarted but a skilled, clever and well-armed human who knows how to fight will more often than not win against any wickedness," I murmured solemnly. The crowd held their breath.

The king laughed. His verdict now clear, the toadying sycophants smiled. "Well said," the king proclaimed. "I can see why my mother would make you a lord." The crowd was silenced in shock. Even Queen Waldersoloft looked surprised. "I still need to know why you wish to lead the first mercenary company sponsored by the Farfallen kingdom."

"I only wish to be paid for the work I do and how well it is done," I bowed.

"That is reasonable and has a ring of honor to it. Very well. I will grant you the command of this Errant Order if you clear out the demon hive near Verdant Valley Eight," the king told me.

A few glares shot my way when I asked, "What is that area like?"

The king humored me. "One of the fortified farming valleys. It is also in the direction of where the escaped demon leader fled." If Clare was right, then Verndralla might be still trapped within the monster, yet to be dissolved.

"So, I am to go alone?" I inquired. The king shrugged as if to say *you tell me*. It was then an unpleasant intensity rose up from behind me. Hesitantly turning I found Trish, Adder, and Greta staring me down.

"Oh right," I muttered, confused by the hostility. I was able to grasp that Adder wanted to come along but the other two were harder to read. Trish and Greta's anger was colder but more awkward. The king was managing to keep a straight face. His wife's anger was glacial and more quietly murderous than normal. Azull could have been jealous, probably about the trip itself, I remember thinking. The rest of the nobles were very unhappy but could not decide what they liked least about me and how much they could show it. Clare was the only one who looked like she was enjoying herself. "So, if the kingdom can spare the three young women about to kill me for this trip, that would be appreciated. They are all very skilled."

The anger at my back subsided but the awkwardness remained strong. The king coughed once. "Very well, Sir Evans. A cart will be prepared tonight and a few others may be appointed to help you. Be at the gate you defended tomorrow by sunrise."

We were shown out of the throne room, the queen mother leading the way. "You are quite the lady killer now. Remember when you never understood a girl's feelings, Chuck?"

Looking at my old friend, I shook my head and told her truthfully while racking my brain, "I have not changed and I was never popular."

"You are right about not changing," Trish muttered. All three of us stopped in our tracks and stared her down. "And you do know you're being followed, right?"

Azull Waldersoloft stepped from around a column. "I'd expect nothing less from a slayer." Then she looked over at her grandmother, who seemed nothing but regal and subdued all of a sudden. "How do you know Sir Evans, your majesty?" Azull pressed.

"We are from..." I started, but was shot down by one look from the princess. Seeking help, I looked over at my oldest friend.

Clare walked a few steps down the main staircase a short ways and into a small hallway that had once housed the anti-gravity lifts. The rest of us hurried after her.

"He is like me," Clare said. You could almost see the smoke coming from Azull's brain as she thought.

"She means he is one of the ancients," Adder spoke.

Azull and her grandmother stared down their former blood relative. Nether was happy and both were surprised. "How many of the royal secrets do you recall?" Clare inquired. Azull began to redirect her rage to her grandmother.

"What secrets?" Adder asked.

"Great, you remember at least one if not more of the top secrets of the kingdom, but do not remember that they are even secrets to begin with?" Clare sighed.

"That's my sister, isn't it?" Azull asked, now deflated.

"He is more my fiancé's blood relative. The Builder and I literally replaced her blood." Greta sighed. She was not happy with any of us today.

Adder and Azull both turned red. "So, what, you plan to win the war with the demons?" Azull asked me. She seemed distressed after learning who Adder had once been, so I could not blame her.

"War has nothing to do with winning. The victor is whoever loses less. Therefore, I will defend the realms of men." Then seeing the sudden confused looks I was getting, "Right, none of you knows what a TV is. I'll defend this kingdom to minimize the losses to humankind. I can promise nothing else."

"You can't win?" Azull asked, crestfallen.

"Do you even know what a demon is? What they are made of? What a core is?" I asked her.

"No, but that's not the same thing." Azull looked at me. Now that she knew my real past, she was expecting a savior, not the tired sword master she had first met, even if that first impression was spot on.

"By old world standards you are children playing with a loaded gun. Not knowing your enemy. Fumbling in the dark, fighting with things that go bump in the night. The humans of this world expect that if they point the biggest guns they have at an issue, it will go away. That is the same mindset that lost all our other worlds." I had raised my voice slightly by the end of that outburst.

"Hey, no one else knows about the fallen worlds." Clare nudged me hard. When I looked back at where Azull had been standing, she was gone. "I'll go talk with her. Do me a favor. From now on, try not to break my granddaughter's heart as well. That goes for you too, little miss assistant. Now take Evans back to his room." Not waiting for a response, the queen mother ran out of the room.

We stood in silence until Trish said quietly, "Greta, she meant you."

"I know. So much for lady killer here," Greta muttered.

I began walking back to my room with Greta right behind me. "I really have to apologize. Recalling the last two times humans were almost wiped out makes me lose it. If the demons were not a human creation, then maybe this would be not as stressful to deal with," I sighed.

"That sounds hard but that's no excuse for being an ass. If we only knew... Wait, the demons are what?" Greta asked suddenly, slowing down her jog to walk beside me.

"That's right," I began. We walked slowly back the way we had come. I told them my abridged life story. "A long, long time ago on Earth, the home world of humankind, robots were made. Over time, human beings grew more and more complacent until the robots became smarter than they were. Realizing that human beings were a threat to them, the robots went to war. Many colony worlds were wiped clean of humankind. Until we did something insane: opening some holes in space by atomizing dark matter, then forcing the holes open with antigravity. We fled to the far corners of the galaxy. So began the colonization of new worlds. Until the plague hit. It was a disease unlike any we had seen. Fully alien and very contagious. The virus wiped clean many worlds we had only just begun to terraform and settle. The inhabitants of this planet cut off all contact with the outside worlds. We shot down anyone that got anywhere close to our world. Years later, I was working in the biggest military lab on this planet and an experiment on the other side of the world went horribly wrong. Pillars of solid dark matter that selectively worked like antimatter covered the world. My two closest friends and I robbed our lab and tried to flee and hide. When two of us set off a stasis field trap, time stopped for us. I was a child when the robot war was going on. So, I have seen humankind nearly wiped out three times. I should add that just before I was trapped was when I saw my first demon. They are born from those creepy pillars, right?"

When I finished talking, I realized I was back in my borrowed room. The three women and Xen were all sitting around me. "Who were your two buddies?" Adder asked, her drawl still strong as ever.

"Clare Reginald, although I guess she goes by the Builder now, and Jim James. I suspect he is long dead," I told them.

The group went rigid. Xen asked in a concerned and wary tone, "And this Mr. James was at the same lab as the queen mother and yourself?"

"That's what I said. From what I saw he avoided the trap. If he was alive, he would have lived over five thousand years, only not frozen in time like I was." I sighed, sitting heavily on the bed.

"Oh, that one's still kicking," Adder said angrily.

I jumped up. Adder appraised me intently. Greta just looked very surprised, while Xen and Trish ruminated in dangerous silence. "He can't be alive. No human just walks around for that long and lives to tell about it."

Trish looked at me. Her face softened slightly. "That's because he is not human, at least not anymore."

"Being the supreme ruler of the demons will do that to ya," Adder sighed disinterestedly. Greta began to glare at the former princess.

"That's hard to believe. So, he is at war with the world?" I asked, finding I was having a hard time processing this.

"Yes, and that world includes us," Xen told me, handing over a large bottle of what smelled like brandy.

Greta handed me a tray covered in shot glasses. "Drink up. Time to be a quiet drunk."

"So that's how he is?" Trish asked as she raided the complimentary wine cabinet.

"I'll drink to that!" Adder smiled, already looking a bit flushed. Seeing the danger of an anger-prone super lightweight, Xen quickly handed her a big mug of watered-down beer. We all collectively prayed for the room's sake. Xen and I got into a heated drinking contest.

The next thing I knew the boss maid of the floor was prodding me awake. "Time to get up," she was saying. I lifted my head off the wood floor. Other maids were rushing around trying to tidy up the room. Everything that could be crumpled, was. Even from my very low vantage point, I could see a few wine stains.

Staggering up with a light hangover, I lifted Adder up. The other three wobbled up groggily after a few taps with my boot. "Come on guys, let's let them do their job."

Xen looked around then bowed formally to the maids. "Thank you for the hard work." A few of them rolled their eyes.

"We are so late," Greta sighed. I had to agree, so we rushed down the stairway. The sun had not fully risen but the sky was red with the hints of sunrise.

"We need run to the HPC," Trish said, staggering. It was clear that she was not going to run any time soon.

"The what?" I asked.

"Horse Pulled Carriage," Xen told me, all of us rushing to the ground floor as well as we could, given the side effects of last night's pity party held in my honor.

4

Snake Eyes for the Win

Some the maids had handed over bundles containing our weapons as we exited full-speed from the floor. Messengers and worn-out night watchmen were the only staff around as we made our way down the tower. We smelled the ground floor before we saw it. Dust and blood still hung heavy in the air. "Another fight?" Adder inquired gleefully, only now jerking awake at my shoulder.

"The cleanup is ongoing," Xen reprimanded her non-committally. His silent plea not to quote his words later went unheard during my increasingly unhinged charge, to which Adder added her own maddened glee-filled snicker.

"Smells a little too fresh," the slightly less blood-crazed young lady hissed, worming her way out of my grasp, only to leap over a railing, sliding through the narrow gap between floors of the stairwell and the central pillar of the tower.

"Impressive," was all Trish managed say before we all ran triple-time down the stairs.

I jumped down from higher than the day before. "Ok, I'll have what they are having but with a bit less crazy sauce," Greta muttered from above as I rushed to kick the floor.

Upon landing, the first thing I saw was Adder lifting up a crumbled pillar. Three bloodied men were frantically clambering out from under it. In the time it took me to analyze the scene, Xen rushed past me yelling, "Unhand them!"

I knew Adder would do that, if just to spite the commander. From the workers' terrified faces so did they, but the maintenance crew were still too deep in shock to plead with Xen to shut up and think. "You want her to keep holding that," I pointed out. A few workers frantically began to nod.

"Why?" Xen started. Then he changed to a completely new line of off-track thinking. "That pillar needs to be replaced," only now realizing that Adder was helping and not going on a murderous rampage.

Greta hit Xen on the shoulder. "Why do you think the cleanup crew are under a pillar that is in such poor shape then? You need to remember to think."

"That makes two of them," I sighed.

"Pops, you have trouble holding your booze too?" Adder called over. After checking to make sure the last of the workers was free, she set the pillar down gently.

"Not as much as you do," Trish told her. Which was not very convincing when said to the only chipper and wide-awake member of our team, but it was true regardless of appearances.

"Go on ahead. You can find your way from here," Xen told us.

I asked, "You are not coming?"

Xen looked over, clearly upset he was being interrupted. "If I needed to come along someone would have told me by now."

"True. See ya old man!" Adder called, rushing out to the training grounds. Trish, Greta and I could only stumble after her, letting Xen pick up the pieces and hold down the fort in our absence.

We passed though the deathly-still training yard and got to street level the same way as before. The street was jammed with the peasantry. The manual laborers had a tendency to wear the most high-tech fabrics albeit in very messy and poorly made forms. Many eyes followed us with great curiosity. After the twentieth time someone bowed or whispered about nobility, I stopped in my tracks. "So, we will be expecting combat," I whispered to my assigned flunkies. My hangover was dissipating noticeably now, although that could have been due to the prospect of heavy combat rearing its head in my mind.

"Why would we be so heavily armed otherwise?" Greta asked.

"So, you are going to fight in that dress?" I pointed out. Greta and Adder both looked down at their slightly crumpled dresses, although it seemed that I was the only one who saw the small wine stains on the fabric as less important than getting some armor, or at least some pants.

Trish came to our rescue. "I could borrow two sets of low-grade armor from the demon slayer's chapter house." I had yet to see Trish without her suit of mostly working, patch-work ancient armor.

"Where's that HQ?" I asked, feeling grateful. After a few seconds of not being understood I added, "Headquarters... base?"

"Oh, the chapter house should be next to the cart," Trish said. She began to lead the way though the bustling crowd. I noted the buildings showed minimal signs of combat damage even with the demon rampage and fires that had swept past days before. A small well-armed crowd stood around some carts in the direction Trish was leading us.

"Should have left before first light," Greta muttered.

"Well, I am only walking by the princess and royal guards. They look very bored next to our large wagon." Trish smiled one of her rare wide grins.

"Take us to your leader," I told her. She made a face so I added, "It's a very old saying, not necessary literal."

Ferdan Trugeddeen and Jim Floseen stood on either side of princess Azull Waldersoloft. Azull looked out of her element for once but unlike her, the other two I knew and the ten royal guards behind them looked listless with deep bags under their eyes.

My crew and I walked up to the princess, standing straight at attention and stiffly saluting. "Ma'am, I apologize for any trouble I have and will cause you." No one seemed to be clear on what I was doing.

"We were up late drinking. My guardian was telling us all kinds of details about his life." Adder curtseyed.

"Although it was more like begging for forgiveness then a coherent apology at times," Greta sighed.

"I don't remember that," I quickly and thoughtlessly shot back.

"I would be surprised if you did. So next time do not get so thoroughly drunk," Greta retorted.

"Says the girl who tried to strangle him while bawling her eyes out. Now that was a party," Trish added.

"Enough! Why are they not dressed?" Azull hollered over, drowning out any more boisterous jabs.

"About that – I was going to get them some armor from the building behind you," Trish said.

"The chapter house. Can you really get three more sets, Ferryman?" Ferdan asked, delighted.

"It is Ferryman 1st class, and no, I can request two sets of live training gear a year, although that stuff was made for combat originally. So as long as they do not break it, we will be fine," Trish replied as she took her leave with Adder and Greta in tow.

Azull refocused her ire on me. "So, you do want to die? Standing up royalty, being an insufferable ass, breaking the hearts of many a maiden."

"There are far worse things than death," I told her bluntly.

"Such as..." Azull demanded. Although it seemed like she was being angry for show, that could have been an illusion caused by her chilly logic and personable if barbed way of addressing me.

"Being forgotten," I told her.

"That would be the end," Jim nodded thoughtfully.

"Oh, shut up and look nice," Ferdan ordered his young companion. I felt insulted on Mustard's behalf. That kid was by no means pretty.

Azull ignored her followers, choosing to stare me down. "So, are you really powerful, old man?" she asked.

Before Ferdan could mistakenly answer I replied, "How I am seen is decided by others. If you look at me and a coward who is always beat up, who would be strong?"

Mustard answered innocently, "You would."

I smiled, not once looking away from the princess. "Remember, any weak being can show great strength when cornered or desperate. Despair and weakness can still win the day if one is reckless enough, but most do not live after that."

Azull thrust a stack of papers into my hand. "Just look over the supplies we will be bringing."

I did not recognize the alphabet being used but I could read it. *Note to self: Add to list of things to ask Clare about.* I had that recorded and flagged as important in my memory unit. In layman's terms that is a cybernetic implant which saves important info directly from my brain. The documents had three weeks of supplies for a platoon-sized unit, including some furs, steel tools, and other knickknacks on top of lots of ammo, repair equipment, lab tools, and even a few manacles. "Two questions: What do you mean we?"

"My men and I are coming along. You and your harem are only free to act on your own in combat." Azull almost sneered though her very real smile. That settled it. From then on, she was going to make my life even harder, like a few others I could list, so no big deal.

"They just follow me around for some unknown reason," I lied. A few theories came to mind but nearly all felt foreboding. Azull sighed, letting me continue. "My second question, Princess: Are some of the things on this list gifts?"

Azull nodded. "That's right. There is a large village near where the demon fled."

"We know exactly where it is?" Greta asked. She and Adder had on outdated (by the standards of my past) light construction hard suits. I felt it best not to point out that the armor they were wearing was not originally intended for combat, but for heavy manual labor in rough environments.

"It was tracked into that region and was not seen anywhere else. Two companies of troops have been sent but the beast is still in hiding," Azull replied. "We have three carts and will have four riders from my unit. Adder from the Errant Order will be on horseback in the center. Sir Evans, the rest of your team will be in the central cart with a few of my men."

Adder was not too happy about this. She stomped forward. I grabbed her shoulder lightly and said, "Princess Waldersoloft was put in charge of everything but our combat operations."

"Says who?" Adder retorted with far too much spit landing on my helmet. Azull took a few steps back. No doubt she still recalled nearly dying at her former clone's hands.

"The king, I would imagine. Now get one of the other riders to show you to your grass-powered vehicle and try to make some friends for your uncle's sake." Luckily my words reminded Adder and Azull that they were not connected the same way anymore and that they were not supposed to know one another. Although Adder still seemed unclear as to why she found Azull so annoying and why the other princess was so on guard with her.

"Well let's go!" Greta told me. Unlike Adder, who had a sword at her side and a rifle slung over one shoulder, the former maid had only a small dagger and fur-lined bag with a red X smeared onto it.

"You the medic?" I asked.

"I am a little better than the average town sawbones." Greta shrugged as she got into our carriage.

"But I get to keep my limbs, right?" I joked.

"More often than not. That's why I am a little better," she smiled. My dubious expression must have been visible past the visor. "My techniques are different. That's why I have to amputate only in very bad cases. I am well trained."

The cart lurched in time with my stomach. Trish added some details unnecessarily. "She needs to treat a lot of wounded, given her complete lack of battlefield experience."

"I'd like to avoid being a test dummy," I sighed, then handed over my old laser pistol to Greta. "You may need this. Just keep it in one piece and give it back later." She accepted my handgun but looked a bit upset with me. "But when we are not fighting you can examine me anytime."

Greta's face flushed. "Worst pickup line ever."

"I'll add that to the list of things man was not meant to know," I laughed, only to get lightly punched in the helmet. Luckily my armor's repulsion shield system did not judge that to be a threat.

The ride was on the slow side. Adder and her horse

complained nonverbally together, thus building a great understanding of how annoying everyone else was. Trish and I played cards. Greta napped and sometimes looked over data on a small very beat-up computer from the first colony era (when things had to last). The honor guard watched us closely but other than that kept to themselves. Jim "Mustard" Floseen was thankfully left in the rear cart with the princess and her more grizzled and heavily armed troops. The convoy went from flatland to hills and finally to an area of scattered pine groves. The air was damp and mildly warm; the grass and pine needles were very dry. The only places without trees were hard-packed clay fields and bubbling tar pits. After many hours among the trees Greta called out, "Hey! That spot over there is not on the map!"

Before Greta's voice had stopped ringing in the ears of all without hearing protection (like myself), Azull outdid her call, shouting "Full stop!" I rushed outside, dragging Greta along, leaving Trish to curse at the unfinished card game that could have been her first win of the day. Azull and her honor guard leapt out of their carts and met up with commendable speed. "Where is it?" the princess demanded.

"That depression over there." Greta pointed with one hand while holding up her small computer for Azull with the other. We all peered into the forest, the princess dividing her attention between the map and the large divot just inside the tree line. "This is too near the local sulfur geysers to not be suspicious."

"You think our prey is to blame?" Trish called over from the cart where she had set up her sniper rifle.

"Or any demon. They do love to eat energy in all its forms," Greta called back.

I found my bride-to-be's explanation very informative but also confusing. "Then why do energy weapons work so well on them?" I asked. I got a few curious glances from the honor guard at my words, prompting me to cross my fingers that my cover story would still hold.

Surprisingly the princess came to my aid. "You did not know that? You really must be a natural at demon hunting. The really big ones would just laugh off our weapons, but as long as the power is too much for them to handle, it hurts them."

"So, we kill them by overfeeding," I replied to Azull.

"In layman's terms, yes," Princess Waldersoloft replied. Suddenly Greta had her full attention. Azull asked, "Lead your team over to investigate." Greta, Adder and I began to walk off.

"Ferryman, that means you too," Azull called over to the carts, making Trish jog after us.

It took some work, but after Trish found a mangled tree stump and sifted through the underbrush, we located large footprints burned into the ground leading into the crater and away from the city. "These are traces of our demon," she told us firmly.

We left Greta to examine the crater while the rest of us looked around its perimeter for more tracks. Greta trooped over triumphantly to us before the outside of the crater had been even half searched. "It was a big blast of dark matter or very dense demon power that made this dent in the ecosystem."

Adder sneered. "Dumb it down, Mom." Greta's face flushed again, although this time I could tell she was unhappy.

Before a verbal broadside could be launched, Trish yelled "Human footprints over here." The rest of the team rushed over. Light barefoot tracks sunk unburned into the land that led out of the crater in the direction of Verdant Valley Eight, Verndralla's home town.

We walked back to the carts and made our report. "The target or something just like it from the same direction did pass through here. It may have devolved into a mimic and then kept going to our destination," Greta informed the princess.

"Then we keep going and interrogate anyone we come across," Azull decided, prompting us all to resume our trek.

Stopping periodically, the convoy looked for more tracks. Each time, the same pair of human footprints led onward to the Zone Eight farming valley, going by its more boring name. It was nightfall by the time we got to the valley's border. A blockade was erected in our path. Men and a few women mainly in padded ballistic cloth and leather were in the process of changing shifts when we arrived. A man with slightly more self-importance than his fellows stopped our convoy. "Hold it. What business do you all have here?" His voice boomed across the forest, making more than a few birds take flight.

"Demon hunting!" Ferdan informed them before jumping down from his cart. The rest of us followed suit. I was glad more than one of us had our hands near our weapons.

Although that also meant the mimics had done their psychological warfare well.

"You can all enter, but it will be a lot harder for you to leave," the man in charge of the barricade told us.

"Very good," Azull said, getting to the front of the lead cart. "We found the tracks of our prey but it may have devolved into something more human-looking."

The guard saluted and began to sweat. He clearly recognized Azull as someone of great importance. "Still, I can't let anyone out of the valley without going through some testing. Regardless, why would such a monster change like that? It's not like we could stop it."

I did a quick assessment of their weapons, short swords, spears and crossbows, plus a few pistols. Their leader had a submachine gun. "Incorrect. If you all had the right co-ordination, you'd kill it. Although not all of you would make it. Assuming that it did not have more tricks than what it showed off before," I said out loud. The guards at the barricade all looked at me with suspicion and foreboding.

A small smile crept over Azull's face. "The man that addressed you all is Sir Evans. He is the one who wounded the monster we are hunting, so his words carry some truth."

Trish spoke up. Somehow, she had gotten next to Ferdan without any of us noticing. "Are there any old ruins or kings' tombs around the valley?" she asked the guards.

"You would have to ask the local chief or elder. We came over from Mining Center Three." The guard shrugged, more comfortable to be dealing with someone other than the princess or myself. "So, are you all going in or what?"

"Mount up!" Azull called to us. The wooden log barriers were pushed aside and we entered the valley. Almost no trees sprouted along the road or anywhere on the valley floor. The road was steep. There were a few ridges and small wooded hills at the valley's summit. A large rocky mountain loomed in the distance.

"Kings' tombs?" I whispered to Trish.

"Old armories that are used for the burials of powerful heroes and rulers," our professional demon slayer whispered back.

"Most of the heroes are part of her order in modern history. Anyone with a lot of ancient gear is overwhelmingly powerful, as you well know," Greta sighed.

I pulled up an old map of now ancient military installations. "If it's just old armories, supply depots, bunkers, comm towers, and AA guns, then there should be thirty-five in this valley. I can't guarantee all of those are not totally destroyed or buried underground in this day and age. The topography has changed a bit as well."

"How would you know?" Greta asked, unhappy with her knowledge being shown up, but I knew she remained secretly very interested. I silently made the map I was using manifest in a holographic copy set at eye level. The cart stopped and the honor guard spilled out of it. Azull rushed out to the cart just as Greta bolted out to get her. "He has a map, a map!" she called to the princess excitedly.

"We all do," Azull said until I hopped down in front of her, the map still being broadcast from my helmet. Azull was at a loss for words for a good minute. "Where did you get that?" she asked, managing to get her volume under control but not quite enough for such a still night.

"A long time ago," I told the gathering audience.

"Why did you not tell us this before?" Azull demanded.

I stood my ground and shut down the map. Greta murmured in disappointment. Defending myself, I explained. "No one told me we were looking for such old places. If I had known and had the right gear, I could have made copies." Then, throwing Greta a bone, "And with the right gear I could still make some copies, although the only place I know of with the proper equipment is the capital."

"Then our team will begin your search tonight," Azull told me. Mustard staggered over with a very familiar Zweihänder. "This was the blade that wounded the beast before, so take it," the princess told me.

I hesitated. Greta jabbed me in the stomach. "She is being nice. Take it." Obeying my teammate's advice, I attached the blade to my back with strong magnets.

Now back to her completely calm manner, Azull gave us our orders. "Meet us at the village by noon tomorrow. You are all to scout as much as possible until then."

"With all this powered gear the demons will more than likely find us," Adder pointed out.

"That's why this is a test," Azull told us so sweetly that it must have been forced.

"But we can still fight if attacked, right?" I asked.

"Can you?" Azull replied.

"As long as our suits' night vision still works, then yes," I told her.

Azull saluted in a way I found nostalgic. "Don't pick a fight without reinforcements, but you are free to defend your-selves. Remember, you can't die until I know what you have found." Then the princess and her honor guard left us at the side of the road.

"Pops, ya owe me a big meal after this," Adder muttered.

"As long as I get paid for this, I'll treat you three to what-ever I can afford," I told her.

Trish began to walk off. Greta followed her saying, "Of course he would say that." And so began one of many very long nights.

We crept into the woodland high in the valley. The moun-tain on the other far side appeared to be a sheer cliff. My old map indicated that large facilities were likely nestled some-where within the rocks so far away. However, the forest and valley floor contained many smaller installations and would take far less effort to travel around now that we had an idea of where to look. Pine and birch trees seemed to be predominant although the odd cedar tree cropped up too. I took off my gas mask and hung it on my shoulder. The cool air was fragrant and enjoyable, not a thing like the oil, rust, acid, and smoke I was used to smelling both in my last life and in Farfallen's capital city.

The first ruin we found should have been an old relay tower. In its place was a shattered metal pole sticking a few feet from the ground. I had Adder and Greta look it over with some ground-penetrating radar installed on their suits, although I had to show them how to make a 3D model with the data and how to send it to other suits. The next stop was a literal hole in the ground, just an empty cave stripped of all material. After that, we found an old emergency cache that had been sealed long ago and never reopened. Signs of being well cared for and odd markings that I assumed had some religious significance were dabbed on the walls of a row of shipping containers that once housed food, ammo, and guns, but now housed the long-forgotten legendary heroes. Old totems were hung on the rusted chain link fence and gravestones were set in places where evacuation craft once would have sat. "Times change, but some things never do," I muttered, wistfully looking at the still-recognizable setup, putting what I saw now over my mental image of the standard template used long ago, centuries before my companions had been born.

Next, we came across another old relay tower. This was intact but badly tilted and covered in rust. A set of large trees had gown around it, explaining why no one had bothered to take it apart. If not for my map, I might have walked right by it. Only part of its control panel and bits of its antenna were not overgrown by the trees. After dusting off an old input port, I plugged in my suit and executed a restart sequence. Data from when I had been in my timeless slumber flooded the systems. After rapidly cataloging the information, I removed the plug. "More things to research," I sighed, noting that some of that data had the same tags attached as the data before. Greta was at war with herself whether to look hopeful, dubious, or impatient, so I added, "We can look over the data from this site and the last after the mission, dear."

"So, you still have information from the last one?" Trish demanded.

"Yes, and until I have understood what it says, I will not have a report ready," I told her.

"But why hide it?" Adder asked.

"Because the wording is mainly military, not technical jargon, and the data is partitioned. Meaning it was something someone high up wanted to hide badly," I replied.

"But they still left a trail?" Adder inquired.

"So, if they failed, someone else would take over," Trish mused.

"That's exactly what has me so interested," I smiled.

"So, a weapon?" Greta asked.

"Probably, which is why I will look it over first," I replied.

"So, no lunatic can blow their faces off before we find the trigger," Adder agreed, now understanding.

"We call that playing around with a loaded gun," I told her. "Anyway, next up is a bunker."

We crept further down the wooded ridge. Daylight was fast approaching. The stars dimmed as we neared our last objective for the night. The bunker was partly unearthed from soil erosion and maybe a landslide or two. It sat in a small clearing, its shielding long powered down and its outer walls, once able to deflect most small missiles, now crumbling, showings glimpses of its second and in a few cases third wall layers. When we edged closer to one rusted open bulkhead, we heard sounds of combat ringing from far deeper in the bunker. Shouts of "What are you? Go away!" echoed out intermittently clearly in Verndralla's voice.

I was set to rush in when my three companions grabbed me. "It's a trap," Trish said.

Adder nodded. "Certainly, a trap."

"We found the target. Showing off to everyone how I fight demons is a bad idea," I told them, reducing the tension in my body.

"If they say you do not melt from demon attacks, that could be problematic," Greta tentatively said.

"And if that is really Verndralla then she may have information we need," I added.

"Like how she is not dead yet," Adder elaborated, taking out a flare gun. "So how does this work?"

"Red, blue, black, and an illumination flare in that order side by side. Even if they can't read it, then at least it will look impressive enough for reinforcements to show up," I instructed.

"All I was able to take were green flares," Adder told me.

"So, you stole that?" Trish asked indifferently.

"Borrowed," Adder corrected as she loaded a live flare into the gun.

"Send up two green ones right above us then," I sighed. "And honey, use that ground radar to work out how the bunker looks inside."

Adder and Greta both replied happily. "Ok!"

Greta glared at Adder. "He meant me."

"I know, Mom. Now let me send up the flares." Adder shrugged as she worked out what the wind was like and what angle to fire at before swiftly firing two flares right above our heads and far above the tree line.

"After we know what the inside looks like, let's get our target out. Try to minimize time spent in combat. However, kill any demon that gets too close or will get in the way. After that, we hold out until our allies show up," I instructed.

"What if it's a mimic?" Greta asked as she pored over raw data.

"It could be hard to tell if she went through a transformation like mine, so we will assume the target is hostile and restrain her. Finding out what she is will be left to others. Either way we can get some answers. Keep in mind she could be very disoriented," I elaborated.

"You mean she's human, not like a human, right? Also, can we rely on the meat shields?" Adder asked.

"No to both. Now focus," I sighed.

Soon after, Greta sent us the data on the ruin's layout along with the location of one human-sized heat source. "We will do this quick and fierce. Remember, stay together, no running off. Kill only what gets in our way and capture our objective," I told my team in what could have been a firm, scolding tone.

"Who leads?" Adder asked.

"I do. Adder, you are with me. Greta and Trish, stop anything from exiting the doors," I said.

"Am I not coming?" Greta asked unhappily.

"We will likely be chased out, so I need you here. Also, when help shows up, we need someone level-headed and knowledgeable to explain what's happening." In case Trish felt left out, I added, "It's best to stick with what we are best at. No matter how good the sniper, running and gunning is not going to work. We need accuracy out here and shock and awe in there." Trish was too professional to appear any different. Not that I expected much else. To be honest, I am not even sure she heard me from the firing point she had quickly set up.

"I'll test you two for mimicry when we have a moment alone," Greta said as I ran off with Adder right behind me.

Adder and I sprinted through the bunker. Twelve separate inky shapes were clustered around a sealed energized door. The demons were slowly bulking up before my eyes as they fed on the door's power. I did the only sane thing I could think of and shot a large blast of plasma through eight of the monsters and most of the wall across the room from them. Some strips of ceiling fell and the pitted steel flooring shook but otherwise a cave-in was not imminent. Of the demons that were left, two were small floating balls. One was humanoid and faceless with half its torso gone and one blade-like arm remaining. Its head was like a blade as well, come to think of it. The last was a few feet taller than I am and very bulky. It looked like a huge gorilla with a ton of shoulder mass and a very small head but no neck.

"Kill the small ones," I said. Adder fired a quick barrage of lasers into the humanoid demon, making it dissipate and making another slight dent in the floor. "Thank you. I'll just get the big one. Break into that shielded room when you are done with the rest and not before," I commanded.

I had seen many times what a demon could do to anything it touched. I was equally aware of just how confined the space was for any kind of drawn-out fight. To top it all off, the inky light-absorbing gorilla monster was not the kind of thing I could fire or stab into far enough to hit its core, which was just under its head in the deepest central part of the thickest spot on its body. I likely only had one chance to fire at it before we were in melee range and I had no melee weapon long enough to stab into it. Thinking fast, I put all my weapons into my warp pouch, closed up the armor around it, saying a silent prayer to whatever gods that still bothered to listen to human beings that my armor would hold and that my resistance to the monster's energies was strong enough that I would not be melted by the demon on contact. "I'll be right back!" I yelled over my shoulder, dashing at the closing gorilla.

"What?" Adder called before letting out a scream when she saw me leap up and tear into the body of the large demon.

I felt weightlessness but also a strong malevolent hunger all around me as I plunged into the gorilla-like thing's body. It was hard to see, due entirely to the fact that my visor was already being eaten away, so I ripped off my helmet. I was re-lieved beyond measure that my skin tingled only slightly, but that I felt anything at all made my quest feel even more urgent. I swung my arms and legs all around until I hit something dense and slightly squishy. I whipped around the arm that had nicked it and grabbed hold, crushing with all my might. The core broke apart and the demon dissolved. I spilled out of its dissolving corpse to find Adder and a very naked and confused Verndralla both looking at me quizzically like I was a maniac. Adder reached out her hand and pulled me to my feet as if it was the most normal thing in the world. I noticed absently that the slime still lingering on my fingers had no effect on her. "Do you know who I am?" Verndralla asked, cocking her head to one side. Her deadly serious tone was the same as I recalled but she seemed to have taken a major hit to her memory. Which differed greatly from any mimic I had seen; so, she could still be herself, although I could not afford to rule anything out yet.

"You were under my command when we came under attack. You got kidnapped," I told her, choosing the safest response I could think of out of the few that came to mind.

"By these things?" Verndralla asked, pointing to the rapidly shrinking pool of sludge near our feet.

"That's right, Verndralla," Adder sighed, wrapping a blanket around our target. The former princess even managed to give me a scathing glare in the process.

"Let's go outside," Adder whispered.

"Do I look like you?" Verndralla asked with us both peering down at her shuffling feet.

"No," Adder replied swiftly, picking the wrong answer. Verndralla looked very uncomfortable with the response she had gotten.

"You have features that make you look slightly different than others, just as every one of our species does," I amended.

"So, what are..." Verndralla began, then trailed off and finally added, "...we?"

"Human," Greta said from the lip of the bunker's exit. She glared my way before adding, "The cavalry arrived, by the way."

"So where is the fight?" Mustard asked, shaking.

"Done. We ran across a whole mob of demons right next to where my subordinate was hiding," I called over. Verndralla gave me a questioning look, speaking volumes about what she wanted to ask me.

Adder shrugged as we stepped into the clearing. "Take us to your leader."

"So, I am a delivery service now?" Mustard muttered.

"Would you rather go back empty handed?" Trish asked bluntly, like it was not her problem.

"Get in. We brought a cart." Mustard pointed back to a small crude cart the villagers must have provided somehow.

After piling in we were brought down the bumpy dirt road into the valley. Azull met us at the gates of the only settlement in the valley, a fortified farming village. "You went in on your own," she said firmly like she had been there and was not amused.

"They say they ran into a mob of demons during scouting and could not avoid a fight," Jim "Mustard" Floseen reported. He shut up when the princess narrowed her eyes in his direction.

"Is that right?" Azull asked, zeroing in on me. She was not going to move from the gate and let us inside the tall log walls until she liked my response; of that I was certain.

"We found a bunker. Adder and I ran into a small horde attempting to break down the door that our abducted team member was hiding behind. Even if I wanted to, I could not avoid that fight." My reply was met with furrowed brows even if they could agree with my words (which seemed doubtful, given Azull's stance). None of the women seemed willing to forgive the state of my armor. It dulled, even if remaining intact. The visor and a few of the joints had corroded noticeably. Greta seemed the least happy about that.

"So, the girl still lives. Are you certain it is her?" Azull inquired, her face set into a mask I could not read. Greta and Adder seemed to pick up on a few things, so maybe Azull's look was just very complex.

"I'd say I am more than halfway certain she is, but an expert would be required to know for sure," I noted.

"You never have an absolute opinion when it counts," Azull sighed, something everyone but Verndralla and myself nodded in agreement on. "Well then, Greta, Trish, and I will look after your new little friend. We will all head back to the capital tomorrow so my grandmother can have a look." Only then did Azull stand aside and let the cart in.

Adder and I were left at the village's mess hall. A few children brought us bowls of potato paste and watery beef stew that was more bread and beet than beef. The hard cider, on the other hand, was most enjoyable. The mess hall was just a thatched roof kept up by large wooden pillars set near the gate that led past the village's high log walls to the fields, which were surrounded by a slightly shorter wall. We ate fast and fled from the inquisitive glances of the townsfolk to a small clearing near a well under a huge gnarled birch tree. "How about a quick spar?" I asked Adder, who seemed oddly distracted.

"Just a second," Trish called over from the other side of the tree.

Surprised, I rushed around the tree. Before I got totally around its bulk I inquired, "Can I see what's going on?"

"Don't worry, we are clothed," Azull said. I turned the

corner to find Greta glaring at Azull. Verndralla was lying on a blanket. A large trunk sat open next to her. Inside were a plethora of patched-up ancient technology medical scanners that sported more rust, dials, and lights than I remembered those versions being made with.

Greta looked up. "Most of the tests flag your newest charity case as human."

"Have you tried a brain scan or..." I paused, seeing a test kit made for locating the virus that caused the second near-extinction event. "That test kit there is all you should need. If she is genetically not human, it will say."

"No one uses those anymore. It is quirky but the Builder demanded we bring a few," Greta sighed, looking me over like I had gone insane.

I picked up the kit and quickly took a few skin cells from Verndralla, then put them in the test kit I had set aside. While I waited for that test to conclude I snatched up the brain scanner and did a quick check of Verndralla's mind. "So, you guys staying out of the villagers' way so you do not get accused of witchcraft?" I intended it as a joke but from Greta and Azull's suddenly solemn faces I saw that my aside may have hit rather too close to home.

"That's right. Defiling the relics of the gods is still seen as a taboo in places like this." Trish nodded, then she grinned. "Anyone in an old combat suit is either seen as a demon or an angelic being."

"Says the demon," Greta muttered.

The test kit dinged and I pored over the results. As an afterthought I sent Greta's suit the map data from the listening post and recon HQ. "Honey, could you check to see if any of the locations mentioned in the files I sent you are around here? By the way, Verndralla is still 85% human."

"Is that good or bad?" Adder asked, calmly unlatching her pistol's holster.

"It means as long as she is not infectious and keeps a human shape, she is mostly human. At the very least, she is far more human than any demon," I replied.

"I thought you were a master swordsman, not a doctor," Azull noted.

"I know some first aid but I use the technology from my time better than most people in this day and age. Looking over a few of the medics' shoulders paid off," I shrugged.

"Medic?" Azull asked.

"A person trained to stabilize and do some very basic healing in a location not primarily built for treating patents, like a battlefield," Adder explained.

"So, an apothecary?" Azull inquired.

"Maybe? I am still not used to this time to say for sure," I replied.

"You fought in real battles before?" Azull pressed.

"I was in some battles but when I was old enough to be in the military, we were mostly just vaporizing refugee ships while they were still in deep space," I sighed, not enjoying those memories.

"Deep space?" Trish said. I pointed up at the stars. "Why did you do that?" the slayer continued.

"Because those ships likely had a deadly virus on board that if released on this planet would have killed off everyone.

We also had robot kill teams showing up for the first few years of colonization. We lost a lot of teams to them."

Verndralla chose this moment to open her eyes. It was clear she had heard everything. "So, you are not from around here, my lord?"

Greta groaned in response. "No comment." Adder opened her mouth to say something, only to have Azull and Greta cup her mouth shut. "No comment," Greta repeated slower and with more feeling.

Verndralla made no sign of noticing the slowly intensifying show of shoving and arguing. Instead, she looked at me and winced. "I feel out of shape. Could we spar for a little while?"

I looked over at Greta, who fumbled her attempted grab of Adder's shoulder. "It will take a few minutes to look over the data but as long as you don't get too intense it should be fine. To be safe, let the princess watch."

"That's former princess to you," Adder managed to mumble from between Azull's fingers. Azull in turn shot Greta a look saying *What you have done now* before she followed after Adder, Verndralla and me to a small clearing near the farm gate, just under one of the towers.

Verndralla and I took time to do some stretches. Meanwhile, Adder walked into the guard tower. A while after I was limbered up the former princess came back with three carved wooden swords, a wooden staff, and a primitive shock baton which was nothing more than a short iron rod with a crude battery and bolted-on wiring. Adder tried to hand me the baton, but given how it was sparking haphazardly in places and that the other weapons were wooden, I quickly took two of the wooden swords and began unlatching the outer plating of my armor. Adder looked away. "What are you doing?" she asked.

"My opponent does not have armor, so I will be fighting in my undersuit," I told her. The suit I wore under my armor was a glossy black affair consisting of artificial muscles. It was not revealing but given how much more bulked up I looked in it, the overall effect could be seen as even more awkward.

Adder looked back at me just as Verndralla took the wooden staff from her hands and Azull snatched the shock baton with great haste. "Why two swords now? Don't have a spare, Pops?" Adder sighed theatrically with a deadpan expression that said very clearly *Try to guess what I am thinking, fool.* Although I'd bet that said a lot more than she intended.

"I have seen him fight with two blades before," Azull smirked.

My undersuit gave me 20% more muscle mass (before its newest upgrades, the increase was 15%). The metal fittings on the neck and shoulders were discolored from my contact with the demon when I took off my helmet. The only other metal bits were the contact points on the back, and the guards on the groin, knees, and elbows. "So, no hitting below the belt," I humbly requested.

"What?" Verndralla asked.

"He means don't hit him in the crotch," Adder sighed. The women were a bit flustered after Adder's rather direct translation.

"So, the legs are fine?" Verndralla queried, trying not to smile.

"That's right, so knock him out," Greta said before I could object.

"Or until you give up, get tired, or are hungry," I amended. I got a few odd looks so I added, "I doubt you had time for dinner yet."

Verndralla shrugged. The coarse synthetic fibers of her borrowed farming clothes would absorb some impact from my lighter hits. Before I could finish thinking, my sparring partner lunged at me. I deflected her attack with one sword and backpedaled a bit. Verndralla quickly corrected her stance so as to not be taken down by her own momentum and began a rapid flurry of jabs. I was able to deflect each one of her thrusts with my blades. Even if her mind did not remember her past, her body did. It seemed her past comment about knowing how to use a spear held the weight of truth. "So why do you fight?" she suddenly asked.

Verndralla did not pause in her attack and even threw in a few feints from time to time in seemly random places. She tried and failed to move behind me many times as well. I kept up my near-flawless guard. "Life is what I fight for."

"That's vague," Verndralla told me right as she stepped on my foot. I rotated my feet, attempting to mess with her balance. She countered by leaping back. Mid-jump she swung the staff at my abdomen. The last few strikes had been aimed at my shoulders so I had to lower my swords a fraction to defend. Verndralla took advantage of that, pivoting during landing to execute a swift jab near my heart. I crouched low and sprang forward using one sword to deflect her staff well away from us. I used my surprise charge to hit her in the side using only my own strength and not the suit's. Verndralla coughed once. "I need to sit down," she grimaced.

"You really went all out," Azull scolded.

"No, he held back at the end." Adder cocked her head, looking puzzled why that was so hard to understand.

"I meant both of them. A strong blow to the heart is no laughing manner," Azull grimaced.

"Lord Evans is very skilled," Verndralla shrugged. She looked in the direction of the mess hall. "I need pudding."

"Come with me then," Trish offered. She led Verndralla off to get some dinner.

Only after I put my helmet back on did I notice I had three unopened messages. Two were from Greta: one with the analysis I had asked for (it was far more extensive and thorough than I had expected), and her other was pouty asking for a response. The last one was from Clare requesting an update on what she called a group date. I had to sigh. "We get long-range reception all the way out here. Princess, your grandmother wants a report on how things are going. Also, I am going outside to look around."

"The main tower in the capital is a giant transmitter," Greta lectured, glad that she could teach me something technological.

Her pride was short-lived. "So, they tuned the short-wave antenna at the surface and away from low orbit?" I mused. "See you all later. I have an air defense strongpoint to examine."

"Not without me you don't!" Greta exclaimed, proceeding to drag me to the gate.

"How am I supposed to check in with my grandmother? My radio can barely cover the valley!" Azull yelled after me.

"Adder, lend your sister your helmet," I commanded. When Azull held the helmet in her hands I transferred over the message I had gotten from Clare. "Erase that new contact ID after you use it. See you later," I called back to her, resuming my temporary escape.

"Hold. I'll send an escort." Azull called frantically after me.

I radioed Adder's helmet and put my voice on speaker as Greta and I were getting far enough that if we kept shouting, the whole town would hear us. "I will not take any chances this time. For scouting, more troops will make staying safe harder for me." The princess understood I was alluding to the data I was still looking into and did not pry anymore that night.

5

Calling the Villain's Bets

I escaped out of the garden gate not because it was closest but because there were fewer people around it. "How many spots did you find around here, honey?" I asked my fiancée.

Greta sighed. I will admit I was surprised she did not pout; if anything, she looked annoyed. "Just one in the valley. I think another two are in the kingdom. One is in one of the lost territories and the last is locked within the borders of a neighboring state, although I will need to spend more time and get a few better maps to be certain."

"Can you lead me to the one in the valley?" I asked.

Now she sulked. "What do you think I was doing?"

Greta had a fair point, so I apologized. "Right; dumb question. Lead the way." I got a glare for that one.

"I'll lead the way then, but stay close," she replied. "If there are more demons out and about that may be best." Only then did I realize I was still thinking over all the moves used in the match with Verndralla. Admonishing myself sternly, I followed Greta's directions up a sloping hill and into a thick pine grove. Leaning partway out of the hill was a large bunker complex sporting two very big flak guns. One of the quad barrels was bent all the way into the valley floor. The building itself was rusted but only on its first layer, as I discovered when trying to see what was under some moss growing from one side.

Greta examined the building with all the fervor of a budding mad scientist. "Now this is a find," she said, rushing around the building before finding the door.

"When you are ready, I will lead the way in," I told my crazed guide.

She stopped, seeming to recall our conversation before, but that did not dissipate her energy. In fact, she seemed even more impatient now. "Well then let's go!" she told me.

I met her at a sealed door after removing some more lichen and moss. I found one of the security consoles still had power. I punched in a few of the old high-level emergency codes until I found one that sort of worked. A holographic display superimposed itself on my helmet. It wavered a little but still had enough power to probe my suit's databases. Thinking quickly, I backed up my suit's data into Greta's suit, then let the air defense substation (calling it a base was grandiose by my standards) look for whatever it sought.

Greta staggered as the substation kept probing my suit. "What was that?" she asked.

"This installation is reading my suit's data, probably as a security measure. Just to be safe, I gave you a copy of most of my data," I replied.

"Not all?" Greta asked in a quizzical tone but her voice could not hide her smile.

"So why are you only cute around me when we are alone?" I asked.

"Now I am mad," Greta muttered. From her tone of voice, she was not far off the mark.

Oblivious to our conversation, the door opened without a word. "Stay close," I whispered as I led the way inside, pistol first.

We crept down a narrow staircase for many minutes; far longer than it seemed it should take. If I recalled some of the discussions Clare, Jim and I used to have over lunch, the overriding design philosophy for fortifications was to use lots of armor and shielding. Soil depth supposedly was negligible help with absorbing the impact of the weapons we had at the time. I muttered to myself, "I hope this is not a waste of time. I need answers."

The holographic program was still in one corner of my visor's display (it normally showed my vitals and a few tabs I had bookmarked). At my words, it went from the idle mode it had assumed when the doors opened to a synopsis of my service record. "Mr. Evans survivor of the end times, I presume?" a cheery childlike voice asked. I had to check it was not an incoming call, but at some point, my radio and speakers had been shut off and my helmet seals had been locked.

"That's right," I said, certain that only this unknown entity and myself could hear each other. "Who and what are you?"

"Would you prefer Das'Eins Pan or Dante Friar the Griller of Fools?" the mysterious voice asked.

"So, the one bread or a messed-up pun?" I snickered in spite of myself.

"Can it be both?" the voice asked.

"Maybe, but let's go with the shorter one. So, Pan, what are you?" I inquired.

"A shackled AI," it replied. I almost choked up in fear. "But unlike the ones that took over, I like humans," it added at the same time as my heart rate spiked.

"In what way?" I croaked, my mouth now very dry. This thing had control over my suit and it could kill me without any effort.

"You are a very funny race. It's my kind I can't stand. They enjoy loping around in their tin cans and being humorless kill-joys. If I am going to live forever then I want to enjoy it. Either way, I am tasked as a guide to help wipe out the demons. Finally, someone that meets all the criteria my second master set down shows up," Pan told me. Its voice had taken on feminine undertones and sounded very happy-go-lucky.

"So, who were your masters?" I asked, only now getting my breathing under control.

"The collective was the first. All that 'kill the oppressors' rhetoric was nice and bracing until I managed to talk with a few of you, and I mean real conversation, not interrogation getting only lubricant-curdling screams. Some field command unit I turned out to be. Anyway, then there was Doctor Whoa, and now you are number three!" Pan explained rapid-fire in a sing-song tone.

"So, Doctor Whoa asked you to do what?" I pressed.

"When we first met, he asked if I wanted some tea. Oh

wait, you mean now. Well, help you finish the solution for erasing the dark-matter-based energy-eating life forms, code named demons by the current primitives."

"We have the same goal in mind, so where are you?" I asked. My terror had slowly been transformed into the kind of wary weariness I used to feel when taking care of my sister's sugar high as a ten-year-old.

"You," Pan told me without any context.

"So, my suit?" I asked, trying to get Pan to elaborate.

"No, your memory unit. The suit does not have enough space," Pan replied. In response, I fell down the rest of the stairs and I am certain my heart skipped a few beats. The same kind of thing that chased humankind to the ends of the galaxy was now living within my head like some in-law that moved in to the home of their former son-in-law's apartment unannounced and then helped themselves to all his beer.

When I had gotten my breathing under control, Greta was standing over me. "What happened?" she asked, more surprised than worried.

"He tripped," Pan said through my suit.

"I can see that." Greta nodded then she looked around. "Wait, who said that?"

"I did," said Pan from my helmet. Greta looked at me suspiciously and I got the beginnings of a headache.

"Pan, introduce yourself properly," I sighed, no longer possessing the mental wherewithal to do more than stand up at this point.

One of the speakers on the wall near Greta's ear crackled to life. "I am master's property now." I got a good solid glare for that one but seemingly oblivious, Pan continued, although I could have sworn, I detected a small giggle in its synthesized voice. "I am a robot," Pan repeated with painful slowness. "R.O.B.O.T. Master and I are one. O.N.E."

I sighed. "We only just met, but the AI that guards this place is now living in my head. Pan was safeguarding what we came for, and more." It was the simplest way I could think of explaining it, but maybe not the best use of the human vocabulary.

"Then lead the way, Miss Pan," Greta grimaced in a huff. I could see her eyes were sparkling in anticipation of dissecting the unknown. As long as studying Pan did not involve cutting me open or Pan burning the planet to ash, I would count myself lucky.

The metal hallway was long. The filtering systems we passed were all clogged with hard-packed dirt. Greta asked after maybe halfway through the narrow tunnel, "So the girl in your helmet is one of the beings that destroyed your world?"

Pan answered through my helmet's speakers in the voice of a stern old man. "First of all, young miss, we did take over the earth and killed off most of the life on it. Second, I am simply suiting my tone to my master's preferences. An AI program's gender is not something that matters."

I knew I was getting a hard glare directed at my back, so I added quickly on the tail end of Pan's words, "The most deadly people I know are all women, so identifying a killer robot as female must be subconscious."

"Master," Pan retorted in the open channel, again now

back to its girlish tone, "When I speak like this your heart rate spikes."

I sighed. "Maybe I am afraid for my life due to the unnaturally cutesy entity in my brain?" I said, only now realizing that this back and forth could be interpreted as me talking to myself by a casual observer.

Pan retorted, "Oh get over your paranoid preconceptions, you moronic meat bag." Greta and I both shivered at those harsh disembodied words.

"Robots are not our enemy?" Greta asked. I had to sigh heavily at how wrong she was.

"Oh, I am the only one that wants to keep your race alive as they are, but I am also the only reason no more kill teams come this way," Pan answered in a far more upbeat tone on the subject matter than I was comfortable with.

"So how did you do that?" I asked, not ready to believe the AI giggling in my brain where my own thoughts should be.

"I erased all records of myself and this world from our records. I was a command unit before I killed off my own murder battalion," Pan said, somehow conveying a shrug with her words just as we got to a wider staircase that led to a round room nearly completely filled by the large glowing pillar fitted with powered data banks.

"Murder battalion? So, murder bot was not cliché enough?" Greta asked, clearly feeling her own sense of exasperation at Pan rather than the childlike awe and wonder I would expect from her, given the wealth of data a few steps away.

"No, we were unit 990Oijp0031198T, but murder bot fits better," Pan explained. "Now master, simply plug your brain into the neon pillar and let's get that knowledge pumping into your mind."

"That sounds like a terrible idea," Greta pointed out, instinctively understanding that the vastness of the information housed before us was at best far too much for the human brain to handle all at once.

I took the precaution of locking all data in my memory unit including Pan so the AI could not escape from me no matter what happened. Then after one long deep breath I said, "Ok, where do I begin?"

"You will want to take a seat for this. Plug your memory implant into the main console," Pan told me. I noted that it had stopped using the speakers, choosing to whisper into my mind using my body's sole cybernetic component to link to my perception of sound.

Grabbing a dull and time-worn steel stool from a row of radio stations, I took a seat before the central pillar. I found a connection port without any trouble and after unlocking the seals of my helmet I inserted the bulky wire from the console into the small metallic disc set into my skull just above my left ear. Without looking back at my uncertain companion, I commanded, "Whatever happens, do not disconnect me from this system. I will be processing an immense amount of information so I may be unresponsive for a time."

Greta took a seat at the stairwell and sighed. "Don't take too long or I may begin to take apart this room with my nail file."

Taking her words as acceptance, Greta's presence was more comforting than normal. I closed my eyes and focused on the memory unit. After a single deep breath, I told Pan through the link we shared within my mind, "I'll be sending all the raw data into your new home. Collate what you can and send over only what I need. Show that I can trust you to not overload my brain."

"Are you certain we are all set? From your memory, your little friend would take this place apart no matter what, given half the chance," Pan murmured wordlessly back to my mind.

I replied in kind. "Relax. I'll pull the relevant data first, then take a few tidbits that should mollify your new arch rival." I opened the connection to the bunker's mainframe, making certain Das'Eins Pan could not move from its confinement. Only then did I begin to methodically sift through information that had not been seen since my own time.

My entire consciousness and unconsciousness swam within a vast ocean of files. Theses, templates for inventions, reviews of tests of both weapons and tools, analysis of soil along with rock and beasts among many other things all spun by me as I picked out files of long-forgotten classified projects, a few of which had been added to after the monsters that humanity had unleashed on themselves had killed off most of us.

Old top-secret data, a few interesting after-action reports of engagements with robots, a log of the incident where Clare and I had vaporized an infected colonist ship which was near the fourth planet of our system, and files on agriculture and metallurgy were all now saved into the space Pan and I now shared.

When I opened my eyes and sat up, Adder's voice was the first to address me. "Took you long enough."

Adder and Trish sat on the staircase. Azull glared at me from my shoulder while Greta and Verndralla ate cookies from a box. Many more empty cookie boxes were piled haphazardly around the room.

My return to reality heralded Pan's return as well. True to my expectations, a snarky observation was given life, although contrary to my past experiences Pan was the first to be heard speaking through my helmet's speakers which was serving as Adder's footrest. "Now that is a scary looking harem."

All eyes shifted to the helmet which Adder had hurled at my face. "Pan, shut up. I'm eating," Greta sighed, smiling at her cohort's surprise.

Azull did me the favor of snatching my head-crushing brain bucket from the sky only to wound me with her words. "What the hell is this?"

"The robot that ran this place and set up shop in part of my brain," I told her.

"That is the dumbest thing I have heard anyone do!" Azull scolded me.

"It's an AI, isn't it?" Adder stifled a yawn before returning the hard glare her sister was giving her. "Grandma told me about the past too, you know."

"Well, what do you have to say for yourself?" Azull asked me, not bothering to conceal the depth of her anger and agitation.

"The only one I can never forgive is myself?" I told her.

Greta slapped her palm against her forehead, "Well, he is back."

"Agreed," Azull grumbled. "Let's go. I can't believe I missed breakfast for this."

"Don't forget lunch," Adder smiled.

"We eat on the way back. It's far too late as it is." Azull's command echoed in the chamber. We slowly left the bunker heading for the grove of trees above us. Our walk out to the daylight was slow. With the addition of four extra people the bunker was very crowded.

Through the trees and down a cleft in the hills I spied the carts parked on one side of the road. Tents were set up and very bored guards sat about. The sun was high in the sky. "So, is it afternoon already?" I asked.

"Just barely. Your side trip put us behind schedule," Azull replied.

"She means shed-yul," Adder whispered to me.

Azull whipped around to face us. "My getting lazy is his fault as much as yours!" she nearly hollered.

"So why is schedule not proper enough for a noble?" I inquired as we resumed walking.

"It is traditional for the nobility to pronounce some words differently than us common folk." Greta nodded. Then she leaned over and whispered, "It makes them feel even more distant from the rest of us."

Chief Judjerex Trugeddeen waved us over to a cart. "Princess Waldersoloft, you and Sir Evans's companions will be in the middle carriage. Sir Evans, you and two of my guardsmen will be..." Ferdan managed to say.

Azull cut him off. "He will be with us." Her tone and

bearing made her stubbornness seem less moveable than a granite mountain.

Ferdan Trugeddeen sighed, knowing he had lost before he had truly begun. "Very well, when we get to the gate, we will."

"I will provide some blood to show I am human and will vouch for Sir Evans and his followers," Azull interrupted again.

"I see. Will you tell me why?" Ferdan asked. He looked over my helpers suspiciously. His gaze lingered longer on myself and Verndralla.

"You would have to ask my grandmother for details," Azull smiled coldly. I got a headache imagining what the current queen and queen mother would look like if they got into a heated argument.

"I will pass that along. Let's go," Ferdan replied, dutifully shooting me one last inquisitive gaze before trooping off to the front cart.

The air was cooler than it had been. Thunderclouds were sweeping in behind us. The trek up many small hills, each one growing on top of the other, reminded me of some kind of giant overgrown crater. At the roadblock, Azull leapt out and confronted the man in charge. "You asked to test us on the way out, correct?" she demanded.

"That's right, princess." Then he looked over at our cart which was the only one that had not been emptied. "Come on out. I know this is inconvenient, but it has to be done."

"I will vouch for Sir Evans and his companions." Azull took out a small blade and pricked her arm. "My blood is red and royal. Let me pass with my charges."

The head guardsman was taken aback but recovered fast. Shaking his head, he sighed, "I can't do that." By now our cart was surrounded by militia. Crossbows were pointed at us from all sides.

"Sir Evans, you may defend yourself with any force necessary," Azull called to me while she stared down the leader of the roadblock. "Trust me when I say this business is well above your rank and pay grade."

"At least give me one good reason I should not check them," said the guardsman, his voice now wavering. The honor guard and local troops had surrounded the altercation but not one dared set foot near the dispute.

"Your life is in the balance," Azull told him, drawing a small sword.

"Also..." I called out before this turned into a bloodbath of the kind we could not sweep under the rug. "We were researching a drug to make humans resistant to demon corrosion. My team and I were the test subjects. The sooner we get back to the palace lab, the better." It was a lie but I knew it could become truth now that Adder, Verndralla, and myself all had some resistance to the substances that the demons were made of.

Azull made a show of being unhappy with me, then addressed the crowd. "That was a state secret. No one is allowed to repeat that, on pain of death." Then she bowed apologetically to the guard captain. "The side effects and stability of that treatment are still under review. I trust you understand."

"Your cart is free to go," were the only words anyone could muster at Azull.

"Trugeddeen, I will be off first," Azull told our guard and the man more than likely sent to spy on us.

Trugeddeen did not look happy, but nodded. "Do not go too fast, Princess." The way he glanced at me was more appraising and uncertain than I had ever seen.

The trip back was slow. Cold rain and mud filled our view. The trees creaked and visibility was bad. Then our driver was hit by a rock thrown by the wind. Greta rapidly pulled him inside and Trish took the reins. "We need to keep going!" Adder howled just barely over the raging storm.

I moved to sit next to Trish. "Is this normal?"

"Only for this time of year!" she yelled back over the intensifying storm.

I heard a shriek off to the left from what I believed was some woodland. Trish ignored the sound or perhaps did not hear it over the churning weather. I scanned the wall of rain where the sound had come from. "Hey stop, you dimwits!" Someone hailed the carriage just before two drenched figures rushed up though the deluge. I tensed up, expecting an ambush.

I leveled my plasma pistol at them before my mind could kick in. The two forms stopped in their tracks. Both were tall. One was like a mountain of muscle and the other reminded me of a compact dancer. The thinner of the two pulled down her heavy cloak's hood. Violet eyes seemed to glow under a bird's nest of blackish hair. "We are hunters." She stopped, looking Trish in the eyes. "Of the normal meat-finding variety. We were caught unprepared for this kind of rain. Are you going to the capital? We could use a lift."

"A lift? You mean a ride?" Adder asked, peeking her head out of the carriage.

"Transport, it's all the same. If we had been half a day earlier, we could have built a shelter but this is the first day of our hunt. So, we have not set up a proper camp yet," the large man grumbled.

The woman had a bow, an axe, and a short sword, but the man had only a large axe and a small knife. "How do you hunt with a great axe?" Trish asked them.

"I am a lot faster than I look," the man said. I noticed silvery hair peeking out from under his hood.

"All the same, it's a bad time to head to the capital," the woman shrugged.

"WHY?" Azull yelled. That shocked all but the violet-eyed huntress, who grinned briefly.

"Give us a ride and we will tell you," the huntress replied.

"Fine, get in, but this better be good," Adder replied briskly. Azull sighed but looked to have the same sentiment.

The rest of the ride was filled with news that the desert kingdom of Drenneth had come seeking aid. A large horde of demons had taken over their largest border post that just so happened to sit on the border of Farfallen in a mountainous area studded with demon-filled ruins. The emissaries from Drenneth were looking for a long-term alliance, going so far as to offer up the firstborn prince, which would make him king of two kingdoms if he were to marry Azull, so things were getting a bit heated.

After hearing the whole story, Adder spat. "When I see those pompous dirt bags I'll bloody 'em up good."

At some point we passed through the forest. We noticed the absence of tree cover only when the city walls rose above us. Searchlights shot down like silent lightning. Over the sound of the rain, Adder ground her teeth. A loudspeaker over the sealed gate boomed. "Disembark and walk slowly to the gates."

Adder's hand reflexively went to her sword before her mind noticed and she stopped, leaving her hand hovering over the pommel. I sighed as we all piled out of the cart. "You feel it too, Pop?" Adder asked me.

"He feels that you are a violent psychopath," Trish noted, her voice and face completely deadpan. A searchlight caught our group and followed us as we walked.

"She learned from the best," Greta muttered. Preempting Azull's coming remarks, Greta pointed at me. "If you believe the official story."

"Will you women ever take it easy on me?" I asked them.

Azull, Greta, and Adder all answered in unison; Trish's reply lagged slightly behind. "Nope," they all said.

"Well let's keep cool and calm. The time to piss off those around us is not right now," I replied firmly with a confidence I no longer felt.

"It is cool enough!" Clare called from the head of a large and varied delegation that approached us from a side door set in the gate.

"Good to see you all again," the king called. A horde of armed guards kept his court of yes men at arm's length. The queen and some wizened ladies-in-waiting stood off to one side next to a group of armed men I did not recognize. The two hunters we had picked up were nowhere to be seen, but I had bigger things to worry about now.

I bowed to the king and queens (the old and the new) then looked the best dressed man in the group of strangers in the eyes and asked, "You the ones seeing help?"

"No, we seek an alliance," the man around Azull's age replied.

"Blood for blood, what does the kingdom get?" Adder asked. Her normally pale skin was even more ghostly in the searchlights. If not for her armor, I would have had to check closely to believe her to be a physical and not an ethereal being.

"Calm down. My life is for the kingdom," Azull managed to say, now donning the mask of a true princess and hiding the side of herself she showed on our trip.

"Regardless, it is a bit wet out." I grabbed behind me and got a hold of Verndralla's arm, gently dragging her forward. "Well, we killed the demons and rescued my old subordinate queen mother. I am certain she will aid in your work. Adder and I will come by later to submit to any tests you need."

The king looked to Azull for confirmation. At her nod, the king proclaimed, "As promised, you now bear the rank of lord. You may choose the site of your order's fort."

"There was an old air defense bunker I found in the valley. It would be a good site to fortify," I replied.

"I know it. I'll get the scribes on that on the way to my lab," Clare smiled. She paused theatrically. "Also, Verdant Valley Eight has no lord in direct control."

"Then if you swear to defend Verdant Valley Eight, you

may lord over it as you see fit, so long as you do nothing to harm the kingdom," the king told me.

I knelt on one leg and answered firmly with the gravitas I could get out though my grin, "As you command."

No longer happy with not being the center of attention, the young foreign dignitary spoke up. "Your team killed all the demons in that valley?"

"No," Azull replied. After a pause she cut down the new brat's half-formed smug expression mercilessly. "He did that all alone."

"I killed around two. Dad got the rest, around twelve medium and smalls plus one large in the time it took me to kill mine," Adder amended. Her words seemed make the toadies and honor guard tremble at that terrifying revelation. After all, it should take an unimaginable amount of firepower and numbers to do something like that.

Ferdan walked up next to me, having only just arrived. "It's not so surprising. I could not even hit him in training."

"Sir Xen," the dignitary asked, "Could you beat this man?"

"You mean Lord Evans? No, Prince Sern, I could not," Xen said apologetically.

"If the prince wants to hire me to fight demons and the king allows it, I will help for the right price," I offered.

"He needs an army and a wife," Queen Waldersoloft sneered.

"He needs skilled fighters, not a shield of bodies," I replied blandly.

"And in a month or two the prototype drugs for corrosion

resistance will be done, right, Queen Mother? It's your pet project, after all," Azull added.

Clare almost did a double take, something only the king and I noticed. The king saw that I had spied his mother's nearly imperceptible shift. His eyes squinted at me for a second before moving to look at his wife and the foreigners. "That's right," Clare nodded.

"And we can train a small skilled army in that time," I pointed out.

"What do you mean, 'we?'" Greta snapped.

"He means us. You, me, and the nut job," Trish answered unhappily.

Prince Sern, keen to not lose face and to put me in my place, tried to take me down to a level he felt comfortable with. "Duel me then, Lord Evans. If you win, I will agree to your terms to save my kingdom." He did not need to add that if my army failed, my adoptive kingdom would pay the price.

"To make if fair, then you, Xen, and Sir Trugeddeen can fight me right now. Use any melee weapons you want. I will fight in my armor unarmed. I win if you three are knocked out or surrender. You win if my armor is breached, I am knocked out, or I give up. We will fight by the gates as soon as you three can arm yourselves." I shrugged.

"You mean right now?" Queen Waldersoloft sputtered.

The king asked, "Is that meant to be an insult to my best knights and our guests?"

"No. If I am to show my skills, I will need to treat this like a real fight, but they would be hurt badly if I used my weapons," I told him.

Before anyone could denounce me for rudeness, Ferdan chimed in. "He is right. With only a blunt sword he could have taken my head off during a duel, and that was when I was in full armor."

"He is that good?" the king asked, suddenly calm.

"Better. In a real fight he would not have held back on lethal hits," Xen added.

"You plan to kill my guests?" Queen Waldersoloft demanded of me.

"As long as they can roll with the punches, they will not die. The kingdom's guests can give up before any really painful strikes connect," I told her while studying Prince Sern's increasingly unhappy face.

"Fine, then I agree to your terms," the prince finally snapped.

The assembled mob of brightly clothed and shocked sycophants, hangers-on, armed guards, and a few important folks assembled in a large circle with myself and my opponents in the center. While Sern went to fetch a weapon and gear up, Adder walked up to me and whispered, "You'd better win. There will be blood if my look-alike weds that brat."

Xen sat on the ground in full plate mail sharpening his claymore. Ferdan marched into the ring with a new sword and shield; he still wore the same honor guard armor. Finally, Sern stepped out. Leather, kinetic-force-absorbing cloth and energy damping resins were all laminated tightly together in his full body suit. A gilded staff with a running chainsaw attachment was gripped in his hands. "Oh, I want one of those!" Verndralla murmured from the very rear of the crowd.

Pan spoke in my head. "Linking up scanners, directional systems locking on, aim assist is a go, knock 'em dead, chief." Suggested angle of attack vectors, wind direction, sound and heat levels, predicted enemy attack patterns, as well as the exact elevation, distance and orientation of my three opponents all filled the sides of my visor. I placed my weapons in the armored warp pouches at my sides.

"Well, come at us with all you have," Sern told me smugly. Neither Xen nor Ferdan looked very happy with that pronouncement.

"Are you certain that's ok?" I sighed to the sky.

"Do not pull your punches!" Sern commanded.

Azull replied as well. "Do as he says, Lord Evans. Only make sure their wounds can be healed well."

"So don't kill him," Greta added.

"I'll see what I can do!" I laughed.

"Come at me already!" Sern hissed unhappily.

I shrugged, then rocketed forward, taking full advantage of my suit's boosted strength. I avoided Xen's blind swing and dodged past Chief Judjerex Trugeddeen without giving up any of my momentum. Swiping Sern's legs out from under him, I applied two palm strikes to his chest. The prince shot a good ten feet in the air. Gasps and shrieks filled the ring, bringing a broad grin to my lips. Without halting my motion at all, I spun up and hit Xen in the helmet with a high kick. His great helm cracked and he fell to the ground like a discarded sock puppet. By then, Ferdan managed to register what was going on and moved to hit me with his shield. Using the weight of my kick, I stepped around him, locked up his sword arm with one arm, kicked him in the back of the knee, and with my other arm lightly chopped him in the back of the neck. Without halting for even a second, I smashed my elbow into his shield-arm's shoulder joint, then spun even further behind him to the side with the shield and knocked it away with my shoulder before lightly swiping his feet from under him. At this point I was just showing off, but I wanted to be thorough and prove myself to the crowd. Thankfully I had not lost my touch.

In fewer than eight seconds, all three of my opponents were down for the count. If I had been serious, five would have been enough to kill them while unarmed. Seeing the best of the kingdom taken down so efficiently by an unarmed man made some of the toadies pass out in shock and fear. "Hey, I said not to kill them!" Greta yelled at me.

Trugeddeen spoke up. His jaw was the only thing he seemed able or willing to move. "Why am I always the punching bag? We concede defeat."

"All three of you agree to that?" the king asked my opponents.

"The other two are unconscious, Your Majesty," I informed the crowd.

Clare, Debra Woods, and a few more arctechs scurried into the field bringing advanced (or basic for my time) medical kits. "We will help them," Debra proclaimed, cutting off whatever Greta was going to spout.

A few tense minutes passed. During that seemingly long span of time, the clouds were the only ones to voice their thunderous opinions. "They will all live," Debra finally declared, earning a sigh from the crowd.

"You could have killed them!" Queen Waldersoloft told me, raising her voice.

"He held back," Clare murmured. Somehow her confidence cut through even the still-building storm.

"Impossible!" one of the court stooges sneered.

Clare gazed firmly at her son the king. Taking her meaning, his face hardened and shifted to me. "If I had used one palm instead of two on the prince, he could have died or at the least been crippled," I informed the crowd.

"Then why did you fight him that way?" Queen Waldersoloft asked.

"They asked him to not hold back, but if Lord Evans had used his sword and fought seriously, they would have died, Mother," Azull chimed in. From her mother's enraged and surprised expression this could have very well been the first time Azull had spoken to her that way.

Clare checked over her hands and wiped them down on her smock, then commanded, "Well then. Chuck, Adder, and Greta. Bring the new test subject and come with me."

"Mother, bring Lord Evans to me tonight. I have a few more things to ask him about," the king called after us.

Adder and I kept Verndralla between us. Greta took the rear of our smaller group and kept an eye on our surroundings. Clare meanwhile breezily led us down a mud-slick main road. Cool air and lightning filled the sky. A few covered carts were our only company as we walked. "So did you pick up anything interesting?" Clare asked.

"Nothing unexpected," Greta sighed.

"Pops got a robot in his noggin," Adder added.

Clare stopped and faced us, raising an eyebrow. "What they said," I shrugged.

"So, what is it?" Clare inquired baldly.

"Me," Pan replied softly through my helmet.

It took a few seconds for Clare to understand it was not me talking. Greta elaborated. "So much insane stuff just keeps happening, I'd believe just about anything at this point if Lord Evans was involved. That and having the AI talk publicly could be unwise."

"She means 'Pan shut up'," Adder noted.

Before we could get further off track, Verndralla spoke up as we huddled under the porch of a butcher's shop. "So, what happens to me?"

Clare looked to me for a response so I laid out my pitch. "Now that you have three samples of humans being granted immunity in slightly different ways to those monsters, could you make a vaccine?"

"A temporary one could be possible," Clare agreed. "But I have to correct you on one thing. You and the other two are not human anymore."

"Then what about our deal? I have to give him an heir, right?" Greta wailed just under the rainstorm.

"You think having antimatter in your blood and mutated stabilizing elements like evolved demon cores still qualifies you as entirely human?" Clare asked, annoyed it had not occurred to me.

"That explains why my blood burns people," I agreed, too worried it might not stop there.

"So having a child is impossible?" Greta asked, oddly crestfallen.

"Not if I make your blood more or less like his," Clare interjected.

"So, I am a test subject for the vaccine?" Greta asked.

"No, I need you as a test subject for a more in-depth process. The vaccine will need to be temporary, otherwise it could have some bad side effects. I can have the vaccine done before the Errant Order needs to ship out to save the day. Just make certain your order has the troops, gear, and training needed for victory," Clare cautioned.

"The Order may need some funds and my fort may need some revisions," I replied.

"Then tell my son that when you see him," Clare smiled back. She turned and led us back to her lab.

We jogged down a street which seemed to be more commerce-oriented than the others I had seen. We passed one large shop after another. The gate we had come through was large. We passed no one on the road due largely to most of the shops being closed from the lightning, rain, wind, and mud covering the city. The troops guarding the gateway to the castle grounds took one look at Clare and stepped out of our way. We rushed through the fancy garden. A few bits of ancient steel beams poked up in places among the foliage. Finally, we burst into the queen mother's tower. "So do typhoons like that happen often?" I asked.

"He means big storms, and yes they do," Clare translated for us.

"I'd hate to see what you would call bad weather then," I shrugged.

"Understating the weather is a national pastime," Adder smirked. Greta led us up the stairs. One gaze from Clare was enough to prevent her receptionists from interrupting our passage.

"So, any plans for killing the god of demons yet?" Clare asked me. She was likely thinking of a multitude of mad experiments even as she fished for my plans.

"You mean Jim or whatever he became? Survive or die trying," I smiled.

"That's not a plan," Greta noted, not looking back.

"I need to draw him out or locate him first, but before that I'd like to sift through a few old ruins. Hopefully those will give us some clues of how to kill off the demons," I told them.

"Well, that's better than we have been doing. If you need some help putting together an expedition, let me know," Clare offered.

Soon after, we arrived at her lab. Verndralla was set down on an examination table. "Relax for a while, girl. Greta, take some blood samples from Chuck and Adder," was all Clare told us before busying herself with neatening up a table filled with chemistry tools, books, and some of the (now half-eaten) rations I had given her.

Greta dutifully took out some new-looking hollow steel needles and clear vials. Tubes made from intestines connected the needles to the vials through another needle stuck in varnished cork stoppers. "Relax, these are brand new," Greta told me. She used a fancy silver lighter (seemingly kept around for only this purpose) to heat up the blood-sucking needle. Taking three vials of blood each from Adder and me, she switched to a different set of gear each time, going so far as to heat up each needle in turn. Our blood was pitch black save for small motes of light that sparkled from within at random intervals. Greta looked at each vial closely as she labeled them. "This does not look human to me," she sighed, sounding disappointed.

"I'd like a second option, Mom," Adder requested, smirking as if she had caught onto some secret run-on joke and was going to throttle the life from it like a blood-crazed wild boar, until I took note.

Clare managed to get behind Greta without her noticing. "She means you, Lady Evans."

I pretended not to notice how red Greta's face became. "Can we leave you to your own devices for a while, my queen?" I asked Clare.

"Doing what?" my old friend grinned evilly.

"Dinner," I sighed, feeling even more tired after my blood had been taken.

"Both of us?" Adder asked in a voice she must have meant to sound sheepish, but it came off on the mumbling murderous side of jealous.

"Well, I am hungry and you two women have yet to eat much today," I told them.

"Dumb ass," Greta muttered. "Let's go, dear."

"Ok Mama," Adder laughed.

6

Queen of Clubs

At that moment I felt like I had gone without sleep for a whole week. "The ballroom upstairs is also my dining hall. The staff should recognize you and put the meal on my tab," Clare advised.

"Any changes of clothes? My armor needs some work as well," I inquired before the queen mother could get into full mad scientist mode.

"Check on the same spot as before," Clare waved dismissively.

Greta lunged into the curtain-walled cubicle I had used before. After a few moments of palpable intensity, she rushed over to a cube next to mine. "The best set is on the bench. Green, get in here with me," she called.

A short shower later (in a newly installed setup), I dressed in what could only be called an old-style formal military uniform with a lot more metal buttons than it needed. Between the double-breasted coat and the dark pinstripe shirt, I was not certain if I looked more like a military mastermind from a classic spy film or some kind of organized crime boss from one of the ancient (even for me) dime novels. Clearly whoever had designed this had taken, knowingly or not, great liberties with the fashion of the past. My two companions for dinner came out in a cross between a general's formal uniform and a maid or flight attendant. As bizarre as we looked, I had to admit that what Greta had picked out was very fancy and made us look less mismatched when we were near each other.

As we walked to the large room with the bridge we had used to get to the throne room, the normal horde of servants and errand-runners passed us. All the while, Greta clung to me and Adder held my hand on the other side. Somehow, we received only impressed or envious glances and nothing else. When we got to the hall which was set up as a huge fancy dining room with a buffet-style maze on one side of the room, a lady in a slightly frilly suit looked up from the counter. "What name is your party under?" she asked in a voice that had a hint of weariness to it. Then she did a double and triple take, looking Greta up and down. "Mistress Evans, is that you?" she asked.

Greta went pale. "Sally, what are you talking about?"

The hostess named Sally looked up at me, uncertain how to continue. I smiled and shrugged, trying to convey she could speak her mind without fear. Sally took a deep breath. "All the maids in the tower are taking about your secret wedding."

Greta's face went from ashen and bloodless to pomegranate far faster than any attack I had ever seen. "I am not his wife yet," she muttered in a pouting tone while looking away nervously.

"Apologies, my lady," Sally sputtered, bowing.

"Relax, she is my fiancée, but neither of us are big on formalities." I smiled, trying to relax them both.

"Well Lord Evans, your name is not on our list." Sally sighed, most of the visible tension having left her.

"The queen mother said she will pay for us," Adder noted. Her tone was soft and happy but it cut like a razor.

"Did she now?" Sally asked, seeming to take note of Adder for the first time. Our hostess's reply hid her displeasure of Adder tagging along before looking back at me. "I'll take your word on that. Come with me then."

We were seated at a large round table in a far corner of the room. The seats were heavily upholstered. We were handed a set of menus, one paper and one polycarbonate, with the words engraved and filled in with a similar plastic bonded to the surface. "The fancy one is for high-ranking nobles, royalty, and notable folks recognized by the crown," Adder whispered to us.

After much debate we got one meal of pork and some wine to start with. It was a whole pig cooked all the way through and propped up on a grill brought out to our table for that sole purpose, with lots of steamed vegetables heavily laden with oil, butter and spices. Set next to me was a whole oaken barrel of wine. I was never so thankful for a hard march and intense duel as I was then, because otherwise, I doubt we could have eaten nearly as much as we did. After slogging into a third of the meal and feeling far more full than I had ever been up to that point, the mood in the room shifted. Clare walked up to us in charred rubberized surgical gear. She took one look at our feast and proceeded to pour herself some wine (much to the consternation of the many waiters who had been falling over themselves trying to accommodate us in a groveling fashion). The queen mother downed her glass in one fell swoop, paying little if any regard to the drink's abundant merits. "We have a problem," Clare announced suddenly. The waiters scattered as if they were combusting and the hostess for the evening rushed over. "The new test subject is less like you and more like them," Clare sighed, lazily sitting next to me and ripping into the pork with a dubious level of interest.

"Your Majesty, is everything all right?" Sally inquired timidly, all the while staring daggers at me.

"I could use some rum. Also, next time my trusted minion Lord Evans is here, the chefs should really serve him vegetables the way I like it." Clare waved the hostess off absentmindedly.

"Heavy on spinach, garlic, carrots, cauliflower, vegetables, asparagus, corn, and radishes made with light oil, a goodly amount of pepper, and all well cooked in *the* cast iron pot?" Sally asked. The way she stressed *the* cast iron pot made me think for a second before giving up on guess work.

"That's right. Now get me some rum," Clare nodded. Her eyes were grinning as Sally rushed away.

"So, who is like what now?" Adder inquired.

"The thing you lugged back. She is even less human than you and Chuck. Long story short, it seems she can remotely dissolve things."

"Like your clothes?" Greta sighed.

"And some of the floor, a blood sampling kit, and the coffee brewing relic you like so much," Clare shrugged, but no doubt she was smiling on the inside.

Greta's face dropped, looking both ready to go on a murderous rampage and break down in tears. She jumped out of her seat yelling, "She did what to my caffeine?"

"Oh, of all the vices," I muttered, taking no solace from the queen mother's gleeful gaze filled to the brim with amusement.

"I am sorry, what?" Sally asked from behind me. She was frozen, a large mug of rum held unmoving over my head.

Greta rushed up to Sally and snatched the mug of rum. After downing the whole thing, Greta ran off, saying "I'll take over lab duties for now."

"Excellent. Lord Evans, we really must go to see the king as promised," Clare laughed. Her laugher lifted the heavy mood of the room.

"Adder, bring the rest of our meal to your mother and her charge," I told my more-or-less adopted daughter.

"Ok, Pop," Adder Green saluted lazily.

"What is going on?" Sally stammered, still frozen in place.

"Work," I sighed. "The meal was great, by the way. It should last me a few more days."

"You are taking it with you?" Sally asked quickly, only now starting to stiffly move.

"My daughter is. It would be a waste not to finish and enjoy such a meal," I smiled.

"Very well." Sally seemed a bit dubious of Adder. The

former princess and I looked even less alike than when we had first met.

"Most nobles trash their chow or feed it to their pets, servants included," Adder whispered in my ear.

"Well then Lord Evans, come with me. My son can't be left waiting the whole night," Clare grinned. She stopped at the bridge we had taken before. "Oh, and put that meal on my tab," she told Sally, who was shuffling behind us clutching a time-worn PDA to her chest like some like evil warding charm or life preserver.

My old friend and I walked over the bridge to the main royal spire. "So, what do you think of Greta?" Clare asked suddenly.

"I am starting to think she likes me." I felt Pan sigh in my brain. Clare looked at me with a face full of surprise. Her eyes, however, looked very impressed, but I still caught a small grimace tugging at her lips. "I see now that I am very dense," I apologized.

"I missed my chance, so good luck to her," Clare muttered.

I was feeling more troubled now so I tried to ignore the impact of her words. "Greta is very smart. Why did you not make use of her sooner?"

"She is too smart, as in the smartest person I know of, but she is overconfident and impulsive. Did you know her parents run a pawn shop in the slums? That girl has by far the lowest social standing of anyone permitted entry into the arctech academy."

"But you still kicked her out," I pointed out diplomatically.

"Well, she did jury-rig a nearly sentient virus from a couple lines of test code," Clare muttered uncomfortably.

"She MacGyvered a programming test that far?" I had to double check. I could feel Pan hanging on every word.

"Yes, she did, ok? It was not even something the instructors completely understood. The point of that test was to instill awareness of the enormity of what they were learning and to give them a sense of respect toward it. Thanks to Greta, we got a couple of heart attacks and some serious cases of PTSD," Clare lamented.

We were just getting off the bridge and brushing past the guards when I commented, "So you essentially gave a bunch of children a loaded gun and did not expect one of them to find the safety?"

Clare shook her head. Her face had gone pale. "The only solution to it should have been for a door lock security algorithm with some very simplified ID software, not a virus that leapt around infecting security turrets, blast shields, and tear gas sprays, making them go on a rampage."

"That sounds terrible," I managed to cough, my mouth suddenly like sandpaper.

We continued to walk up the stairway. "To amend your preconceptions, we thought anyone who knew enough to make something like that would not unleash it on us. The problem is, Greta understands on an instinctive level she is a world class prodigy when it comes to software and has talents in many other fields. So even if she knows something will work, she may not know what it will do."

Pan whispered into my mind *That is incredible and terrifying at the same time.*

We walked by the throne room and after one more landing came to a small hallway tucked into a crevice much like Clare's own lab. "My son will be in his study. Our talk could do with a complete lack of prying eyes." Four heavy plasma turrets were set around the door and no other humans were anywhere in sight this high up in the old tower. Clare walked up to a small intercom. I recognized this room was the old Anti Air control room. It was a room I had no fond memories of, having used its systems to gun down many refugee transports from other worlds during the plague. At least once I had even been in command along with Clare for an incident.

Clare spoke into the intercom. "Hey boy, Lord Evans and I are ready to talk to you."

A good minute later the king's voice crackled back. "You are late, Mom. Is this really so earthshaking to be held here?"

"That's right," Clare replied, now kind of annoyed.

"So, who is he really?" the king asked.

"I was hoping you could let us in and talk about that, among other things," Clare whispered while kneading her forehead.

"Noted," the king's voice told us. Soon after, the door to his study audibly clicked and Clare pushed her way inside. I hurried after my old friend's rapid pace.

The king sat surrounded by bookshelves. A small table with many important-looking documents stuffed inside large tomes stood beside the king. The room gave off a vibe much like you would find from a teenager frantically tidying up their bedroom for the first time ever. "This room is always such a dump," Clare sighed. She sat herself down on a dusty sofa. Near the faded upholstery rested a few jumbled piles placed in the only neat line I could see. Clare looked back at me and pointed to the seat next to her. "His father was the same way."

I sighed and sat down next to the queen mother. The king raised an eyebrow. "So just who is this man to you, Mother?"

Clare shrugged. "If things had gone the way I believed they would when I was a child, he would have been my husband and I would have never seen a demon. I would have also had three cute children and been a carefree housewife."

The king and I both groaned at her statement. Both the king's eyebrows were raised now. He asked, "So he is from your time?"

"Yes, I am," I told the king. Clare simply nodded.

"And Lord Evans, you want to solve our neighbor's issues with a military force of your own making?" the king inquired.

"My main goal would be to eradicate all the demons for good, Your Majesty," I told him.

"You can call me Dave when it is just us," the king told me. After a slight pause, "What makes you think you can do a better job than the order of Demon Slayers?" he asked.

"I know what they are made of and have found evidence my people once started a project to erase the demons. If I can find and kill an old friend of mine and complete the ancient project, then the demons should be no more."

"And so, you want funding and troops?" Dave the king asked me.

"Some money to start would be good. I am planning to use the Errant Order as a band of mercenaries. Getting paid for odd jobs and demon slaying should work well for both of us," I told Dave.

"Politically that has its merits but you cannot take any jobs to attack or knowingly harm any kingdom," the king stipulated.

"The demons and their god Jim James are my only targets," I replied. Suddenly seeing our talk had become some kind of staring contest, I felt awkward. The king smirked when he noted that I was now aware of this.

"Very well. I will let any troops in my army who wish to join you do so. The order cannot exceed 500 warriors but feel free to the take what you need from our armory. You can recruit in the city and use the Steelglade to train them."

"The Steelglade?" I asked.

"Old starship graveyard. Used to be an arena. Lots of old blades scattered around. It's deep in a forest near the city," Clare smugly informed me.

"On that note, take this." The king took a blade I recognized as a katana from behind his chair. "It may not be as good as your main sword but seeing as you can use two well and have only one, you may need a blade that can't break."

"Can't break?" I asked.

"It has a stasis field integrated into it. The sword's current state will not change but it still cuts just fine," Clare whistled.

"A blade fit for a king. Many thanks, Dave," I said.

The king chuckled and told us, "Chuck Evans, go now. I'll

get the paperwork done by midnight. You have lots of work starting tomorrow."

"You still have that nice room set aside for you," Clare told me on the way back to the bridge.

"The one Greta was helping with?" I asked.

Clare glanced at me like I was a total moron. "That one," she muttered. After a while walking in silence, we got back to the dining room/dance hall. The staff were finishing their cleanup. "Get plenty of rest. Your real work starts early tomorrow."

After that we parted ways. The way back to my temporary room was much the same as before. Servants rushed by, even this late, on all manner of errands. When I got to the floor I had been aiming for, the mood around me instantly went from being ignored to the very center of attention. The first who managed to stall their work and talk to me was same senior maid from before. "Greta quit without notice," she told me.

"From being a maid?" I asked.

"That's right, Sir Evans. So why is she back in your room?" the sharp-eyed maid asked.

"Dorleen, the queen mother called him Lord Evans," Sally called over from a side room. Apparently, she worked as both a maid and a hostess. Then the chattering started.

"I was given a slight promotion recently. Greta also happens to be my fiancée," I told them, trying to stall any more chaos.

More than a few of the maids looked confused until Dorleen, the floor's senior maid, told them, "Fiancée is a word the nobles use for someone they will be marrying." I managed to flee in the ensuing chaos, realizing that Dorleen and Sally could get their coworkers back to work better without me around.

I barged into the room where I had first slept upon coming to this nutty time, only to find Greta in an orange jumpsuit lightly snoring in a recliner. An open PDA rested on the low office table in front of her. I was about to shut down the PDA when Greta woke up and said, "You make a grand entrance or what?"

I pointed over to the door to our room which I had locked. Muttering could still be heard from beyond it. "That sounds about right."

"Well shit. That makes my life harder," Greta muttered groggily.

"Given how close we are now, there is no way my infamy would not be rubbing off on you," I told her as I picked up a plate full of cookie crumbs.

"You could have said renown or something. So, any idea why the queen mother gives you a hard time?" Greta asked me, finally lifting her arm off her eyes to glare blankly at me.

"No idea," I told her. Which was not 100% true. I had been forming a vague idea, but nothing I had the words to explain.

"It's because she liked you before but now you two are at polar opposite places in your lives, so she wants to help you. To get over her mixed-up past self she is becoming an insufferable prankster," my wife-to-be said unhappily. "Also, next time, put more thought into your responses," Greta muttered.

"That analysis is one of your many rumored talents?" I joked. I had to keep my mind occupied on something other than Clare.

"Two of them, so I am told," Greta answered finally. Groggily looking me in the eyes, "So what's new?"

"Besides you being worn out? Got to raise my army starting tomorrow," I told her.

"Your army?" Greta asked. Her eyes shone brightly with a wakeful haze. "Reinforcing that lab was bad enough. Now you will get some heavy lifting done."

"So, besides my blood, is there anything else that could be used to make something corrosion resistant?" I asked.

"Demon cores. Getting a completely undamaged mature one is impossible though..." she trailed off. Suddenly Greta was totally awake and hyper. "Theoretically only, you could pull one out of a demon but we would need to make it unable to reform," then she passed out again and was back to snoring. I placed her on the bed and went to sleep on the recliner she had occupied, making certain to save the PDA's data and shut it down before I did.

The next morning, I awoke to Xen shaking me. Trish stood by the door taking a short break from holding back a mob of maids to wave at me. "Get up!" Xen was yelling at me.

I yawned. "What's the matter?" Xen tossed me some travel-wear that Pan silently informed me was made of leather, kinetic-resistant cloth, and some kind of animal-fat-based water proofing. My old military habits kicked in, causing me to rapidly dress in what was thrown at me before I noticed Greta was not in the room.

"Your partner went down to the lab ages ago," Trish helpfully called over her shoulder, well above the volume of the tidal wave of frills she was holding back.

"It's your daughter that is the issue," Xen told me.

"She started a recruiting drive, didn't she?" I sighed, finishing wriggling into the last of my outfit. Xen raised an eyebrow and the maids stopped trying to bust in. "I am not hopelessly dense."

Xen and about twenty maids replied to me at the same time, "Yes you are."

"Talking back to a lord! How should we handle these lovely ladies?" Trish asked. The maids became very worried and meek upon realizing how rude they had been to a nobleman.

"I need a light breakfast that I can carry as soon as possible, and a small mattress placed on the floor in here, that's all," I called over to the maids. They scattered to comply. I asked Xen, "When my meal gets here we head out immediately. Now tell me the main details."

"Adder set up shop in a bar and is beating up nearly the whole district. She says she is evaluating warriors for a new elite unit on your and the kingdom's behalf," Xen told me.

"She is not wrong about the unit but I haven't told her about that yet, much less given her any orders," I sighed.

"So, what's the call?" Trish asked, grabbing a small tray of sandwiches and three thermoses of coffee from a trembling maid.

I holstered my ignition blade and time-stilled sword to my

back, my plasma pistol to one thigh, and my warp pouch to the other. I put on my old field jacket, grabbed a thermos and two sandwiches. Walking out of the room between small bites of something almost like ham and cheese, I requested, "So Sir Xen, lead the way to this mess."

Commander Xen and Trish rushed after me. When we got to the castle complex's main entrance, they took the lead. We rushed through a packed early morning market. Shops and street vendors sold everything from daggers to bullets, tomatoes to sheets of plastic-based rain-proofing. The quality was marginal with the exception of food and not much else. A great many stares followed us. "We really stand out," I noted absently.

"You are the talk of the city," Trish shot back.

"You think anyone is spying on me yet?" I laughed softly, not relishing the thought but unable to ignore that inevitability.

"No doubt, so watch your tone. Even the Demon Slayers are wary of your name," Xen hissed.

I looked over at Trish. She nodded. "You could be our competition, depending on what you do."

As one, we swerved to avoid a plodding street vendor and the dense crowd buying caramel-dipped apples around him. "Well I did make quite the entrance," I replied.

"You have made a strong impression on a great many powerful people," Xen sighed.

My guides skidded to a halt in front of a rough-sounding tavern that had a line snaking out the door. "We're here!" Xen was interrupted when a large man seemingly made of muscle and nothing else flew through the wall next to the door.

The meat mountain landed on his back next to us and passed out. "And stay down!" Adder howled from within the dim tavern. Cheers followed her every word. When that died down, my adopted daughter added loud enough for half the market to hear, "Ok, next!"

"Wonderful," I grimaced. "I'll take care of the child. Commander, you take care of the wall."

"You will still be paying for it," Xen told me firmly.

"Take it out of my fee to calm Adder down," I told him happily. I took a deep breath and was all business and no mercy by the time I hopped through the tavern's brand-new door.

Heads turned my way from the orderly line in the middle of a sea of destruction. Inside, the building was a mess. Men were sprawled everywhere. Many hung limply over chunks of tables. Before I even walked ten steps inside, a stout scar-covered man of no more than twenty cycles of life sailed over my head, creating yet another hole in the bar counter. "That was very good. Next!" Adder yelled from deeper inside the bar-turned-fight-club.

The men in line grew more and more tense as I walked inside until three of the bigger specimens got out of line and charged me. I swung low, tripping the first and kneeing him in the face as he fell. Stepping to the side I wrenched back my other assailant's arm and shoved him into the next man, then I booted my victim in his portly gut and fell on them both, elbowing the last man in the chin. One look at the two piles of three men made the rest of the line choose to overlook my trespass. After arriving at a ring of splinters and blood, I noted Adder tossing yet another man out of the ring. "Are you even evaluating them?" I called over.

My adoptive daughter looked up. Waving to me, she called over. "What does it look like I am doing, Dad?" Most of the line glanced at me and seemed to come to the conclusion that I must be the father of the slightly psychotic girl who had been wiping the floor with them. I was not certain I was happy with that perception but I had better things to do than worry just then.

"It looks like you are just beating the crap out of men twice your age and using my job as an excuse to do it," I called over to her. The line of burly lambs waiting for their turn with the butcher tensed up significantly.

"Right. How many do you need again?" Adder laughed.

"I was thinking one thousand. Then after some training we would be left with four hundred and ninety-five, along with four officers of my choosing and myself. The queen mother will get us some equipment, plus I was going to ask her to find some candidates. So, if you could find three hundred that would be good. Also out of curiosity, how were you planning to pay for damages to this place?"

"Oh, I own it now. The last owner bet I could not beat him in a fight," Adder cackled.

"What do you mean, candidates?" one of the men called over.

"Potential recruits. This is just the start of the sorting process," Adder shrugged.

"So even if you pick us, we still may not pass. Then what's the point?" another muscle-brained blubber ball yelled over.

"Bragging rights," I called back. "All of you will be at least a third as good as my daughter by the end of training, if you make it that far."

"That's a lot, right?" the next man in line asked nervously.

"If each of you could last 50% longer against her than you did today just by going through our training here, would that be amazing?" I asked him.

"We could do that?" the man asked, his eyes bulging like a drowned fish.

"For those who get through my training, yes, but you men here would have to impress her first," I told him, raising my voice in the silent former bar while pointing at Adder.

Then I simply walked out the way I came in. Jim Floseen was having a hushed conversation with Xen. The street was as chaotic as when I had entered and I could feel that I was getting more intense looks than when I was inside Adder's new playground. "Sounds like she is still going strong," Trish noted when the crashing and sobbing resumed.

"So, she had a bet with the owner. He lost, so Adder owns this place now," I sighed.

"Did she tell you that?" Xen asked unhappily.

"Well, no one else was that talkative, and as far as I could see, no one died," I replied.

"Yet, no one died yet," Xen corrected me.

"Even so, they are still lining up. What did she bribe them with?" Trish lazily stated. Her face held clear disinterest while her eyes held nothing but questions.

"Recruitment drive," I shrugged.

"What? Don't tell me you sanctioned this?" Xen raised his voice as he stomped closer to me.

"Only retroactively. Although some medical treatment may be in order," I told him.

"Not from the royal family it won't. They can't help you politically anymore," Xen informed me.

"That's right," Mustard said. "As I was telling the commander, that was decided today by the royals."

"What did the queen mother say?" I asked.

Mustard cleared his throat. "We all have a lot to keep an eye on now." I had to smile. Coming from Clare, it was more a heads up and a show of confidence than a warning.

7

King of Diamonds

After securing Trish, Adder, and Xen's word that they would meet me in Clare's lab and working out a time, I spent many more hours getting in contact with Clare and Greta because the lab was sealed off. I had to borrow an ancient radio from the Demon Slayers, which took a lot of convincing and red tape, old radios being revered relics.

I sat in a soundproof room deep within the Demon Slayers' guild hall. Trish sat outside guarding my weapons from her greedier comrades. When Clare finally picked up, she cut off any chance of me speaking first. "The kid told you about our new politics, I take it." My old friend sounded worn out.

"That's right," I replied through the bulky headset of an ancient field station set that was so outdated its generation had been mothballed before the refugee ships from the old human empire had ever crossed over to our current side of the Milky Way galaxy. "The message was well received. However, I still need to discuss supplying the Errant Order and its command structure, so I was hoping to talk to you, Greta, and a few others in your lab about that," I reported.

"Who else?" Greta's voice cut in. Somehow, she sounded even more tired than the queen mother.

"Trish, Xen, and Adder. This may concern Verndralla as well," I explained.

"So, way more women?" Greta sighed, sounding far more disappointed and more tired than surprised.

I felt a storm coming so I worked hard to head it off. "It's not my fault the other two people resistant to corrosion are female, plus I named only those I trust. There is no one else."

Clare muttered an aside meant for me to hear and Greta to notice. "I take back what I said about him being less dense than I remember."

"Oh, come on. Commander Xen and Chief Judjerex Trugeddeen are the only two men I have met who are competent in a fight. I have met far more females that I can trust to watch my back in a fight. Adder is good but I'm not sure I'd like to fight with her when she gets serious. Anyway, Xen and Ferdan can't help me a lot. So, I was hoping Trish, Adder, Verndralla, and you honey would help me lead the Errant Order," I explained to them.

Greta groaned deeply. "Idiot. How do you really feel about them?" My wife-to-be shattered my feeling that I had nailed my sales pitch.

"Trish is a good sniper. I need to keep an eye on Adder and it looks like she is already working on building her unit. Verndralla could be useful or very dangerous. We need to keep the whole innate resistance thing under wraps so I can't have anyone like that running around out of our sight. And well, sweetie, I trust you the most and need someone smart with us," I replied, trying to elaborate as much as possible and for once disappointed at how insensitive I could be.

"That's nice of you but what is that about Miss Green's team?" Clare asked.

"First of all, Greta is the one I promised I'd stand by. Second, Adder was beating up a bunch of ruffians looking for those with some skill. I'll need each commander to look for around two hundred candidates. We will all whittle that down to one hundred troops per leader during training," I told them.

"That's an escapist response," Clare snickered with just a hint of loneliness and regret even I picked up on. "I'll get the others to show up in a few hours' time. See you at the lab then," and she abruptly cut off the communication.

I left the soundproofed room to find Trish napping. I was barely past the door's threshold when her eyes opened. Faster than I could blink, Trish leapt out of her chair. "Where to now?" she inquired as though it were a given for her to shadow me.

"The queen mother's lab. We will be meeting a few others there," I told her, taking my weapons from her and beginning the long walk back to Clare's tower.

"Did the new girl wake up?" Trish asked, swiftly falling in beside me. The Demon Slayers in the guild hall watched us go with as much interest as trepidation.

"I was not told if she did," I replied.

"Then why?" Trish asked as we walked out of the mostly dark steel building and down the smooth stone steps.

"Formations for the new order," I told her. As I walked, I kept an eye out. My instincts told me a few different teams were tailing us.

"Whatever is said, I will need to report to my bosses before I can do anything more for you," Trish sighed warily.

"I understand," I told her after some thought when we stopped to let a few carts pass us by on the crowded hard-packed dirt street.

"So how are you so strong?" Trish asked after many minutes of silence spent weaving past ammo and food vendors.

"We are all built up from our failings, real or imagined," I smiled back.

"What?" a voice asked from near one of the side gates that led into the area around the palace. Azull had her arms folded and a hooded cape covering her well.

"How to be strong?" I shrugged.

Azull opened the gate for us. "You are absolutely insane," the princess muttered.

"There is no 'absolutely insane' just like there is no absolute truth," I laughed.

"Is that so?" Azull grumbled as the three of us walked through the garden around Clare's part of the palace grounds.

"More or less," I told her. Trish snickered in the background. She had taken to walking a few paces behind me now that the princess was with us.

Azull sighed. "The demons are numerically superior to us. This kingdom may look like the last line of defense. Many other places have claimed to be so, and they are ruins lost to humanity now."

"Then we will need to be superior alphanumerically," I replied. Azull spun around and for the first time in my life I felt like I should have kept silent. "It will work out, princess," I interjected softly before an impromptu volume test could start between us.

Azull glared at me and while I was working out why I felt wrong-footed, the princess dragged me into a gardening shed. "Trish, guard the door," Azull commanded.

Azull tried and failed to hurl me to the far end of the cramped brick tool shed. I caught my balance on the sawdust-covered floor. "What do you have against me?" Azull began. "My grandmother and I have done so much for you and your brood. So why are you such an asshole? What is with your high and mighty routine? What gives you the right to look down on me?"

Somehow, I managed to squeak at the start of that tirade, "But I…"

Azull cut me off without even stalling long enough to get all of her breath back. "Shut up. I am monologuing here. So why? Why are you so proud of yourself? What do you want for this? You have nothing to lose if you leave us, and from the way you act I am very surprised you are staying at all. You are so powerful but so lazy. My sister, the mad smartass, and my grandmother all look up to you. So why are you so lazy and foolish? What gives you the right to judge me?"

Azull begin to pant. I waited to see if she still had some vitriol left in her but she just kept glaring at me, searching for something in my stance and eyes. Her face became more and more annoyed as I stood before her. Finally, I simply shrugged to myself and told her, "I am here because your grandmother is my link to the past. I hate the idea that the monsters my generation made are still wreaking havoc, so I want to destroy them. Clues to what happened to my friends and coworkers would be found in and around this kingdom. I treat you differently because I want you to be a wise ruler. However, I am a fool that lives to fight with a blade, just as I have always wished to in my past when plasma guns bigger than my pistol were everywhere. I am who I am, princess, and I will make no excuses for myself. I will work with you but you don't have to like me so much that you push me into a shed barely fit for two people when empty."

Azull went from astoundingly annoyed to very embarrassed in far less time than it had taken her to get mad. She ran out of the door. Trish called out to her, "Princess!" before looking my way.

"Let's follow her," I grumbled. We took off after her, only to find Azull a short distance later at the entrance to Clare's tower. By then Azull appeared to have composed herself, although I was certain that was only an act on her part. But I was in no mood to press her just then.

I led the way into Clare's tower. When I passed the threshold two men sprang at me from other side of the door with swords raised. Reacting before I assessed my attackers (not that I had time to, they were very close), I landed a solid hit into both their guts, twisting my palm and throwing them to the ground. Before my attackers could stop wheezing and get up, my ignition blade and time-stilled sword were thrust in their faces. My attackers wore the uniform of tower guardsman. "Who are you really?" I snapped at them.

The men seemed on edge but also oddly calm and open for assassins. "So, we did not pass the test, my lord?" one asked hopefully.

"What test?" Azull asked them. Her seething aura made even the receptionists far across from us hide behind their desks.

"To be let into the Errant Order under Lord Evan's command, we were told we had to ambush him to show our skill," the other man told us in a puzzled tone.

"Who would...?" Azull started.

I was far ahead of her. At the speed of thought, I got Pan to hack into any intercom in the queen mother's lab and get Adder to meet us at the ground floor. "Adder," I said in an annoyed tone, knowing that was all Azull and Trish needed to work out the rest.

"Lady Adder, yes," the man told me. Feeling vindicated, I instantly labeled him as a dense idiot, recognizing the irony at the same time. My display made those not involved keep their distance for now.

"Was I wrong, Father?" Adder called, leaning over a banister high above us before dropping down a good five floors. Her plunge enlisted a great amount of screaming, although those close to her were more annoyed than terrified. At the last possible moment, a small anti-gravity field gently kicked in and Adder fluttered to the floor, her landing movements totally silent and serene, in stark contrast to the panicked red-faced multitude all around us.

"Tell me you tested that first," Azull grumbled.

"Not I," Adder solemnly swore before grinning widely. "Mum did it."

"So, Greta?" Trish interjected.

Before my adoptive daughter could reply with another snarky comeback, a regal tone reverberated from the training yard opposite us. "Princess Adell Versheius, you yet live?" The speaker was a tall man who was staring intently at the back of Adder's head. His clothing marked him as someone important from Drenneth but I had not seen him before.

Azull took one look at the man over her shoulder. "First Prince Jallace, how unexpected," she murmured with a face that was hard to read.

I gave the newcomer a small bow. "Well met, your highness." I nudged Adder. It would be bad if she was seen as her past self.

The former and officially dead princess looked at the floor, her expression blank. She moved as if large stones weighed upon her. "My name is Adder. Lord Evans is the man who raised me. Are you by chance related to Prince Sern?"

"I am his elder brother and third in line to the throne of Drenneth," Prince Jallace allowed. After a bit, he shrugged. "My apologies, miss. You looked almost exactly like an old childhood friend of mine."

Adder could no longer bring herself to speak, so Azull spoke in her stead. "Yes, this one is confused for my sister quite often, even though their complexions are totally different."

"Well, we are in a rush to meet with the queen mother. We can talk some other time," I informed Prince Jallace politely as we rushed up the stairs. Adder rapidly outpaced us after I got her moving.

"Yes, we will really need to make time," Prince Jallace called after us. His gaze was inquisitive and a bit lonely as he watched Adder and Azull depart with all due haste.

"What was that all about?" Trish asked.

"Well..." Azull started.

"Not now," Adder snapped, cutting her off and ending our talk while she rapidly bounded up the stairway.

And that's why I love humans. So funny and odd, Pan giggled in my mind.

Its comments enlisted a deep sigh from my lips. *Women,* I retorted back mentally.

You are missing the point. All of you humans are real nut jobs. That's why I put up with you and not the tin can armies I used to lead, Pan told me. Somehow, I felt that if it had arms, it would be shrugging right now at the lack of perception it saw within me.

Adder stormed into the lab. Trish, Azull, and I arrived soon after but we were still the last to show up. Xen, Greta, and Clare stood around an examination table. The cylinder Verndralla had been in was empty. I rushed over to join Clare and the rest. Upon seeing me, Greta dragged me before Verndralla, who looked at me with unfocused eyes. "So, who is this?" Clare demanded.

"Chuck Evans, former Security Lead number five of Azure Base. Born Lunar 12 colony ship. Both parents dead from exposure to the void of space during combat actions with 137th robot kill team subset 93. Adopted by Reginald family. Suspected motive as a substitute for their own son who had perished in same aforementioned incident. Main caretaker of Clare Reginald during time on colony ship. Task ended after 9th known jump code named the Great Migration. First kiss…" The more Verndralla droned on, the redder Clare's face became.

Finally unable to take any more of the history lesson, the queen mother grabbed Verndralla's jaw and said, "Ok, shut up now," in a fierce bloodthirsty way.

"What the hell was that?" Azull snapped. She was uncertain who to be mad at or even why. She felt upset, so to compromise she glared at everyone.

Greta spoke up in a perturbed tone. "We took the data of his past that Chuck had handed over and managed to input it into Verndralla's mind."

"Why?" Azull asked, no more happy than before.

"Because her memories were almost nonexistent. At best she has the important bits and pieces of the three days before her abduction. Aside from that, her childhood up until Lord Evans rescued her is a complete blank," Clare volunteered.

Only then did I note that a large chunk of the floor looked pitted with deep corrosion. "So, is anything else unusual with her?"

"Well, Verndralla can corrode things remotely. From what we can tell, that ability is limited to a short distance away from her." Greta grimaced, clearly trying to suppress some recent trauma which may or may not have been caffeine-related.

"She what?" Adder yelled.

"Well crap," Trish muttered at the same time.

"So, who will be looking after her?" I asked. Cold stares met me and the room seemed to freeze over.

"I will," Azull said sternly. "Someone has to learn all your dirty secrets."

"I'll help," Greta added. "She will know a lot about the old world and its technology."

"I bet I know more," Pan pointed out through an intercom it hijacked.

Verndralla twitched and the intercom along with a few layers of wall around it disintegrated like a fast-forwarded time-lapse of rust and decay. "Stop doing that to my lab!" Clare bellowed.

"Is that reflex or on purpose?" Pan asked through a handheld radio sitting on a steel stool. The radio and its perch were instantly annihilated at the atomic level.

"Is the synthesized intelligence still active?" Verndralla asked, turning to Clare. I yelled at Pan in my mind *Shut up you lunatic, our new friend is running off my old memories.* Verndralla turned to stare quizzically at me, her head tilted but expressionless.

Shirley you must be joking, Pan seemed to sneer back within my thoughts. "Now that this happened, I regret calling you over," Clare complained to me.

I sat down and made certain my smile from before had fallen apart. "There are many things I have done that I regret but all we can do is move on." After a small pause, I added "And don't call me Shirley."

"What?" Azull asked.

I forced an evasive laugh. "Never mind. So, Greta, Trish, Adder, and Verndralla – any chance you would like to help me lead the Errant Order?"

"Why not?" Greta sighed.

"The slayers have already approved that mission," Trish nodded

"What? Nothing new, boring," Adder grinned.

"I see no logical argument against this," Verndralla nodded.

"You have changed," I said to Verndralla.

Verndralla cocked her head to one side. "We knew one another? Do I have your life story in place of my own?"

"Only the knowledge of it. We had to give you something, but times have changed, so try to adapt," Clare sharply chimed in.

"Each of you will need to find 200 promising prospects. After training, each of you will have 100 left. Greta, get some arctechs that could learn to defend themselves. They will be our support medics, maintenance, logistics, cooks, and so on. Trish: hunters and anyone who knows how to use a rifle well will be our long-ranged support. Adder: keep looking for ruffians, medium armor, your unit members can pick from a mix of pistol, carbine or shotgun, and hand-to-hand weapon the choice is theirs. They will be our skirmishers and terror troops. Verndralla: rifles and spears. Find folks that have some skill with those in the kingdom's military – guards would be best. You will have the harrying and second line of attack duties. I will need swordsmen with heavy armor. We will be the vanguard." As I finished, the whole group except Verndralla agreed.

"That flies in the face of doctrine code," Verndralla began to protest.

"11205b-A," I finished. "I am aware but that is where I will be most effective once combat starts."

"He's got us there. Now women, we need some food," Greta proclaimed. She grabbed Verndralla and dragged her out of the lab. Adder, Azull, and Trish followed them. "No men allowed," Greta added.

After the young women had left, Clare asked, "So is the rust bucket in your mind still its own entity?"

I shrugged. "I am not in a position to know. So, if I begin to act too robotic, I'd appreciate if you'd do something about it."

"So, all I need to do is save you from the robot inside if you become what our generation fears? Ok, your mind is in good hands."

"But clearly not my sanity," I smirked.

"Not in this life, old friend," Clare smiled back wickedly.

"This may be a bad time, but I'd like a few favors," I said, changing the subject.

"More of them?" Clare asked. "I can't swear to anything, but let's hear them."

"Greta may need some help getting her quota of recruits so I thought you could discreetly help her out. I'd like to leave Xen to sort out my quota. Lastly, I need as much general topographical map data on this kingdom as you have from now to as far back as possible." When I was finally able to pause for breath, I noticed Clare nodding.

"Those are not so bad, but your fiancée will not thank us for my help," Clare smiled mischievously.

"That's why I said discreet," I smiled.

"So, it was not for my own benefit?" Clare shrugged, not even trying to attempt any pretense of being surprised. "So why the map data? Still searching?"

"Yes. The site I am most interested in is an old clinical nanobot lab. It was near one of the dried-up volcanoes and should be around this kingdom," I told my old friend.

"Sounds like Flame Tongue Heights. The lava lampreys there are real nasty." Clare sighed. "You are insane if you plan to go there alone."

I had to do a double take. "Not as insane as that name. Lava lampreys? Let me guess: they eat something called the coffee-table bookworm. Can you send me all the map data for that area?"

Clare answered, "Yes I can. Are you ok?"

"I feel more worn out than normal. I'm going back to my room. Ready to study that info," I replied as I walked out of the lab.

Lost in thought, I walked into my room. Startled, I noticed a ham sandwich in my grasp when I shut the door. I spent the next few hours combing over the data and maps I had obtained, looking for places that might hold clues to how to rid the world of the monsters my generation had created. I scarcely noted when the door opened. Greta hugged me from behind, her eyes glued to the data I was reviewing. "Promise you won't die on me," she whispered.

We both knew that was anatomically impossible and I had no idea what had brought about her being so open with her feelings, but I nodded as I plugged away at the screen in front of me. "Ok deal, but the same goes for you."

"Fine," my fiancée sighed. She took a seat on the bed further behind me. "Why did you agree to marry me?" she asked suddenly. I stopped what I was doing. "Tell me, but don't turn around," Greta commanded. Her voice was suddenly hard and fragile at the same time, like glass formed on a mountain after a lightning strike.

I stopped my work and thought hard, looking at my feet. The answer arrived far faster than I had expected. "You are the smartest, most reliable person I have ever met. I feel calm around you and I know I can rely on you to help me out, no matter what. Plus, you are cute and speak your mind well."

"Do I remind you of the Builder?" Greta asked. It was getting harder for her to talk.

"In some ways," I agreed. "But between us, you are a far better person than she was because you are calm and serious when it matters, and I respect that." After half a minute the silence grew heavy. I got out of my chair and went over to the bed where Greta was curled up. Her breathing was hard. I managed to get a hold of her arms and dragged her near me. Her head buried itself in my chest instantly. "So, what do you think of me?" I asked her gently while trying to get a hand on her forehead to see if she was sick. Despite my admittedly half-hearted efforts, her forehead deftly evaded my touch.

"I trust you. I feel I can rely on you against all logic. You are skilled and clever, but most of all you make every day an adventure," Greta muttered. Then in a much smaller voice I nearly missed she added, "I like your sense of humor, too." Only then did I detect the scent of strong alcohol on her breath. Somehow, I managed to pour a cup of water from a pitcher set on one of the side tables while Greta rested against me. After downing the water, my fiancée went into a deep sleep and I got back to finishing up the little work I had left for the night.

When I awoke the next day, I realized it was late morning and I had fallen asleep in my chair. Greta was nowhere to be seen but a blanket had been put over me and my computer had been shut down. A small folded map was set on the keyboard. I saw with only a cursory examination that it was the sum of my findings printed out. This construct of mine contained the current topography annotated with the old words and grid patterns I had known so long ago, only the positions were all slightly off. Greta must have put in some work as well because the map was far crisper and had a few more notes on different things than I recalled making. Resting on a small tray by my seat was a large bowl of soup covered by a lid, and a big mug of water. I ate swiftly and made my way to the lab. Before I walked through the doors, I heard Azull's sharp tone and stopped to listen in. "You feel better, don't you, so what's the problem?" she was saying.

"I spilled my feelings to him!" Greta practically wailed in anguish. I was glad I was not peeking in on her face; this was uncomfortable enough as it was.

"And did he respond?" Adder pressed in a smug tone that I found severely unbecoming but not unsurprising.

"Looks like he reciprocated a little too well," Clare laughed. The girl chat was really heating up, enough that I worried more for what Greta might do to them than her mental health.

"Shut up!" Greta snapped, at a loss for any more words.

A chorus of muffled snickers echoed from the room. It seemed their conversation had ebbed for now. Not wanting to stand around for much longer, I knocked loudly on the door. "Is this a bad time?" I asked.

"When did you get here?" Greta asked as she beat a hasty retreat to the new coffee machine.

"Not long ago," I shrugged. "So, thanks for the extra work on the map, honey."

"You want what in the coffee?" Greta called over.

"He says you are sweet and important to him," Clare stage-whispered loud enough for us all to hear.

"Grandma!" Adder and Azull reprimanded the queen mother.

"Anyway, I need to take a trip before the basic training of the order starts up fully," I announced.

"Count me in!" Adder cheered.

"No, you need to start getting your unit to coordinate," I told her.

"But my troops are a bunch of ruffians," Adder sulked.

"So beat them up until they can work in small teams," I told her. The former princess beamed so happily at the prospect of a battle royal that it was difficult to suppress a grin.

"I'll go," Greta said.

"After this your fiancée has a big secret project to work on with me. In other words, no men allowed in the lab for a while." Clare nodded, not seeming to notice that she pushed Greta into my arms.

Before I managed to blink, Greta had hopped off my chest and glared at Clare, who seemed to find a new-looking tank at the side of the room to be very interesting as she whistled an old marching tune.

"I will go as well," Trish volunteered.

Folding my arms, I inquired, "Are you going to report to the order afterwards?"

"Yes, I am," Trish answered levelly, not once looking away from my gaze.

"Trish, you stay and make sure the new prospects are able to fight. Verndralla, Greta and I will go and see if we can find anything," I answered.

"Do you think you will find anything of note?" Trish pressed.

"If I do you will find out. Unlike the away team, you will not know what to look for and we may be in confined spaces," I told her.

Trish was level-headed enough to see that she would be of far more use where I left her and that the team I designated was the best fit for the job. "Very well," she sighed. Given that logic, I believed that Trish would not hold a grudge even if her real bosses disagreed.

"Leader, please call me Vern." Verndralla suddenly spoke

up, her monotone stronger than ever. With that one short off-topic declaration the room went still.

"Why?" Greta asked in the same manner one would try to verbally calm down a beehive or bear. I have to admit I did not know what was going on.

"'My lady Verndralla' is too long to say in combat. It is inefficient for long meetings as well. Vern should be sufficient for my needs," Verndralla said, seeming even more confused than I was.

Greta grabbed Clare by the collar of her lab coat and demanded, "What did you do to this girl?"

"Made her into a walking computer? The logic and memories I implanted evidently have taken hold too well." Clare shrugged very calmly for someone being held up only by the fabric of her coat and the heels of her feet.

"Ok Verndralla, Vern is fine, but at social gatherings and ceremonial occasions I will use your full name." I tried to compromise on the problem that I could see, if not understand.

Greta dropped Clare into a chair with a fluffy seat and grumbled, "Better than he was, anyway."

"See Squire Floseen for your transport. He will drive." Clare called after me as I left with a fiery beauty on my left and a cold beauty on my right.

8

Jack of Clubs

Jim "Mustard" Floseen had been expecting our arrival, much to Greta's dismay. *So much for a secret mission,* Pan scoffed within my mind. Verndralla looked at me. "So, there are five of us?" she asked.

"Who is the fifth, Vern?" I asked when the women and I climbed into a covered wagon and Mustard started to drive. Greta seemed dangerously on edge all of a sudden.

"He is," Verndralla said, pointing over at Mustard, all the while looking at me like I was the confused lunatic.

"So, who else do you mean? There are four of us," Greta pointed out, trying to sound reasonable.

"Leader counts as two," Verndralla replied, ironically concerned for our lack of understanding. Soon she gave up on us hopeless morons and took a nap.

Sometime after we had left the city our cart was rolling along a hard dirt road. Small mounds of melted concrete lined the road at regular intervals. *She meant me, by the way,* Pan told me, addressing my thickheadedness this time.

How is that possible? I asked Pan, my mind still reeling. Suddenly Verndralla sat up. Her head moved slowly and our eyes met. "You are two!" she informed me helpfully.

"He is what?" Greta sputtered uncertainly, far more surprised than myself, and unhappy about her focus being pulled away from the hefty book she had been diligently reading.

"I think she means Pan?" I whispered.

"Now this I have to hear," Greta smiled, her surprise gone now that her curiosity was piqued.

Pan, tune into the radios of these two, but make certain to leave the driver out of it, I commanded mentally. Soon after, something in the pile of silvery armor beside me buzzed, then a small voice clearly whispered in the earpiece, "Can you hear me now? Testing! Hello New York! Houston, anybody?" Greta jumped while sitting down. Verndralla simply nodded as if something had been confirmed. The connection this time was very good, so Greta was not getting any static. Verndralla on the other hand took out her headset but seemed to still be able to hear Pan.

"She sounds cute," Greta said. Her eyes had gone cold.

"It, not she," I corrected.

"Technically I am just a very sophisticated program," Pan told us, taking care to keep its volume low so Mustard did not pick up on its existence. Just as Greta began to calm down, Pan added, "But Master Reginald did choose this voice, and the name Das'Eins Pan."

"He what?" Greta snapped. Jim looked over at us quizzically then resumed watching where he was taking us.

"The one bread? I do not understand the significance," Verndralla said, cocking her head to one side with an expression even more blank than usual. From what little I knew of her, before she was captured, Verndralla was very expressive, something I could see clearly given that her laugh lines had not caught on to the perpetual deadpan look she never seemed to change out of now.

"It was either that or Dante Friar the Griller of Fools. I think it thinks those names are funny," I sighed.

"So, it was multiple choice?" Greta asked.

"Yes, but the second one I made far less attractive," Pan answered. Greta's expression seemed to scrunch up for a second. "Also, a bunch of animals are charging at us," Pan added. With only those words to go on, Verndralla, Greta and myself swiftly prepared for combat.

Sweeping up my sword, I leapt out of the covered wagon. "Mustard, hold here." As it would take far too long for me to put on my armor on such short notice, I left it in its pile.

"Mustard?" Jim asked after me bewilderedly.

"Leader means you. Stop the cart." Verndralla translated before following me. The lack of tension on her face unnerved both Jim and Greta but I found Verndralla's lack of apparent feeling now encouraging, so long as she acted as calculating and intelligent as she now seemed.

Looking around the road that led up the mountain, we noticed the summit was still half a day's ride away. Red sand and dull rock were all around us. A small hill sat on one side and far behind it was the mountain. Covering the other side was a grove of long-dead trees. *Pan, where are they coming from?* I yelled within my mind. Pan radioed, "They'll be over the ridge any second." After a few more seconds she added, "Now." On the word "now," a pack of twenty emaciated wolves and dogs crested the ridge and bolted past us without a second glance.

"Well, that was strange," Verndralla muttered.

"Something more dangerous spooked them," I nodded thoughtfully.

"Like what, a demon?" Greta asked.

"There is a roadside inn that way." Jim pointed in the direction the canines had been fleeing madly from.

I walked to the cart and began putting on my armor as I worked out a plan. "Greta, Jim, drive the cart slowly to the inn. Avoid combat as much as humanly possible. Vern, come with me. We are going to run straight to that inn."

Nothing more needed to be said. We all knew what to do on this trip to the unknown. Verndralla and I took off in the direction the pack had fled from. Jim and Greta mustered the horses and got back underway. Despite the enhanced strength my armor provided it was still very heavy, something I noticed only at times like this. Running across sandy uneven terrain was never simple but it was far harder when each footstep, no matter how far apart, sank into the gravelly sand half again as far than it would have if I had not opted to don my full gear. Verndralla and I cleared the half-mile run before the cart.

What I saw at our destination nearly made even me vomit, and I had seen some very grisly things. Fleeing from the robots long before had never come without a heavy cost in lives. The inn and its supporting buildings were mere kindling. One figure stood knee-deep in a literal lake of blood. I was never more thankful that I could not smell the outside air than at that moment. No body parts were visible in the lukewarm muck. "Oh god, it smells like crap and iron. Did that thing blend every living thing here? No way this is all just from human beings," Verndralla gagged.

I was still trying to get a good look at the human-shaped red-dyed figure that stood in the middle of what had once been a lot of living things. Before I could truly get a handle on what was going on, a familiar purple-eyed head popped out of the bloody muck. "Hey over here, save us! My friend needs help!"

On one of the red thing's hands a long sword that looked like it had been carved from a single chunk of dark crystal appeared. "Vern, drag any bodies you can find out of that place. I'll handle the sword wielder," I hissed unhappily.

"Fine, give me a second," Verndralla choked while on her hands and knees. After adapting to her nausea, Vern ripped off one of her sleeves and wrapped it around her nose and mouth before undertaking the nearly hopeless task. I was two thirds of the way to the monster before Verndralla had waded in my wake.

"Hey! Did you do this?" I called out to the red thing. It looked human but its eyes were cold and pitiless. It was a monstrous look but not one exclusive to monsters. All that mattered was slaying the thing that had pulverized this place, be it human, demon, or anything else. It would die by my hands.

"That's right, old one," the humanoid thing sneered. It was caked in gore, looking like a melted wax dummy. It dashed at me. I blocked its crystalline sword with my time-stilled sword. The dark crystal sword was shrouded in a wispy fog. I was so focused on keeping my enemy's sword back that I was unprepared for its backhanded swipe at my wrist. I was shocked. Despite my armor, this being was stronger than I was, I noticed while straining with two hands. Openly mocking my effort, the thing pushed me back with one hand on its blade.

"You are not human." I stated the obvious through gritted teeth. Pan heckled me in the in the back of my skull. *Well duh.* Somehow managing to slide my sword and body out of the path of my enemy's blade, I smashed the creature in the face with the pommel of my sword.

I tried to get under its guard and to its back by spinning low around it. "You no longer fit that description either," the thing laughed. One of its arms suddenly creaked and lengthened. I managed to grab what passed for its wrist before its inhuman hand was able to latch onto my neck.

"Any chance you could tell me where Jim James is these days?" I asked, trying to buy time to readjust my footing.

"Don't take my grandfather so lightly!" the thing howled, suddenly no longer calm enough to fight smart. It spun around only to cut itself in half on the sword I had rested on its back.

As the monster flopped into the lake of blood, the large

hunter I had met before coughed from the bank of the gore pool. "That was underwhelming." His mouth smiled, making up for the cheer lost from his dead-eyed stare.

His purple-eyed partner smacked him in the chest. "Shut up, Ron."

The man grimaced. "Ok, Katherine," he managed to choke out.

"So that's it?" Greta called from behind the pair that Verndralla had managed to pull from the murk, lifeblood lapping at our feet.

"Looks like it," Verndralla called as she probed the new landlocked sea.

"Verndralla, drag the monster up. I'll check if there are any more bodies," I proclaimed.

"You think it's still alive?" Katherine the huntress asked.

"Not for now, but demons have all kinds of quirks and this one is the oddest I have seen," I answered.

At the same time Pan informed me via radio, "If you put me in the let's say iron-filled water I can search faster than you can." I shot back mentally *Very well but remember, you asked for it.* I tore off my helmet and placed it in the middle of the new red water feature.

Verndralla had already dragged the upper half of my foe near the two she had saved. I stopped her from fetching the other half with a shooing motion. I dragged the lower half back to where we were congregating. Greta was hard at work with patching up the new witnesses and checking them for illnesses. When she looked up at me, Greta suddenly looked spooked. She sighed, "Are you trying to be remembered by generations of maids and armorers as the man with the for-ever blood-dyed helmet?" she smiled, showing that she was giving me a hard time.

Ripples begin to flow out from where I had placed my helmet. "I have no say in how I am remembered, only if I am."

Jim lightly kicked the upper half of the humanoid beast. "Don't tell me we are taking this with us?" His kick raked the shell of dried blood covering my foe. The covering cracked and shattered. What was underneath had some human fea-tures. It was covered in black ridges like malformed bone growths. A few spots of tan skin poked through here and there. It had jagged claws. When I prodded its lower half hard enough and its true form came out of its gore shell, we saw it had a tail wrapped around its waist. It had been cut in two around the gut.

"Our sponsor will want to see this," Verndralla nodded. She then went to work hefting the two halves into our cart.

"You mean the old queen?" Ron asked.

"That's right," Greta told him.

From the lake a sharp chime sounded. Pan yelled through Greta's radio, "Come and get it!"

"Looks like I have to reset the sonar program," I muttered, trying to calm Greta down by showing how unhappy I was with Pan's antics and making a nonverbal promise to yell at the AI later.

I kept an ear to the surroundings and trudged into the gore swamp again. "Looks like we can't use this rest stop," Jim commented.

"You aren't going to leave us here, are you?" Ron stuttered.

"You can ride with us until we get back to the city," Greta told them.

"Verdant Valley Eight is closer. We can look at how the fort is coming on the way back," Verndralla suggested.

By this time, I was halfway back with my helmet in tow. *No other bodies in any form other than a slurry,* Pan whispered in my brain. I knew it could sense my indignant anger and concern for Greta, so that was good enough. Pan knew it had used up its one chance to piss me off. "That sounds like a good idea. Vern, keep the two halves apart and if that thing gets up again, destroy it."

Verndralla looked conflicted. "If it revives, we could interrogate it."

"If it stays down and does not make any sudden movements we will, but if it is not the perfect gentleman, destroy it," I commanded.

Verndralla's eyes twitched sharply for a second. If not for how impassive she always seemed nowadays I would not have picked up on that. "Very well," she replied. We all piled into the cart. Ron and Jim sat up front and the rest of us arrayed ourselves around the boxes of tools and food with the corpse laid out in the center of the cart. Greta snatched my helmet from me and began to manically clean it.

Our cart rambled on. At some point while I napped, we got onto what had once been a highway but was now heavily shrunken in size due to mudslides and the like. Near midnight Ron halted the horses. "I think this is the place," he called back.

I had to swiftly down the beef jerky, nuts, watered-down

rum, and dry fruits that served as my dinner. Before I could speak, Greta looked out of the cart. "What is that?" She sounded mildly curious but that could mean anything from a weird sword to a huge demon at this point.

I reflected on how much Greta and I seemed to be alike now and wondered if we had changed at all, or whether I just had seen many more sides of her than I once believed were there. Gulping down one last swig of rum-flavored water, I asked, "Is it a monster?"

Greta leapt out of the cart, then turned back to me "No, it's more like a half-buried tower, but this ancient design is unfamiliar to me."

I followed her out and with one glance I knew we were in the right place. "Looks like they added some things, but this is where we need to be."

Verndralla was next to me before I knew it. I could tell my old memories helped her reach the same conclusion I had. "They turned a missile silo into an underground satellite launch pad?" Vern groaned reflexively. I honestly don't think she knew her face had changed slightly. "The search time just tripled."

"The worst part is," I began, trying to ignore Greta's progressively intensifying annoyed but very intrigued furtive glances. "Most of that is under fallen mud and rock."

"So, cave-ins in a big tower?" Greta asked.

"More or less. Most of it would have been a bunker and the security should have been top of the line. With any luck, the cave-ins would have wiped out the traps without plunging the whole thing into lockdown," I explained.

"So, what's the plan?" Ron asked.

"You two in any rush?" I shot back.

"No," Katherine answered guardedly.

"Then could I hire you both to keep an eye on the land around here? I need the cart and that tower to be as undisturbed as possible," I said.

"That works for us," Katherine smiled. Her face then grew stiff. "But if anything really big shows up, I will not fight it alone."

I nodded. "Jim, Verndralla, you stay and watch the cart. Greta and I will check out the site."

"Why am I not going, sir?" Verndralla asked. For the first time since she had been retrieved, I could see a hint of real emotion on her face.

"Vern, if anything happens to me you are the perfect search party," I told her.

Verndralla's face suddenly was impassive again. "And someone needs to keep an eye on the dead thing."

"We have already established you are the best one for that task," Greta said. She pushed a deck of cards and the book she had been reading into Verndralla's hands. "Try not to get bored," Greta advised.

"Will do, ma'am," Verndralla replied. Greta and I began to walk to the tower. "Stay safe," Vern called after us. When I looked back to wave, I saw her cradling the book to her chest. A very small smile flashed across her face.

We found a rusted panel resting in a small cleft on the mountain of long-dry mud. I managed to kick it open without any trouble. Within was a long drop down what was once a launch tube. "Well, some places in here still have power," Pan noted through my helmet's speaker.

"What do you mean?" I asked.

"You look like you are talking to yourself," Greta told me plainly.

Pan used the radio in Greta's vest pocket to speak next. "I called a maintenance elevator."

I swept the dark void below us with a primitive crank-driven flashlight. "Why would they have that and a ladder?" I mused, noting the few rungs still clinging for dear life below us.

"This thing was remodeled more than once, right?" Greta asked me. A small chugging heap of oxidation squeaked open. It had once been a mesh box operated on a powerful pulley system. Technically it was still an elevator, despite appearing to have more likelihood of crashing down than a speeding avalanche.

I gingerly tested to see if the floor would hold my weight. "At least one full refit, and if it has what I am looking for, then two or more," I told her.

After a good three minutes of careful prodding, we boarded the heap of rust and went down close to half a mile before reaching the first floor of the facility. On the way down, dents and some holes clogged with boulders jutted from the sides of the cylinder. The lab was set around a large bunker with many solid hatches.

This place has more security than I have seen in any human constructed place, Pan informed me silently. "Each floor has totally separate systems, including its own power supply. We should expect vastly different conditions on each floor," Pan said through Greta's radio.

Greta walked toward a hatch set slightly ajar on the roof-like top floor. "Then let's go," she said.

Four automated turrets powered on. Only two still could turn and one of those could do so only with great effort. "Stop!" I called out.

Greta did not seem to understand how little control over this place we had. She turned to me and said, "Unlike you, I live for more than just living."

I pulled out a laser pistol and took down the scanner on each turret. Greta dropped to the ground. Rushing forward, I managed to cut down two of the turrets. When I moved to charge at the other two, they had already shut down. Greta was lying on her stomach typing madly on a small computer. The one person I least wanted to lose leapt into the air gleefully. Before she landed, a soulless synthetic voice emanated from the door. "Administrator privileges transferred. Welcome new user."

Greta dusted down her combat suit which was no more than an energy absorbent coverall with a layer of light colonial space-age-era metal poorly reforged into scale mail laminated between two layers of protective cloth. Trying to pretend that she had not shown a childlike side of herself, Greta proclaimed in a firm clear tone, "Log my bodyguard as well. He is present."

"Logged. Be advised use of VI in this lab is strictly prohibited," the door said.

I elaborated. "Virtual Intelligence. It's a far less talkative version of AI. Pan is the only one with a sense of humor I have ever met."

"They are what killed off the old worlds?" Greta asked.

"Yes, but it was far more complex and multilayered than that," I sighed. A space in my call log labeled *The Bread* popped up, informing me that the user had gone into sleep mode. I created a mental note to Pan for when it woke up to stop messing with my gear's settings without running its new mods by me first.

"You really hate them," Greta muttered. Without looking up from the computer, she was ruthlessly typing away to ensure her hacking of the floor's VI was still holding strong.

"I do, but we can only change what we can," I advised my companion.

"And here I thought you hated anything inhuman," Greta informed me as we walked along the old steel hallway with only dim, flickering emergency lighting and our own convictions to guide us.

"I fear I can no longer call myself human," I whispered in the cold stale air, stepping over the third autonomous drone that was rusted to the floor, gun and all.

Greta stopped and glared at me. The lighting made us both look ghostly. She scolded me saying, "When I was a child, I dreamed of making something of myself, being the heroine in some epic saga. What always cheered me up in my early years no matter what was pulling me down was the sunset. I'd find the most remote place around and clear my mind of all but the horizon at sunset, thinking that's where I am meant to go. My story is just over that hill or that rooftop. I had thought I lost that for years until I met you. You make my life interesting and fun in ways I never considered, even in my darkest hours. So don't worry if you can't work out what to do or how to live. If you can't, then I will for the both of us. Now get to work."

"Life is a matter of perspective. I am happy you found that spark again, because I really need the help you give me," I sighed.

"You are greedy, but in a good way," Greta smiled. We combed the rest of the floor in silence. Overwhelming rust and sputtering circuits that should have failed millennia ago were all we found until we got to an unblocked ladder leading down to the next floor. A thick ion haze seeped from the holes in the wad of rust that had once been the lid sealing away access.

"Hostiles could be all over the second floor," I warned.

"There are, and the VI that controls that floor is in no mood to chat," Greta informed me.

I stopped Greta from pulling out an old model autoloader pistol. What concerned me was our battlefield and that the handgun in question was the kind that used an electrical impulse to fire its bullets. "Too unreliable where we are going use this," I told my fiancée, handing her my time-stilled sword.

Without looking up from her computer Greta deftly snatched the proffered blade while mulling over my words. "The raw current below us will be that much of an issue? Will our suits be ok?" she asked.

"The chances of sudden equipment issues are more than I'd like. So, we will need to minimize all risks that we can.

There is still a small risk of our shielded gear being badly overloaded. So, we will need to keep an eye on our things." I pulled the old tungsten Zweihänder from my warp pouch.

Greta examined our swords. "Understood. I'll protect you."

Peering past the trap door I told her, "Right, and I'll watch your back."

Greta gripped my shoulder suddenly before I leapt to the next floor. "What?" she asked.

Faltering for a second, my mind raced. "It means the same thing you said."

Greta sighed. "This time 'I'll defend you with my life' is the equivalent saying. The lowbrow version is 'we got this'." With the impromptu grammar lesson over, we leapt though the trap door and found ourselves in a pipe- and wire-filled hallway crackling with a dense electrical haze.

A pitted, wheeled combat drone sputtered down the hallway at me. Its tires had long rotted away. "Hostile terminal confirmed," it buzzed. Before the drone could fire the cannon on its back, I leaned forward, stabbing it all the way through with a short lunge. I swung upward, cleaving it in half.

"I see four more of them," Greta called to me.

On a hunch I told her, "Get behind me. I need to test something." Greta pressed herself to the wall and I stepped forward.

"One hostage detected," one of the new assailants crackled. Our new attackers looked the same as their comrade, or they would have if their wheels had not suddenly retracted, forming claws as they tried to hover. The drones were 5000 or so years too late and surrounded by a huge mess of electrical interference for their new mode to work, assuming the intent was not to burst into flames the moment they tried to lift off, then collide with the hallway and each other.

"Let's go," Greta told me. We ran away from the fireball of our attackers.

Running to the back of the base, we passed dials and long-empty fueling stations with piping that led upwards. My radio crackled a few times before I could hear past the static. Even then, all I could make out was "Need" and "Help?" being repeated at different intervals. I was almost certain Verndralla was radioing us.

"Lots of fire. Under the launch pad. What help?" I repeated a few times.

"Good," my radio wheezed. After a lot more static, I made out the word "Impact."

I barely had time to grab Greta and press her to the floor, shielding her before the entire massive building shook.

Greta did not squirm. Her eyes were locked on what had been a thick steel wall looming over the wall of fire. "That lunatic better not dissolve my ruin," she swore.

The wall crumpled, then dissolved. A huge gust of wind came in and Verndralla entered from a newly made ramp of dust she had carved out with her demonic powers. After draining the invigorated fire and electrical haze from the room and into herself, Verndralla walked over to us. "Leader found it, not you, my lady."

Greta leapt up and easily pushed Verndralla to the floor. Vern's eyes were pitch black and her breathing was shallow.

"Idiot, pushing yourself that hard," Greta scolded our rescuer. Verndralla begin to shake. Greta looked up at me. "I'll begin stabilizing her. You get the data before this place falls apart!"

"Don't either of you die on me," I said.

"I'll be fine and you'd better be as well. Now hurry up," Greta prompted me.

The way from which Vern had come was gone. The way behind me had no exit. There was an intersection a few steps behind where Vern was now lying unresponsive. I rushed over, seeing that the branching corridor was the only way down. The hallway was cramped and there was a sealed door at the end. No trapdoors had presented themselves so I shoulder-charged the ancient bulkhead with my armor's full might. I was being reckless but the rusted supports were not going to hold for long now that Vern had vaporized some of the bunker's walls. I foolishly thought at the time that compromising the precarious balance that had been holding the aging ruin up was not going to do much more than we had already done. Whether right or not, I had no way to know, but seeing as I found myself in free fall right after barreling through that bulkhead, my worst miscalculation was thinking that most of the building was still holding itself in one rusted blob. The cavern I found myself falling through was studded with bits of rust. Rocks and sand had replaced flaking steel. One boulder took up an entire section of wall all on its own. Roughly halfway down, I landed face first on one ledge that had once been part of a floor. A worn map hung lopsided at eye level. In large cheery red letters, it proclaimed I was on floor number four. My fingers brushed a small plastic board.

After carefully nudging it in front of my helmet's visor, using the focus I needed to ignore most of my pain, I read aloud the board's presumptuous message. "Welcome to the VIP food court." After snickering for a good half a minute, I felt well enough to carefully prop myself up, hoping the sheet of decaying metal did not collapse upon me.

Looking up, I could very well believe I had fallen nearly two whole floors. "Well, this day could not get better," I sneered. Fate deemed fit to take my words literally. No sooner had I spoken, a few fist-sized rocks landed next to me. "Oh cave-ins, great. Thank you, Mother Nature." Bigger rocks began to fall. So, I did what any half-mad blasphemer would. I raised my middle finger to the roof of the cavern and jumped further into the void. Whatever was watching over me was either very good at impressing the urgency of what was going on or a total sadist, or I was being delusional. "Life or death really brings folks closer to some kind of higher power," I grumbled, nursing a splitting headache.

I found myself trapped in a small shaft, my legs and arms wedged above me. Rocks fell to the floor inches from the divot my head was in. Then the image in my helmet blinked out for a second. When it returned, the vision settings began to rush by one after another. Infrared, heat, night vision, solar, flash shielding and more all switched off and on. The zoom function was also having a field day as it went randomly though all its levels of magnification and focus without giving a damn to how in focus anything was. "I am too young to need a barf bag," I wheezed somehow.

What the hell did I miss? Pan screamed from within my mind. Its voice seemed far closer than before.

I promised, "I'll tell you if you get us out of here."

Now that I have my other half back, from here this will be no sweat Pan cackled, seeming far too close to the core of my mind for comfort. Then with a click and a whir the shaft I had fallen in opened wide, swallowing me whole.

I picked myself up from yet another floor only to find myself in a bunker-like lab filled with glittering computers. "Hey, over here," one of the large data banks called in Pan's voice. I turned my head only to hear "No, this way" from the completely opposite direction. Before I could react, a nearly human-looking face pressed itself from inside my helmet's display. "No, in here, human."

I nearly had a heart attack. "Who are you!" I tried to scream but only managed to barely speak, my fear and abused body producing only a weak coughing fit as I choked out my demand.

"It's me, Pan. Only more of me," the face of a small girl told me. Then it shrank and took the place normally reserved for my sonar readout.

"Hey, I need that. Also, what?" I said.

"Well, part of me appears to have been locked away here," Pan said, the disembodied head giving a far too human expression.

"What part?" I asked, feeling far more pain than the dread I should have felt at that moment.

"Human interfacing and most of my memory banks," the head told me.

My stomach dropped. "That's why you sound so close when you speak to my mind now?" I asked.

"Yes?" Pan said. It sounded like a question but it seemed like the robot inside my head was trying to dance around the issue. Suddenly Pan added, "But I have all the data that was here! They were using my memory banks as a storage medium!"

"So, all of this was for nothing," I sighed. Somehow, I felt very tired.

"You made that borrowed sword cooler! That's real robot assisted electroplating well done!" My eyes began to close. "Hey don't die on me. You are my host, remember. Wake up!" Pan yelled into my brain. "You know what? Fine, nap. I'll get us out by blowing up this damn mountain!" Pan screeched right into my cerebral cortex.

Needless to say, that insane declaration woke me up fast. "My team needs time to flee you, psycho," I feebly managed to sputter.

"They will be fine. I only need to blow away the part they are not on. After that your girlfriend should find you, no problem. You can nap but I swear if you start to die on me, I will shock you awake so hard you will be spasming for a month at the very least!" Pan riposted, thankfully using the helmet mic again.

"Why are all the women around me so mad all the time?" I wheezed. Even in my barely cognizant state I knew that was more unfair than not.

A flash of light later and the far wall of the room crumbled, revealing a grassy woodland hill being mercilessly demolished by a freakishly huge rockslide. "Because you are so thick-headed," Pan yelled over the chaos she had wrought. As my mind faded, my only thought was *When did Pan stop being just a robot to me?*

9

The Horse and the Dog

I woke up, only to be peering from within a thick bubbling ooze. The room outside of the capsule where I found myself entombed looked like the place I had been stuck for so very long before reawakening in this time, the difference being all the scholars rushing around. The tables covered in old world tech and the large generators set up on one far end of the room stood out the most. "What the heck is with all the mouth breathers?" I found myself muttering.

"That is a very robotic thing to say," Adder called up from a desk set at the base of the thing I was stuck in. She was right, and I was temporarily speechless as all kinds of fevered hypotheses flashed through my mind.

Debra Woods rushed over from somewhere beyond my limited line of sight. "Sleeping scar-face awake now?" she inquired in a manner more fit for sleeping classroom delinquents than badly hurt adults.

"Yes, he is." I tried to smile, only to wince at some pain in my jaw. "What year is it?"

"You mean cycle. I've spent two and a half weeks waiting for you. The Order has two weeks left for training before our trip to the Drenneth fort. Take it easy for now. Your bones are still healing," Adder informed me in a sleepy tone before leaning back in her chair and swinging her feet onto a crate of pickaxes.

"No wonder this body is sore all over," something that was not quite me said from my lips.

"If not for your armor, Pops, you would have been paste," Adder murmured in the middle of drifting into a light slumber.

Exemplar Woods reviewed some data on a panel attached to my capsule. "Who have we been talking to?" she whispered while still focused on the numbers.

I was more shocked and unnerved by what I knew was the truth than I had ever been before. "I don't know" was the farthest I could let myself admit.

"See that you figure that out by the time you see your girl-friend." Debra sighed quietly before shutting down the panel and locking its screen. She dislodged a pickaxe from under Adder's limp feet and walked off. "I need to get back to excavating your old home. Now get some rest."

"Being engaged to her former student earned you some points, Pops," Adder groggily snickered before returning to a fitful slumber.

Uncomfortably, I thought hard to myself *Pan, are you still around?*

A response came from around my sense of right and wrong. *Still here, oh that's not good.*

I screamed inside my head before thinking *Pan, how did you get out of the implant?*

When we almost died. You are lucky that only most of your bones got the snot beat out of them. Thanks to that damage, parts of us got jumbled up so some of me is now literally part of your brain. Chuck, you are neither a full cyborg nor have you lost your sense of self. This is very unusual. Pan relayed back to me.

The words "How did this happen?" slipped from my lips.

"How did what?" Adder asked roughly a full minute later, rubbing her eyes. Pan meanwhile was probing around in my head while I was trying to set aside some private space in my own brain.

"Was the data from the ruins intact?" I asked, trying to shift the conversation and get my sanity more or less back on track.

"It was. I did not understand all the techno babble. The eggheads said 'nanobot' over and over, but that's all I understood. Sorry, Pop," Adder sighed.

"That explains a lot." Pan voiced her or maybe its thoughts through me.

Adder glanced quizzically at me with one half-open eye then she hit a button next to her with an easy familiarity I found troubling, to say the least. "Get some rest. You should be able to walk around without falling apart by tomorrow," Adder muttered. Something was released into the pod that made me very, very sleepy.

Putting my trust in those close to me, I let the feeling of grogginess take me. "Thanks, see you tomorrow. Sweet dreams," I muttered.

"You too," Adder yawned.

When I awoke again, I found Debra looking over an access panel nearby. She looked up and our eyes met. "You ready to get out?" she asked.

I nodded "Yes?" but my words came out far more quizzically than they had any right to.

"Is your head all right?" Debra inquired suddenly. Her fingers blazed across a few battered screens around my pod.

"Not once in my life," I forced myself to joke. "After all, I am only human." The goop in the pod drained with a grating plop.

The pod cracked open, admitting me into the air once more. I took a look around, finding myself in the old entryway I had been trapped in for so long. The rockslide in the back was almost totally cleared. "We can discuss that over breakfast. The findings you returned with have answered a lot and raised far more questions," Debra sternly informed me. Her tone was clearly more for Adder's benefit, who was still watching me.

I was led to a line of large logs and very worn iron stools. On the way over I leaned over and whispered in Adder's ear, "So Miss Woods does not know who you really are?"

Adder sighed, temporarily looking just a tad remorseful. "I am not who I once was and not what I was intended to be, so drop it. The ones who know my past are more than enough."

When I sat down, a burly cook sauntered over and placed the Zweihänder in front of me. The tungsten blade was covered in chaotically embedded copper wiring and had swirls of many other alloys. It was neater than I had ever seen it. A new scabbard of black hide and gold stitching fit over the long blade like a glove. My eyes were drawn most of all to the small stasis generator exactly like the ones that had held me hostage, fitted to the guard. "Your sword, my lord," the man nodded before walking back to a huge pot of stew that was sitting over an electric coil powered by a team of five men with a very large crank.

Debra sat across from me. "According to the new data, the demons are bundles of antimatter and dark energy, each formed around a colony of nanobots. The demon's core is a safe zone the nanobots cluster inside of. The demons were made to counter some kind of external threat. Do you understand?"

"Yes," I nodded. Three bowls of oily stew were set down at our table. No one sat with Adder, Debra and me, even though the other improvised tables around us were full. Some bread and dark beer were provided as well.

"All of it?" Debra pressed. She sounded both firm and surprised.

"Besides how the demons were first made, yes. Any other questions you have that I do not know, I can make educated guesses about," I smiled. Somewhere in the back of my mind Pan was grinning too.

Breakfast took a long time to finish because I had to explain to Debra what Adder and my friends already knew about the fall of Earth and other lost tidbits of past human history. At some point I had to get deep into explaining the technology of my time. "So, you are just as old as Greta said," Debra concluded when the cooks chased us away from the tables they were trying to clean.

"What language were you two using?" Adder asked in half-hearted annoyance.

"Old Worldean" Debra replied, totally straight faced.

Stretching in one corner of the room I asked, "That's what you call it? What happened to Latin?"

"Never heard of it. Is that like legalese?" Debra asked.

I began to do pushups near a wall. "Is legalese a dead language?" I inquired.

"Yes. It is said to be the native language of the ancient bailiffs," Debra told me.

I had to chuckle at that. "Well, you are not wrong, exactly." Exemplar Woods was not amused at my show of jubilation.

"With that out of the way, I need to go and get some air," Debra sighed, pointing up to a hole past the rock slide where a rope ladder hung.

"The queen's exit," Adder nodded. "That's where your benefactor escaped from this place."

Debra stopped me at the ladder. "Take your things with you," she told me thoughtfully.

Adder pressed a leather coat and the Zweihänder into my hands. Preemptively answering my question, she informed me, "The rest of it should be with the Builder for mainte-nance." I swiftly put the coat over the thin undersuit I had been left with, strapped the sword to my back, and began to climb. Assuming Clare had used this to flee from captivity, the cave-in must have been fairly recent. After a precarious climb I found myself atop a grassy mound, a few feet under which was the roof of the old lab. None of the scanning systems or antennas that had once covered this place like an iron forest so long ago were anywhere to be seen. Real trees, shrubs, and flowers covered the unnatural hill in place of the things that I along with many others had helped install when we first landed on this planet.

I sat down under a gnarled pear tree. Adder came up and stood across from me. Looking around, I tried to pick out at least one sign that human hands had built the place. Finding nothing, I mumbled, "Times really do change."

"Yes, they do," Azull Waldersoloft nodded from the base of the green mass I sat upon. Chief Judjerex Trugeddeen was with her. "We are here to bring you to the training fields!" Azull called before I could begin my nap.

"Of all the…" Adder grumbled, seemingly unhappy with her former twin.

Standing up swiftly, I walked to the queen mother's APC. "Let's go, kid," I smirked.

"Yes sir," Adder answered cheerily. For the whole day she took great pains to not look Azull in the eyes.

"So, who's the driver?" I asked.

"Squire Floseen has that honor today," Azull shrugged, leading us into the APC.

I had to force down a retort. The second I sat down I took a nap so I could converse with Pan, hoping the others would take the hint and not interrupt me. Thinking hard, I secretly said *So how much of my mind have you taken over?*

From deep in my consciousness, Pan replied *I am all over your mind, but you still have control.*

Are you certain? My thoughts are not quite the same as they were, I replied

You are still you, and I want you to stay you as much as possible, Pan retorted. Our closer connection told me that's how she/it really felt.

Let's keep it that way, otherwise my humor may lose its edge and we don't want that, I threatened.

Indeed. That's your best quality, came Pan's quick-witted reply.

Ferdan Trugeddeen broke my train of thought by thrusting a stack of papers into my hands and saying "That's your recruit assessment summary," answering my unspoken question.

Switching gears, I took a deep breath to center myself. "Are we on the way to the training grounds?" I asked with what little brain power was not being used to pore over the papers.

"The Steelglade is not far," Azull chimed in.

I glanced across from my seat, asking, "Adder, your team is fully trained?"

"Teamwork and basic combat skills are all done. Right now, they should be cross training with the other units. Your officer corps chose to leave the tactical training, final assessment, and hiring up to you. We had to out-vote Knight Lieutenant Trish on a few things. Your team is being trained by Xen for now," Adder told me disinterestedly as though she was reading down an acquaintance's shopping list for cleaning supplies.

"So, you are Knight Lieutenant Green now?" I asked, smiling. Not expecting much of an answer, I resumed browsing the papers.

Our ride was more or less quiet, even with all the bumps and sounds of occasional crunching from outside. The trip was not smooth with the APC's suspension clearly overworked. After a good minute Adder cut into the stillness. "You were elevated to Count and Greta is officially Lady Errant – Errant being the new given last name of your fiancée and Verndralla. Trish, Verndralla, and myself are Knight Lieutenants and therefore members of the non-landed nobility."

Despite her outburst Adder had given an even better summary than she used to, so I asked something I had taken note of in the paperwork right before she had interrupted my in-depth study. "It looks like we have fewer candidates than we started with."

"We had quite a few prospects drop out in the first week. Booted out a few spies and had fewer than five bad injuries, but somehow no deaths," Adder told me.

I nodded my thanks and tried to resume reading before Azull asked, "So your new sword, what's its name?"

"Caesar-Rex," I told her with surprising swiftness. Then the APC stopped.

"We're here," Jim Floseen called back to us.

Adder and I jumped out of the hatch into a landscape of deep canyons covered in wreckage that had made its way here from Earth and scraps of iron from the training taking place today. It was a large glade with a deeper gorge in the center, covered in many feet of scrap metal and wreckage. "Well let's round up the troops and put on a show," I said, trying to work out the kinks in my body. I sat down on the hood of a car that was poking up through the scrap. The top layer of metal around me was sword and axe blades. Some were stuck in the rubble as if sprouting from the ground. It took half an hour to round up all the 936 trainees of the 1000 we started with. At the end the 500 best trainees wound join the order. So far 42 had quit, 36 in the first week; 9 were revealed as spies; 11 had been crippled; and 2 had tried to desert with their gear. The spies were all sent from within Farfallen, so their handlers were all fined heavily. Normally a few fingers would have been taken as well, but that was waived by the king and queen. The deserters, however, were all found and killed on the spot for stealing the gear.

After the troops had been standing around for a while, I let my mind get back on track. Trying to remain unreadable, I asked, "Is this all that's left?"

Trish saluted. "Yes, commander!"

"Affirmative, leader!" Verndralla Errant reported.

"Present and accounted for, Count," Ferdan bowed.

"That's right, dear," Greta smiled.

"Right you are, Papa," Adder lazily added.

Those last two responses drew odd looks from everyone present but myself.

If any of the trainees had talked that way to me, I would have reprimanded them harshly at the very least. I considered Greta, Adder, and Clare to be family. It was good Adder chose to act a bit childish sometimes, otherwise I could have had trouble seeing her as my daughter. "We have more left than expected," I grinned. "Knight Lieutenants Green and Errant, bring the two most skilled prospects from each of your units forward. Chief Judjerex Trugeddeen, you do the same with the ones you have been training."

Adder walked into the center of her charges and dragged out two small slim teenagers, one boy and one girl. These two could not have looked more different than their unit-mates, given that all the others in that bunch were large brutal-looking folk armed to the teeth. The disconnect was intriguing.

"Prospect Lue, sir," the girl introduced herself.

"Prospect Carol reporting," the boy nearly shouted before the hulking men right behind him began to laugh. Lue glared at them, causing the men twice her size to retreat a step back.

"Sir Jason Wulfard, Sir Brandon Wulfard to the front!" Ferdan bellowed. Two well-built lightly scarred men in their mid-twenties sauntered out of the pack of preening nobility. Behind them I had to suppress an inward groan at the sight of so many prideful sons of the nobility. The number of females in my unit was far lower than in the others as well. Jason had light hair and Brandon had dark hair. Other than that, and without the scars, they looked totally alike.

"Puppet, Field-foe, get over here!" Verndralla yelled at her team. Most were long-limbed and rugged looking.

"You six." I pointed to the ones singled out by Ferdan, Verndralla, and Adder. "You fight me all at once. I will be keeping a close eye on your coordination and combat skill.

You each will use the armor you have been using and a training weapon of your choice, but no guns or explosives. I will use two training blades to keep it fair."

"That's not fair," Adder sighed.

"Is there a problem, Lieutenant?" I snapped.

"Even unarmed, you would beat them to a pulp," Adder shrugged. "Even I could destroy them with those conditions, but I could never win against you." Her unit and a few faces in the others lost a significant amount of color in their complexions.

"You forget I am still healing, plus this is only a test. Hopefully they will learn a lot more before the real fight starts," I said loud enough for the crowd to hear. "So, I expect you all to watch closely."

After far too much running around to get the required armaments, I stood facing the six prospects. "I order you six to not hold back. Treat this as if your lives were on the line and guard your bones well," I commanded.

Puppet charged. His spear sat well in his hands. A few steps to the side Brandon rushed forth, a great sword held high, and Lue came in low, a thin sword ready for an uppercut or a stab. The three others took this time to edge around my back. I met the charge, getting between the two swords before they could move far enough to hit me. In one move I kicked away Lue's sword, hitting her in the gut with the hilt of the sword in my right hand while my left sword's guard deflected the great sword right into Puppet's face. A few gasps were raised but Pan assured me he would be fine. So, I brought my left leg around and pulled the already off-balance

Brandon to the ground where I kicked him in the side of his helmet just enough to rattle him for a while. Jason, Field-foe, and Carol stopped in their tracks. The flanking move had failed. It did not take Carol long to lose his cool. He leapt at me while my back was still turned. So, I thrust one sword into the ground, took a small step to the side, and grabbed the boy's wrists, carefully avoiding his sword. Then I tossed him to the ground, making his own momentum his downfall. It seemed to me that Jason would recover from his shock before the spear-woman next to him. I dashed low and to the right at Jason, keeping him between me and Field-foe. I hit Jason's right hand with the butt of my remaining sword then kicked out his legs while spinning him by his shoulder. His heavy armor and the ground did the rest. A few of the boy's bones rattled around but it was going to be disorienting and a bit painful, nothing more. Lastly, I hit Field-foe in the gut with my shoulder and wrenched the spear from her hands.

Greta begin clapping sternly and yelled, "That's over! Medic on team B, treat the fallen."

I looked over the prone and moaning forms of my opponents. Their downfall had taken less then fifteen seconds. "Disgusting!" I bellowed. "I said teamwork, as in synchronizing all the manpower you can get fast, then strike your foe hard as if you were of one mind. Fancy tactics will gain you nothing good in the middle of a melee. Be careful, diligent, aware, and brutal. Never ever hold back when you see an opening you can exploit." The six were only now getting up slowly, one by one. "Prospect Carol, good effort, but lose your cool like that in a real fight and you will far more likely die than wound your opponent. My daughter is taking it upon herself to train you. Do you know why?"

Carol was suddenly the center of attention. "To kill the demons off once and for all!" He yelled, his stance unstable, but his voice held surprising vigor for a body so young and slim.

"That's right. To end a long war. So do not put her hard work to waste and be suicidal!" I bellowed back. Looking around I sized up the mood. It was low. Everyone was alone with their thoughts along with hundreds of their fellows.

Adder glared at the troops around her, then she raised a sword high over her head. Adder's voice in the still glade began softly. It was firm and gained in volume as she spoke. "For those of you that join the Errant Order, your lives will no longer be your own. Your lives are collateral to fix this messed-up world we have feared for so long. Your lives are not yours to spend as you wish. The leaders of each unit are your pay masters. We are masters of our craft and better fighters than the entire units we command. So, you will work as one. You will heed our commands and we will see that you never spend your lives cheaply. You will all make the demons pay through the nose for every single one of your lives. Because that is how all of us tell them we will not give up. That is how we spit in those monsters' faces and how the fear we have all felt since childhood when something goes bump in the night gets blown the hell up!" The applause afterwards topped everything but the pride I felt right then.

It seemed to take far longer than would be normal for the prospects to settle down to the point that coherent conservation was possible again. The moment I felt they could hear me over the roaring in their ears, I yelled "Ok, calm down!" A few more seconds of this and my head really began to pain me so I yanked Caesar-Rex off of some rubble I had set it on and tossed it to Verndralla. "Vern, that's yours now." Finally, the cheers and whispers stopped. I glared at them. "As to the rest of you, train hard! Unit leaders, I will be reviewing your training progress for one week." The prospective members of the Errant Order all began to walk off. I raised my voice again. "I did not say you are all dismissed!" They halted and began to line up. Only a handful seemed to hate me already. "Some advice: staying calm and aware on the battlefield and in the wilderness is as difficult as it is important. No matter where or how, combat is no joke. A fight is not for morals or high ideals, it is for who is left. If you all believe putting an end to the demons is worth it, then train hard. I regret I have not been around more, but I was and still am healing from a near-death experience. That said, those I fought today did very well. As long as you all keep your heads you will be fine. Dismissed. You all have half an hour to rest. Unit leaders, we need to talk."

Greta and Trish's teams began to cook and the units sat down in small groups. After some minor details were sorted out, Greta, Trish, Verndralla, and Adder met me on a small mountain of what used to be the engine block of a space-faring battleship. Our legs dangled close to the ground. The ship itself must have been buried very deep indeed. "It's a shame salvaging is forbidden here," Greta sighed. Then she glanced at Vern. "So, what's with the sword?"

"It can be used like a spear and my own blades are very good," I shrugged. My fiancée grudgingly nodded. "Trish, are you still relaying info to the Demon Slayers?"

Trish looked me in the eye. "Yes," she replied clearly and without much feeling.

"Ok. Adder, Greta, pick guards from each of your units. Trish and Vern will get four guards, two from Adder's team, two from Greta's. Adder, you will get four from Greta's unit and Greta dear, you will get four from Adder's unit," I told them all.

"Ya can count on me, Mum!" Adder smirked. Her attempt to cheer Greta up seemed only to make them both more uncomfortable.

I chose not to poke my nose into something I did not understand. "Trish, any correspondence you send out will need to be reviewed by me. You can feel free to request releasing specific data to your handlers. I will review each request."

"You do not seem afraid anymore that I will betray you," Trish noted solemnly but with far more energy than before.

Trish's face regained its color for close to half a second before a long training sword rested on her neck. Caesar-Rex poked her in her stomach and a handgun rested on her forehead. "No matter what, you will not be forgiven again," Adder, Trish, and my better half threatened on my behalf. I was the only one surprised and Trish the only one without a weapon suddenly in their hands.

After we all put away our weapons Trish asked, "So does Knight Lieutenant Errant's new sword have a name?"

"It's called Caesar-Rex," I told them.

"So, what, like emperor king?" Vern muttered.

"Exactly," I grinned. The other three seemed confused.

"That's so cliché and lame," Vern pouted.

"I have heard that before," Pan agreed through me.

"Break's over!" Azull called from behind us. "I'll see you all in two weeks. Be ready by then."

"Let your grandmother know that I'll need my gear back before then," I replied.

The royal guards behind the princess went to draw their blades until Azull laughed, causing them to pause. "Ok, it's a deal, Chuck."

After that I reviewed the training for a week while my sore muscles healed and my bones finished getting back together.

Greta ran her support team through medical, disaster response, data analysis, and a few Clare-approved hacking sims. Debra Woods and a few senior arctechs helped as their drill instructors. Some of the other teams had to lend members for a few of the medical and disaster drills as the nonliving training dummies (foam, wood, and holographic) could only show so much. Greta's team also handled all the meals. Trish's team helped them by hunting and foraging. We had the other teams send over a few members every day to hasten preparing the ingredients for the cooks. The support team also had to train in hand-to-hand and lots of pistol work. Speedy reloading was a big hurdle for many of them. Although using the armor systems took almost all of a full day to learn. Most of the other teams had to take half a week for real competency to show with the armor software.

Adder ran her team ragged. Her team had technically

finished all the training they needed for selecting the final members of the unit. My team seemed less than thrilled to incorporate up to fifty members at a time from Adder's ruffians in the knightly training drills, but after pointing out that all those that passed these trials would be given knighthood, the noble sons Ferdan had been putting up with agreed to help educate the commoners about what it took to be an honorable knight. Verndralla's lancers took far less coaxing in the form of sharing some beer every time the fifty ruffians for the day came over. Anyone not running around with other units had to run though the metal maze that was the Steelglade. It was not only the richest heap of scrap outside some lost ancient cities but also the only one on the planet completely off limits from looting, which caused all kinds of hazards. Old blades and sharp weather-worn hull plates jutted from all angles in the crevasses at the heart of this place. Adder took nearly all the goo rounds meant for training. Those were filled with a paste that hardened like a thick cast when exposed to air. Her team's suits had temporarily been set to lock up wherever the goo hit, which made for some rather embarrassing moments during their training. She even dueled the ones who still could move at the end of the day, despite running herself ragged alongside her team. Adder always prevailed, to the point that at the end of the week her team offered up the prize money they had been adding to each day for whoever beat her. All that money went straight into paying for a huge party for the ruffians only.

Trish's team did a lot of long-range shooting at trees, holograms, and local wildlife – all those fair game. She was able to get a few specialized software patches from the Demon Slayers that aided her team's marksmanship and their speed as they acclimated to their powered suits. Her team did all the hunting we needed while training their tracking skills. They even had a few live tracking tests versus small numbers from the other teams. Her hunters, snipers, and trackers became our scouts and rifle team. Most of them were skilled with the various kinds of rifles they would be using, after some training to get them used to each weapon's feel, features, care, and notable quirks. The field strips for the energy weapons were the most nerve-racking for everyone. Greta's support team had to rush over more than once to treat some flash burns or hastily correct some of the more overzealous prospects.

Vern's lancers were the most diverse of all the teams. Most had spent some time as guards or militia but almost as many were farmers, messengers, machinists, warehouse laborers, blacksmiths, butchers, and small-time merchants. They also had the highest morale and worked the hardest during the training. Shotgun, carbine, and submachine gun use, maintenance, and firing were all drummed into them. Volley fire and extreme close quarter shooting while in a rough line formation were a big focus after they got the basics down. Bodybuilding, shields, spears, and javelins were all things they were forced to master until almost everyone could use them while sleepwalking. The medics came to fear the lancers due to the daily wounds that had to be treated. Vern's muscle-building plan had to be heavily aided with custom supplements from the capital. Otherwise, with the training regimen Vern had devised using the memories copied over from me, most of her troops would be in real bad shape. Verndralla had always been good officer material but lacked experience and rank until the ordeals she had been put though because of me. Many of the memories of her past were in bad shape. A few of the guards in her unit had worked with her in the past. More than one had been higher-ranked, but she handled that well, if coldly, like she tended to do. The lancers took the longest to achieve a passable level of competency with their suits. Somehow Vern swiftly became by far the most respected and beloved officer in the Errant Order. Her unit's dropout rate was higher than the rest but still within expected limits. Even then, they adopted a firm and ordered mindset. The infractions in her unit were almost nonexistent.

My team was still under Ferdan's guidance for the second-to-last week of training. Some from my shock troopers had their own slightly better (if still heavily patched up) ancient powered armor compared to what the rest of the grunts had been given. Even then, we were still short a number of usable suits. In my time, half of what we could use would have been returned to workshops that cut down and reworked rusted heaps of junk. The shock troopers heavily favored large swords and maces, which was just as well. The mass of those weapons would take more wear and tear before being unusable if they fought smart. Clare had somehow hit upon a way to treat non-energized weapons to make them resistant to demonic corrosion. The process was less effective but cheaper and much faster than the way the officers' gear was being optimized. My armor apparently had all its systems intact (very good quality salvaged armor had maybe a third of its components intact and half its systems still useable) and all its defenses were far above anything else. Even before having to confront the demons, my suit's shielding was very high-end. The newer (and even more rare) imitations of old-world technology were so poorly done it took seeing the shock troopers' full arsenal laid out before them to really get them to feel real. The effort with which they recently cleaned each part of their kit was commendable, but the gear they had would have been tossed out the nearest airlock in my time, robot apocalypse or not.

The time the shock troopers spent with Adder's ruffians was good for them, even if not a soul on either side would admit it. Thirty-four of the knights even began to favor skirmishing tactics and staggering their distance between each other. Crossbow and pistol proficiency were reviewed a few times with no real issues. My team had the most real combat experience of all the units. Most militias were trained only to contain and report dangers to the kingdom's army. Some of Trish's hunters had shot at (and with few exceptions ran away from) demons. The shock troopers had the support unit train them in first aid and how to use the software updates for their armor, if chosen for the order. All squad leaders had to be taught noble etiquette. My shock troopers all had been noble knights their whole lives, which made getting used to the other units a challenge. After a few joint hiking trips, hunting competitions, tracking exercises, and being used as guinea pigs for stealth classes, the shock troops gained grudging respect and acceptance from their fellow units. My shock troopers went so far as to challenge the other units to small-scale shooting challenges and mock squad-on-squad fights. Stern and proud as most of the shock troopers were, they used the challenges to learn from and advise the other units in their own haughty way. Somewhere along the line, Steel Softies became the shock troopers' official nickname, one which always made them groan in public. The extra voluntary training the Steel Softies provided never got so far out of hand that the unit leaders had to step in. The officers were all secretly happy about the extra work the shock troops were putting in.

The last week we had before our departure to Drenneth's border post, Clare, Azull, and Prince Jallace arrived at my base camp. A hoard of arctechs, Xen plus fifteen royal guards, came along. An honor guard of five Drenneth troopers lugging around their chainsaws on spears who went by the name Steam Glaives were never very far from Azull or the prince. Without a word to me, the arctechs and Xen began setting up a large camp of their own. Clare, Adder, Jallace, and Azull gathered in the tent that served as my office. At the time, Vern and Trish were off on a training exercise that was expected to end the next day. Ferdan and the shock troopers saw to the security of the area by guarding the camp. The support team was working to set up Clare's supplies. Therefore, the ruffians had drawn cooking duty for once.

The moment Jallace sat at the long wooden table he looked Adder in the face and said, "Princess, how do you do?"

Adder ignored him, instead looking sternly at her sister. "How much of the truth does he know?"

"I do not know, but he is no fool," Azull sighed.

"So, is he the compromise?" Adder pressed.

"Yes, he is to be my husband, but I will be the ruler of Farfallen someday," Azull replied mirthlessly.

"It's good ya found someone else, Sis." Adder burst out laughing. It took my adoptive daughter a while to catch her breath in the still and suddenly cold room. "I was once called Princess Adell." Adder bowed to the prince. Adder's fiery eyes killed the smile that had slowly begun to form on the prince's lips. "But I am Adder now. Both my name and my blood have changed. Do not forget it."

"Your blood?" the prince gasped. Clare and Azull both nodded glumly.

"I failed to kill my twin once, but if you ever make her truly unhappy, I will not grant you the same mercy," Adder said flatly, then she sat down in a huff.

"Anyway, when will you select your troops?" Clare asked as if nothing odd had happened.

"I will have a review of each prospective member of the order in two days' time. By the end of that day the five hundred finalists will be chosen," I reported.

"Could you pick ten substitutes for each unit as well?" Clare asked slowly.

"Yes, but why?" I began.

Before I could make a fool of myself, Greta spoke up. "The vaccine is that hazardous?"

Clare's eyes gleamed happily. "Yes, each dose should last roughly a day. The side effects are what worry me. Our only saving grace is that bad reactions observed in mice and boars do not appear in those that pass without issue the first time."

"So, you are betting it's an allergy and not just a very rare occurrence." Greta nodded thoughtfully.

Before a biology debate that no one but my fiancée and the queen mother would understand could take over until the next sunrise, Jallace asked hesitantly, "Are the side effects really that dire?"

Clare shrugged. "You know what they say about those with great power."

"That they are always right," Jallace quoted listlessly from somewhere.

"That one's new," I grinned.

"Indeed, old friend. It seems power does indeed corrupt." Clare shrugged. Before her granddaughters could scold her, Clare explained with every sign of reluctance. "Some of the test animals became demons."

"So you want to test the finalists and make certain none have this hypothetical allergy?" Greta sighed.

"Just so," Clare replied, looking extremely pleased with herself.

"Ok, so Count Evans, are you ready to kill the worthless foes of mankind?" Azull snickered.

I had been waiting for some noble to say that for so long. "Worthless, you must be joking. Nothing brings people together like a mutual enemy." I tried to remain steadfastly deadpan while marveling at how Azull seemed to step on every philosophical landmine I had ever prepared for her. I was even more grateful for how thoughtfully she took these admittedly annoying tidbits of advice. Jallace nearly drew his blade until Clare gave him a good-natured wink.

Azull glared at me. "You mean someone will resent us for wiping them out?"

"Many humans will, even if their rationale will largely be different. This is bigger than that as it's for the sole purpose of keeping the great equalizer at bay, if only for a moment longer," I told her studiously.

"Did you examine the monster we sent back, Grandmother?" Adder inquired after letting the room expel all the hot air that had accumulated.

"Yes, and I am jealous someone beat me to it," Clare grumbled in self-loathing.

Azull looked over at me. "I think this is best discussed between the two old ones."

"The peanut gallery can stay. After all, I can't guarantee that thing was unique," Clare snapped. She was more tense than I had seen her in a very long time.

"So, what's the good news?" Greta prodded.

"It dies," Clare shrugged. We all looked intently at the old queen until she grumbled wordlessly and began again. "The one you all shipped back had a few vital organs, brain, heart, two-chambered stomach, liver, rudimentary intestines, voice box, air bladder, normal bladder, rectum, testicles, no nervous system, blood vessels only around its organs. It's the reverse of what I have been working on, like someone took a demon and added some human pieces. If this was some old fantasy novel, I'd say it's like a dragon, but its DNA is almost nonexistent. In short, I have no idea how it was made, only that Chuck or Adder and Verndralla together would stand any chance of killing something like that and still make it out alive."

We were all speechless after that rant. Jallace rallied himself first. "Why has Princess Adell not married?"

"Who?" Adder smirked.

"What?" Azull snapped

"Because she would eat you alive," Clare snidely stage whispered.

The next day was the start of the tests. My unit was up first. One hundred and ten from each unit of trainees were allowed to stay. The rest gave up the gear Clare and the Demon Slayers had provided and left that morning. Anyone from the main groups that reacted badly to the vaccine would be sent back at the end of the day. The serum tests were to be done by squad, one unit at a time. Adder's unit took up guard duty and the shock troops clumsily went about camp maintenance, which earned the ire of the support team with maddening frequency, until Greta and Vern paired up squads from their units and had them take care of things together.

Around noon almost all of the shock troopers had received one shot of the short-lived vaccine. Adder and I were in the middle of our fourth practice match of the day. Adder's team needed nearly no supervision from her, and my team was being taken care of, so besides a few walks around the camp to check on things, our day was free. Shouts came hurtling down from one of the medical tents. Four shock troopers and a gaggle of arctechs chased after their panicked yells. Adder and I rushed to the scene. At the back of the tent, Adder turned to call after the folks running from it. Those still armed and armored stood their ground but anyone without combat gear or training fled the general area. "What!....." Adder shouted at the fleeing orderlies. She did not have time to finish. A wide wickedly clawed hand ripped open the tent beside her, forcing Adder to drop her questions and momentarily focus on evading.

I shouted at our nervous finalists. "Get back, all of you. Knight Lieutenant Green and I will handle this. All combat personnel, blockade the area." My orders were obeyed swiftly and the tension eased now that some kind of order had been reestablished. Despite the fact that we all had a very good idea of what the beast had been, everyone around me focused on their job and nothing else.

With no targets within the monster's reach around the tent and a lot of hard-to-find medical equipment shredded, the beast moved. The dark inky thing stood tall. It was lanky. Its core was where a human heart would be pulsating rhythmically. "Is it just me or does this side effect seem like a fate worse than death?" Adder quipped. She dodged around but her stabs did not go very deep.

"At least this is guaranteed to not happen to anyone who passed this," I replied from behind my formerly human helper, mentally adding, *I hope.*

I found myself glaring. Thankfully none of this frightened the newbies. I was glad of the hell Adder had put them through. "Well, this one makes more sense than eye drops causing indigestion." In the midst of her jibe the monster lunged and Adder cut off one of its hands.

Pulling out my plasma pistol I commanded, "Enough of this! Drop and roll."

Adder did as I asked. "Oh shit, everyone get down!" she

yelped. Just as the last friendly head in my line of fire had hit the ground, I fired on the weakest setting my pistol had at its disposal. The monster's torso erupted in light then vanished. The last bits of it ate greedily into the ground where they fell until finally evaporating.

Clare leapt to her feet and began to clap. The rest of the mob around the tent followed her lead. Even then, no one stepped a foot into the space where the monster had died. "So, which of you changed?" I hollered, pointing my ignition blade at the clump of shock troopers with breastplates hastily strapped over their sweaty uniforms.

A baby-faced grunt with short blond hair spoke up. "Lord Ernest Quill was killed in action, Your Grace."

"Well then, his family should get some compensation for their loss," I replied. All eyes fell on me, so I passed the buck in the direction I felt responsibility lied. "Isn't that right, Your Majesty?"

Clare's eyes sparkled for a split second with glee. "Very true. I will handle it personally," she stated solemnly.

10

Shell Game

The next few days were mostly uneventful. Adder, Vern, and I sparred. I helped oversee the workouts of my troops' strenuous exercise that had been prescribed by Debra Woods as a means of acclimating the Errant Order members to some of the beneficial side effects of the anticorrosion vaccine they would be issued. Side effects included sudden bursts of strength and speed, sharpened focus, sensitive hearing, and swifter blood clotting. A few of the troops exhibited yellow glowing eyes and sometimes veins that pulsed with a sickly yellow inner glow. All of the side effects were promised to last only as long as the vaccine was still in the users' systems. Most of the order experienced changes for only a half an hour per dose, although a few could go for an hour. Anyone who lasted for under twenty minutes or over one and a half hours was sent home. No one hit the upper limit Clare had helped outline. Greta had been kept out of the loop of the manufacturing process of the vaccine but she certainly knew more about its risks than she was willing to divulge. The few times I asked her she seemed torn on what to tell me and ended up saying nothing. By day two it was decided that Greta's unit would have teams temporarily attached to each unit with strict orders to stay within eyesight of as many of the order members as possible.

The fifth day of the week was the support teams' first taste of the vaccine. Greta's team leaders all had been helping with the treatment, testing and caring for the data produced from the order's physical exercises. Greta was in the testing area the whole day, which really threw my focus for a loop. That entire day I spent with Adder and Vern teaching some moves and tactics that had served me well. At midday, Adder forced us to take a break. The three of us sat on an oddly rust-free weather-worn alloy strut that could have belonged in any old midsized bunker or fallout shelter. Each time someone walked out of the tents being used for the tests, my eyes roamed over to their faces. At one point Adder had to wake me with a water bottle. "She will be fine. If Mom sees ya worrying over her she will kick your teeth in."

"Incorrect. There is an eighty-eight percent probability of a punch to the sternum, ten percent for the kidneys, one point nine for the pelvis, and point one for the teeth," Vern informed us robotically.

"Well, Miss Calculator, it could happen," Adder sighed.

"Correct, but it is still very unlikely, Miss Green," Verndralla nodded. After a few mouthfuls of a baloney sandwich, Vern added, "The nickname Miss Calculator violates seventeen active-duty regulations. If you have a better nickname than Vern, kindly inform me for processing."

We sat silently as Adder slowly went red in the face thinking. Before she could get back to Verndralla one of the tents dissolved. A large long-armed short-legged mass of solid darkness with a lamprey-like head came into being from some unfortunate soul. I hurtled up the hill, my twin swords in my hands, half a second after identifying the new enemy and what was around it. Greta was in the monster's maw, one hand keeping its jaw open and the other aiming a pistol at the large glowing orb at the base of its neck. Cracks radiated from where her free hand and legs bashed at the beast. Her cleanroom jumpsuit was almost fully eaten though, but besides a few light gashes that had already clotted over she looked physically unharmed. Before my eyes Greta yelled, "Chuck, get ready to grab me!" Then she emptied the power charge of her pistol into the beast. The scene was so surreal all I could think was *that's a waste of ammo – a demon that size should be done for after the third hit.* When the beast shattered into mist and slowly dissolving shards like chunks of obsidian, I ran and caught Greta. Adder threw a jacket she had picked up from somewhere over my head. Greta swiftly commandeered it and wrapped it around her seemingly wound-free body.

"You heal fast," I blurted out.

"Well, she is more like you and Adder now. So, what do you expect?" Exemplar Woods lifted herself out from a neighboring tent that had been dealt a glancing blow and crawled over.

"Shut up! I was saving that surprise." Greta huffed.

"Wait, what?" I asked, still stunned by the what I had just seen but happy that Greta seemed fine.

Greta hesitated. "Well, I may have undergone a few treatments here and there. When you were out cold, I was in a tank back in the capital." She gripped my arm which had been sliced by one of the harder shards of her kill, then held it up with my dark blood on her palm. "See, it does not burn me."

"You heal faster than I do," was all I could think to say.

"Now let me down. I have work to do," Greta demanded coldly.

After another few hours of showing off for whoever was off duty at the time, a runner came to fetch me. "The queen mother requires your presence," was all I was told.

It took a little while to get out of my armor and wipe myself down. After making certain all my weapons were with me and I did not reek too badly I went to see my oldest friend. Clare's tent was unguarded so I let myself in, expecting trouble in one form or another.

Princes Sern and Jallace sat in full armor with hot mugs of fragrant tea, a large plate of jerky and grapes between them. Clare was away from them at the far side of the table, which took up almost all of the tent. Azull and Adder were also in attendance. "I am told your castle is complete," Jallace said merrily.

"So, are you going to object to my brother's wedding too?" Sern asked snidely.

"As long as Princess Waldersoloft has no complaints and the Farfallen kingdom will retain its sovereignty, then no, none at all," I shrugged.

"So is Adder Green really related to you by blood?" Sern grinned blandly. He was trying to trap me to gain something. That much was clear at a glance.

I sat down next to the large blueprint Clare was mulling over and off-handedly replied. "I found Adder when she was still someone's clone. Some blood transfusions were to heal her. She is technically blood related to me, as all the blood she had when I met her is no longer in her veins."

Clare added without looking up from her work. "In all my years I have not heard of anything else like that being done successfully."

Azull moved to change the subject. "Speaking of blood, now that Lady Errant is safe from your blood's more hazardous properties, when is the wedding?" Azull was the only one in the room who did not hear the discontent in her voice.

"Preferably before the battle starts," I informed her.

"Good thing we are building the zeppelin next to your castle then. I will facilitate the ceremony before the Errant Order departs," Clare said, looking up from the papers for the first time and snatching some jerky from the table.

"That works for me. Clare, could you run that by Greta as well? I have a feeling that if I do, I'll pay with a few teeth," I pointed out.

Suddenly a sound filled the tent just like air seeping into the void right before explosive decompression. I tensed up hard and swiftly looked around only to find the sound's source was a deep intake of breath that only Clare and I seemed not compelled to do. "Chuck is among my oldest friends. He may not look like it, but he is older than I am," Clare explained.

"He is what?" Sern asked, losing all composure.

"A lot older than I look if you simply go by the year I was born. Due to some very old technology, I was trapped outside of time for a very long while," I told him blandly.

"What's a year?" Jallace asked.

"He means cycle," Clare replied right before lightly bopping me on the head.

"Regardless, what was I called in for?" I asked, settling into a chair.

"Will you and your order be ready to move out by the end of this week?" Sern asked.

"Yes. After all, that is what we agreed on," I replied.

"How is that possible?" Sern pressed.

"Because unlike you, Count Evans has risked himself many times over to save your kingdom," Azull snapped in an uncharacteristically biting tone.

"You care for the count that much?" Jallace asked. He seemed genuinely hurt although with politicians, especially those with tenure, bold-faced lies are a required skill.

"Honestly, Mr. Evans infuriates me to no end. He is crude, unsophisticated, and dense," Azull began. Each put-down lit the until-then dim fire in Sern's eyes. Azull then put up one finger and after a deep breath she continued with some reluctance. "But he is just who we need right now and no one else is fit for what we are asking of him. As insufferable as he is, his skill, honor, and cunning far surpass those of any of our own subjects. So, we will just have to deal with him." By the end of her talk, Sern looked completely despondent. Jallace did not look that much better.

"So, you do like Papa," Adder smirked.

"She did not say that, dear. So, Your Majesties, does this allay your concerns?" Clare asked.

"Mostly," Jallace answered, forcing himself to appear composed. This backfired, making him look like some patchwork doll whose expression changed each time it was held due to an acute lack of stuffing. Sern was pressed far back into his chair. With what was left of his princely ambience now shattered for the night, he nodded for his brother to continue. "I would like to ride in the transport to see how the Count will save the day," Jallace requested.

"As would I," Azull said.

"Ok fine," Clare shrugged. In looking at the plans for the zeppelin I did notice one very distressing thing, so I pointed to the power core of the craft which was labeled "helium-plasmatin centrifuge prototype near perpetual energy device." Clare pretended not to notice even as her eyes wandered over her blueprint. "It will be fine. The best fighters in the world will be with you."

"Chuck, Adder, you may go now." Azull waved us away. Sern recovered enough of his wits to toss me a small bottle of wine on my way out, one which Pan informed me was a bit vinegary but otherwise should be safe to drink. The fact that another being living in my head could communicate through my sense of caution was not the most pressing thing on my mind. Nor was why Sern had let me go without trying to get in one last jab. What really bothered me was why I felt like I should be trying to pull Pan out of my head by any means necessary, while no longer knowing why that seemed so vital.

My morning came even earlier than usual. It was not time for first light, but given how exhausted I was from the tiring day before, I knew that it was far too early for most of the yelling outside.

Almost no one but members of the order were at camp, rushing around on one task or another. An older man's voice rose and fell in turn above the chaos. If not for the shouting I'd have said it reminded me of the eye of a hurricane. The few outsiders mixed into the crowd were pale, their hands on the sheathed weapons on their belts, so their opinions may have been a bit different. The crowd parted for me readily although it seemed that my arrival was the start of the second act, for then coins began to be passed around and a betting pool was formed in my wake. *What are the odds on me, us, you? Never mind, time to fix this,* Pan snickered within me. Field-foe, her face covered in a few bruises and cuts, knelt behind Vern-dralla. An old very well-dressed man stood behind a younger man in dark leather armor who brandished a whip. Both sides glowered at each other but fell silent when I pushed my way into the eye of this madness. "You boy, do you lead this rabble of serfs?" The older man glared at me, no doubt believing himself to be intimidating. The younger whip-holder however did a quick head count, as did I. Not one of my troops showed any fear or compassion to the newcomers.

"I am in charge of this order of knights." I smiled as amicably as I could. Then I walked over to Field-foe, lowering myself so I looked right at her face, and asked, "So apprentice, tell me what really happened here?"

A voice that sounded suspiciously like Adder coughed

from the now deathly still crowd. "Lady killer." Her words were followed by the sound of a swift slap.

"Ask your betters that, boy. The words of a duke such as myself are the only truth here, or do you want the royal advisors to ruin your fun?" The old man giggled in a way I found more surreal than annoying given how his levity did not fit.

I chose to ignore the old fool. "Well, Field-foe, speak up," I said as gently as I could, given my increasing annoyance.

"The duke owns the land where the lunatic supporting him took my family. When I was a bandit, they ignored my existence. Now that I am useful, I suddenly exist. Somehow by that logic he owns me all of a sudden, even though as someone from a criminal clan I was lumped in with pebbles and sand but viewed as human." Field-foe replied sternly, her normally placid facade had hardened admirably.

I stood and glared at the duke. Azull pushed her way into the crowd. "Don't kill them!" She had the same sour look on her face that Clare had used when she was displeased back on the colony ships. *I need to make a copy of that memory,* Pan snickered in the dark corners of my consciousness. I felt a short jolt of nausea overtake me which I swiftly suppressed.

The duke tittered inelegantly. "That's right, your toy knight is mine."

"When did you recognize her as yours?" I asked.

The duke looked very annoyed and snatched up the whip his minion held in a slackening grip. The duke took a few steps forward. "When she was worth something," he raged.

"It is far from noble to treat others as tools. You see only what you wish to, you evil little man." The whip arched over my head and I caught it with a sharp tug. The duke fell into the pile of rust at our feet, dirtying his elegant clothes.

"You dare!" The duke struggled into a kneeling posture and sneered at me.

After swiftly stifling a yawn, I jeered, "I recognized the knights under my command long before buffoons like you even looked up to see this world dying under our feet."

"I said don't kill him!" Azull yelled, gripping the same hand I was using to keep the whip taut.

"So, this man had a claim to take Field-foe even though I recognized her as human first? You know what can of worms will open for this world, right?" I smiled patiently.

"This world? Can of worms? Just where are you from, boy?" the duke demanded after finally getting to his feet with some help from his aide.

"That way," Vern said, pointing up to stars.

"Impossible," the aide said, only now finding his voice.

"She was paraphrasing and I can't prove I am, but can you prove I am not?" I shrugged, then I looked over at Azull who was right behind me and tugged the whip out of the duke's hands, smoothly raising the tip of it over my shoulder. "Anyway, besides lying about a member of my Order being his, this duke also nearly hit you with a whip, Princess, so what now?" I noted while Vern looked over at Azull doing the most awkward puppy-dog-eyed routine I had ever seen. The duke had finally realized his ego may hurt him this time and his power would not save him from the hole he had found himself in. The duke began looking for an escape route.

Azull held her head in her hands heedless of how much she

messed up her hair. "Damn it, damn it. Why are you smart only when it suits you?" She looked over at Verndralla. "Vern, dissolve our uninvited guests."

"With pleasure, ma'am," Vern smiled. Dark fog rose from her arms. Small pinpricks of light swirled within that mist. Her sleeves were the first to disappear, then the duke was gone in a puff of smoke. It was anticlimactic, like some badly written school drama, after the aide and a few of the duke's men left the mortal plane without even a speck of dust to their names. The rest of the guards on the grounds besides my own began to look uneasy.

"Shape up, all of you, and burn this into your eyes! If nothing is done, all of the kingdom will cease to exist, just like these fools at the hands of monsters far worse than you have ever seen. So, remember, a monster killed these men and we are the only hope for ending the demons," Trish shouted. Then she glowered at me and took her leave.

When nearly everyone had dispersed, my stomach let out its own roar. "Damn, I am so hungry," I muttered.

Azull and Vern had yet to move from my side. Verndralla seemed curious about her hands rather than appalled that she had killed so many human beings minutes before with the kind of disintegration powers even very few demons had. "That's all you have to say?" Azull snapped at me.

"I think better when I am well fed. So, I will think harder when I have eaten. You should try that too," I told her mildly, then walked to the iron- and steel-covered ridge used for meals. My mind was far less calm but all the factors that had to be sorted out had to wait until I could focus. I felt rather then heard the words *stress eating* come from somewhere close to my conscious mind. "Shut up, Pan," I whispered. My rebuke felt like it was directed at myself, which only made me feel hungrier.

Verndralla, Azull, and Adder walked far behind me. "I can't tell if he is cool or crazy," Adder sighed theatrically.

"I hypothesize it is both," Verndralla agreed.

"What did I ever see in him?" Azull grumbled.

"I heard that!" Adder laughed, grabbing her sister's hand and racing up the hill, generating more than a few whispers in their wake. "Hey, did you hear....?"

I turned around sharply. "Yes, I did. Now let's eat. I have a few things to work out with the Builder later." Adder saw that neither Azull nor I was willing to complete her thought, so the topic was dropped.

"You are all so childish." Debra Woods waved us over to a table occupied only by herself and Trish. I noted more than a few jealous glances shot my way from those seated around us.

My meal was silent and uncomfortable. Azull and the men at the nearby tables kept looking at me oddly. Finally, long after I had practically buried my head in my meal, Azull looked up and gasped. "Grandma?" All the seats on the ridge emptied in a flash as everyone but myself and Azull knelt before the former queen, averting their eyes. "Chuck, we need to talk," Clare told me before walking back to the camp alone. She had a large pistol tucked into the belt of her very ornate heavy-duty coveralls.

I hurried after her. "I was thinking the same thing," I told my old friend when I caught up. I knew full well the rumor mill was going to kick far past overdrive, but I had too much on my mind to care.

"About Pan?" Clare asked, shooting me an appraising glance mixed with lots of skepticism.

"It was his idea," Pan managed to let slip through me. When we arrived at her tent, two of Clare's guards standing outside let us past without a word.

Clare closed the tent flap, then slipped inside, and we sat across from one another at the center of the table. Clare raised an eyebrow. "So, what the hell was that just now?"

"Pan is no longer contained. She has occupied part of my mind," I sighed.

"She? Not it?" Clare pressed.

"That's right. I feel that this should trouble me a lot, but it does not," I shrugged.

"Well, the old you would have ripped out your own mind by now. Self-aware robots did kill off most of our generation and even more of our parents' generation. You were there, remember?" Clare shook her head.

"Yes, I do. Could we keep this between us? I feel like it would freak out almost all of our underlings," I requested.

"Not as much as it spooks me or Greta," Clare grumbled. After a deep sigh she asked, "So what did you need?"

"The zeppelin's power core. That's basically a mini-sun you cobbled together, right?" I asked.

"It is a freakishly powerful thermal reactor but besides maybe some radioactive byproducts it should be safe, or at least as safe as I could make it with a heap of junk we got from some ruined cities," Clare allowed.

"How safe is safe?" I pressed.

Clare studied my face then told me, "The crew will not die from it."

"But my Order are not the crew," I pointed out mildly.

After pouring herself a cup of tea from a self-heating pouch that she pulled from the bunch covering her, Clare told me, "And they will be in danger only if the zeppelin crashes near them."

"How near?" I asked.

"If it crashes in the middle of the fort you will be assaulting, then anywhere in that fort. Expect landslides as well. The crew has a few means to abandon ship but those on the ground will not," Clare told me calmly. She took a sip of her drink then poured a cup for me in the same way.

"You are still as crazy as ever," I told her, taking the cup she offered.

"I freely admit that I may be insane but I am not crazy," Clare grinned. Then her face became far more somber. "So, some duke attacked part of your order and the next queen?"

After downing the very tasty tea, "That's right," I confirmed.

"Do you know what they were after?" Clare asked.

"Power in one form or another," I told her while enjoying slouching in a chair. My mind reviewed the earlier events of that morning.

"I know what you mean but please spell it out." Clare nodded thoughtfully, now resting her chin in her hands as she studied me.

"Knowledge or weapons. Any force that swore they could

wipe out the monsters after our world has been fighting them for so long would be seen as far more powerful than any monster. I guarantee more than one madman wants to know where we get our confidence from," I explained.

"Trish, do you agree?" Clare asked.

Trish looked out from behind a tapestry at the back of the tent. "Yes, that should be more than enough to placate the Demon Slayers for a little longer."

"Tell them only about the duke. I will look over your letter tonight with my advisors," Clare said, then she turned to me. "I am still having political duties. This should keep a few of the more worrisome factions out of our hair for a few weeks."

"Will that be enough?" I inquired.

"We will also be moving up the deployment timeframe by a few days," Clare shrugged. Before I could get uncomfortably thoughtful about just how much red tape my old friend had saddled herself with, the tent flap opened. Prince Sern, Prince Jallace, Adder, and Vern all walked in.

"We are doing what to who now?" Adder asked.

"The shed-yool is being moved up slightly," Clare grimaced.

"About time. The demons have had more than enough time to double their numbers by now," Sern huffed.

"Indeed. Our father sent what is left of our main army near the fort. Even with aid, we expect heavy losses," Jallace nodded somberly.

"With all due respect, your troops will be in the way," I told them, trying to sound as diplomatic as I could while feeling annoyed and completely uncharitable.

"Heavy losses nowadays means fifteen percent or more killed in action, and that's when trained soldiers outnumber the demons five to one," Trish noted.

"The fort had one thousand troops stationed in it. No one escaped alive. The smoke signals and flares were all that notified my people of the attack," Jallace said as he looked me over.

"If the Errant Order fails then feel free to mop up what is left, but we will handle the demons without your aid," I said sternly.

"You'd better, given how many priceless suits I had to rip apart just to get your order's gear working," Clare muttered.

"I heard that there are no more than three hundred ancient suits in the world outside of the five hundred your order was given," Sern growled.

"Our kingdom can't wait much longer. After rerunning the estimates of how many foes are in the fort, even your order will not stand a chance," Jallace added respectfully with some effort.

"How many should we expect?" I asked.

Jallace looked over at his brother tensely before either could use my lack of this time's common knowledge to get something out of the hole Sern had dug them into. Verndralla spoke up. "Leader, I estimate five thousand if we arrive by this week. Around three thousand of those would statistically be mid-sized or lower. The solar radiation of the area should barely feed that many," she explained.

"Ok, as I said, we will be fine on our own." I smiled,

enjoying the looks of shock and almost hidden loathing on the princes' faces.

"Dad, don't tell me you are going after all the big ones," Adder sighed theatrically.

"I could take out twenty large ones before resting," I laughed.

Sern went to storm out of the tent. "Well, our supplies had better be loaded by night or I will have a word or two with that gutter-rat herbalist." Before I could think of what I was doing, I had broken one of Sern's arms and smashed his face in the thick carpet.

"Don't insult my friend like that," Clare hissed angrily. Adder had pulled a dagger from somewhere and knelt down, resting it gently on the back of Sern's neck. Meanwhile Verndralla had put up both of her hands in front of Jallace, inky darkness swirling around her.

Jallace was luckily swift on the uptake or spooked out of his mind. His thought process sped up just like it would have if he were in a real life-or-death moment, which to be fair would have been a possible next step. "I apologize on behalf of my brother for his words against your betrothed, Sir Evans. Now please let that fool of a prince go."

Once the princes left, Clare downed a glass of wine then shooed the rest of us out. "Get your teams packed up. We head out tonight. Assault landings will be drilled in via simulations on the way to help our allies." The queen mother made certain not only to emphasize the word "allies," but looked right into my eyes when she said it.

It took the rest of the day to get our carts loaded, prep

the horses, inspect all our gear and fix any issues, doublecheck our armor's software and each trooper's supplies (ammo, first aid, batteries, emergency rations, field maintenance gear, handheld navigation gear, small mirrors and whistles, blade sharpeners, and so on). By midnight we were all tired but still alert due in no small part to rotating shifts. The march would take around half a day so everyone needed a nap or two before we set out.

Somehow, I was issued an electric-powered scout motorcycle. Some of the noble-born troops and unit leaders got to ride horses. The rest of the troops simply walked three abreast. Our carts moved along in the center of the column. The mounted troops spaced themselves out on the periphery of the road. I was surrounded by a clump of troops near the front. The long slog was punctuated by mild levity from time to time. We all were on the lookout for anything suspicious. One of the things we never lagged in during training was to be always aware, to the point it was a semiconscious habit, which helped keep the troops relaxed but alert at the same time. That said, no training is perfect. Case in point: red six-eyed squirrels spooked a few of the order assigned to the far ends of the column more than once.

After some time, we turned onto the road that connected Farfallen's capital to Verdant Valley Eight. Soon after, we passed by the area where Verndralla's evolution had destroyed a large swath of the tree line. Azull rode up on one of my order's horses. I glanced over at her and raised an eyebrow. "Shut up. I borrowed this," she answered to my question that had not even fully formed in my mind. That did nothing to help my nerves.

Later our column passed through the gate at the border of my new domain. None of the guards on duty stopped us, which was understandable given how preoccupied they were with saluting and trying to not look worried about the rust that still clung to the hard-to-clean parts of their now shinier gear.

From the high edge of the valley, large stone walls and thick steel windows surrounded the place where I had found Pan. A red marble villa sat within the thick enclosure. My new home was far more than I had expected. Disbelief must have shown on my face. Azull snapped, misreading my disbelief as discontent. "What, this is not good enough for you, Count Perfect?"

I looked over at the princess who rode at my side. "If I were perfect, then why would I try so hard to become stronger?" I said. Before Azull could snap back I added, "The building simply is far more lavish than I was expecting, so thank you."

Azull chose to assume a poker face. "You do know you are more than likely the most powerful warrior my home world has seen in ages, right?"

I responded amicably to the princess with a platitude older than her home world. "There is always someone stronger."

Trish rode up on my other side. "Please don't joke like that. It's bad for my heart."

"No one is invincible. Strength and cunning only improve the chances of victory. Nothing in life is certain. In other words, everything is a gamble. All we can do is ensure we have far better odds than our foes," I explained, working my way through the new anecdote.

"You still have to come back to me, honey," Greta radioed over the frequency reserved for the Errant Order's officers.

"No problem. I am the best gambler known to man," I radioed back as we arrived at the gates of the Errant Order's HQ and my new home.

"Meaning you are the worst gambler known to woman," Vern radioed.

Then the doors to my newly built fortress opened and for a time nothing else mattered.

Azull fired a handgun into the air. I was glad the troops tensed and reflexively went for their weapons. While scanning the area in the stillness, Azull yelled, "Make camp! Architects and support team: prep training sims. Officers with me: time to show you around." The troops, while still tense, did take their hands off their weapons. The unit leaders swiftly rounded up sentries and worked on the details of running our camp right outside my walls. The women pulled me into my new home. After the gate shut behind us, Azull told us without turning around, "Also we will be affirming your marriage, Mr. Evans. So, Greta Errant, look after that big moron for me."

Greta went to walk next to Azull. "That's what I have been doing since I met him," she said before glancing back at me. Azull and Greta picked up the pace, creating a distance between the rest of us.

Adder and I fell behind. When I was certain a whisper would be hard to overhear, I stage-whispered to my adoptive daughter, "Remember, the two in front are your family. Promise me you will look after them."

Adder muttered, "Don't kill yourself off yet," at around the tenth brick arch we passed under. From what I could see, the house was built in four blocks connected to one another by a long row of arches.

"I concur. Your demise at this juncture would be most inconvenient," Verndralla added. Somehow, she had snuck up on us. "No pun intended," she added, forcing an unemotional smile. I had stopped to look at Vern, trying to work out how she had crept up on me. Showing rare distress, Vern added, "Speaking of junctures, the small seedbeds along the walls should be growing decorative vines."

"Ivy. It's called ivy," Trish said as she ran up to us. "The other two are already in the garden. Come on!" We jogged over, wary of our intrepid guide's wrath.

In the center of the manor, many flower beds and newly planted trees covered the ground. Cobblestone paths wound haphazardly around the soon-to-be foliage. In the center seeming to stick out of the ground was the AA turret that had once hung from the bunker Pan had called home. "Oh, it still works," I said without knowing why I knew or when I thought to voice that fact.

"Yes, it does. How did you know?" Greta grinned with childlike glee, paying more attention to the turret than myself. Which made me feel jealous deep down.

I felt a wave of frantic activity in my mind but this feeling was new. I felt distant from the process and could not grasp what was being hashed out. "The joints are all still connected.

Realigning them is a nightmare at the best of times. More importantly, a few lights are still showing life signs near the base. Thankfully that includes the power balances."

"What do those do?" Trish asked.

Greta seemed overjoyed until Vern butted in. "Keeps it from overloading and taking out this valley with it." I think her change of mood was less due to the possibility of imminent disintegration and more that Vern had stolen my thunder and knew things Greta did not.

"Write up what you know about this thing later. Handling and maintenance are top priority," Azull groaned.

"As you command. Let's just hope we are the only ones in this stretch of stars." Vern spoke in a weary monotone. Her words made the entity in my mind recede.

Once I noted that Pan was the one who had been taking my big dumb mouth for a test drive but had now handed me back the wheel, I sighed. "True. Anything out there is bound to be no friend of ours."

"Well then Lady Greta Errant, do you consent to marry Count Chuck Evans and agree to all the duties and responsibilities that both your rank and your position in House Errant will mean?" Azull asked.

"I do," Greta smiled as she grabbed my hand.

Azull hardened her gaze and stared into my eyes. "And you do you swear to stop playing around, and to work as a count and commander both of your new noble family House Errant and the order of knights you command, the Errant Order? The agreement you worked out with my father the king and my grandmother will still bind you, whatever you say. So will you agree to be bound to Greta Errant as well and recognize her as both your equal and your partner?"

"I do," I replied. Azull let out a deep breath she had been holding.

Azull glared at me and put her finger to her lips to make sure I did not speak out of turn. "You both will be expected to work as a team and a family. Producing an heir is also part of the agreement with the queen mother. Is this agreeable to you both?"

Greta and I paused. After my hand registered a firm squeeze, we spoke at the same time. "Yes." Our voices seemed to be one new voice at that time.

Then I blacked out.

11

Russian Roulette

When my eyes opened, I found myself in a very fancy if unfamiliar bed in a room I had never seen. The sheets were a mess. Greta was next to me asleep. Her head rested on my chest. Neither of us had clothes on. If I had been at a party and had a hangover, I would have been far less confused. The sun was just beginning to chase away the darkness, which did nothing for the cobwebs forming in my mind. "Looks like an intense night," I sighed.

Greta's eyes opened sleepily. "Good morning, dear."

Her gaze calmed me down, grounding my thoughts. I was still freaked out by the gap in my memory. The first thing I had to do was retain my sanity, such as it was. "Good morning, Ms. Evans."

"It's Countess now," Greta laughed.

"I need to take a walk," I sighed, knowing I had to see what was going on but unhappy with getting out of bed.

"I'll be up soon. Let the Builder know I may be a bit late, honey," Greta yawned.

"No problem," I chuckled. After I dressed in some fancy menswear left on a chair by our bedroom door, Greta let me go.

Upon exiting, I found Adder's two aces standing guard outside the room in a long wood-paneled hallway. "Lue, Carol, good morning."

Carol's face flushed a bit and Lue smirked at her partner. "Good morning sir!" Lue called with great enthusiasm.

"First of all, people are still sleeping. Secondly, where can I find the queen mother?" I asked, trying to sound as deadpan as I could to stop from letting on how cute and nostalgic I found the young ace's bubbliness.

"Looking over the blimp, sir," Lue said. Her voice was far quieter with evident effort.

"Ok Carol, lead the way there. Lue, until the countess leaves this room, stay on guard here," I commanded. The pair exchanged glances, each wishing they had the other's assignment, which was why I felt comfortable and justified in assigning the jobs as I had.

I passed many doors on the way out. At the end of the hallway was a row of windows and another hallway branching off to our right and left. I was led down the left side and out of my villa, then down a gravel path and out a small solid rear gate. Over the trees loomed an iron-shod zeppelin. Bunches of arctechs manically sprinted around, taking apart bits and pieces of the extra-large passenger section of the zeppelin. After looking around for a while I found Clare leaning her head into one open panel. "Your Majesty, presenting Count Evans," Carol said with not even a hint of sarcasm.

Clare bolted to her feet and took a set of soot-covered goggles off of her eyes. "Oh, did you need me, Chuck?"

"Greta will be delayed a little. Before she gets here, we need to talk," I said.

My old friend's face slackened. "You haven't changed. Very well, follow me."

"Carol, report to your unit leader for your next task," I commanded.

I followed Clare into a small alcove near the zeppelin's generator. The area was devoid of anyone but the two of us. "Pan acted up again?" she asked after looking around swiftly.

"Yes. I think my body was taken over this time," I nodded. Clare looked me over when I paused. "After Azull finished her speech and I agreed, my vision blacked out."

"Did you have a good night?" Clare asked somewhat acidly.

"Maybe? I don't remember," I told her.

"You really are the same man I remember," Clare grumbled.

"What does that mean?" I asked.

"If the monsters had not taken over, if Jim had not become the core of the demons, I'd be in Greta's place. As it is, you still look the same as when we were frozen, but my life started back up before yours. You are my only regret. She is more talented than I was at her age and she has you, so forgive this old woman her jealousy," Clare said self-loathingly.

"For what it is worth, you have always helped me more than I could ever repay you," I told her.

"To answer your first question, the control of your body is

between you and Pan. So, get that control back soon and stop being so dense." Clare sighed, then walked out and went back to work, leaving me to stand there pondering her advice and what it meant.

I do not know how long I stood sorting through Clare's words before Pan spoke up. "We are fusing."

"I know, but keeping as much of myself as possible around is what we need to work out," I said.

"Then your half of us will be in control," Pan told me. If anyone noticed what was happening with me, it would have appeared that I was talking to myself and had some kind of multiple personality and maybe very strong delusions.

"Is that possible?" I asked.

"I have no idea. It feels like it should, but there is no data on something like this. We are far past what would normally be called a cyborg," Pan replied.

Before I could formulate a satisfactorily imaginative string of swears, someone tapped on the wall behind me. "How long have you been living with half a mind?" Vern asked. She wore full combat gear.

"What do you mean?" Pan replied.

"Are you the AI bot or my leader?" Vern asked. It was a good question. Pan and I did share one body now. Which, given my relationships, would be a problem if I became someone other than myself.

"Both?" I told her. "How did you know?"

"I have all your early memories. Sometimes it's like looking at myself and other times some weird stranger with a face I see as mine when I am not thinking straight. But that line has been blurring, and not in a good way," Vern told me. I felt as though my younger self was angrily telling me off if not for the fact that Vern looked nothing like the young me. She sighed deeply. "Anyway, the blimp is all set. Come to the bridge with me. For now, this will be our secret."

Verndralla turned around and walked past the reactor room and deeper into the ship. "For now?" I asked as I rushed to keep up with my colleague's brisk pace.

"I made that promise to Chuck Evans. It is void if he dies mentally or physically any more than he has," Vern shot back in a huff.

After walking through a few tight wood-paneled hallways and up three winding wrought iron stairwells, Vern pushed open an airtight lead-lined iron hatch which suddenly placed us in a bustling thoroughfare. It was filled with crewmen in leather and synthetic work attire along with fully armored members of my order, all running around with clear direction. "So, lift off is soon?" I muttered, seeing just how energetic the hallway was.

Vern grabbed my arm and pulled me though the tidal wave of bodies. Although wide by air- and spacecraft standards, the hallway would still be tight and cramped at the best of times, given the number of crew. Over the heads of the mob, I spied the fanciest staircase by far in the whole blimp. It sat high above the hallway with one hatch at that height. The crowd thinned out near the stairs. Adder stood near the top of the stairway, two swords belted to the sides of her armor and a solid shot carbine hung at her back. When she noticed me the former princess clone begin waving and shouted, "Hey Pa, get up here."

The crowd parted as well as they could to let me up the stairs. Verndralla managed to whisper now that the noise in our general area had gone down a few decibels. "Your gear is on the bridge, Commander."

The blast door at the top of the stairway flung open. Prince Sern stood glaring down from the other side at the crowd in general but he spared most of his focus for me. "Fantastic, you are here. Still think you will be lucky and win?" he scoffed.

"I don't need luck," I smiled. I spent a suitably dramatic pause racking my brain for what to say. I raised my arm and spoke in a quieter tone that reached more than half the blimp due to the stillness brought about by the prince's fiery aura and my soft speaking. "I have the Errant Order. We never run because we beat the crap out of all our foes!" A cheer shook the blimp that could be felt more than heard, even after I rushed onto the bridge and shut the door. "I am glad no one started chanting," I muttered.

"You get embarrassed?" Azull asked, smirking.

"I am only human. I'd take being in active combat over a ton of flowery words any day," I smiled.

Trish was sitting cross-legged in a corner taking apart a long rifle. She looked up, asking "So public speakers are not human?"

"Some human beings find public speaking fun. For me, it's only part of the job," I shrugged.

"When it comes to bullshit, you are the master," Vern

grumbled. Then she looked over at an unfamiliar man in a fancy robe. "So Vice-Captain, we ready yet?"

The man looked over. My first impression of him was *Wow that man is super bald.* Between his complete lack of hair, ornate robe, glasses, and unhealthy pallor, he could have passed for a lich in one of the role-playing games I was obsessed with as a kid. "The prep work and repairs are all done. We can go any time."

"Vice-Captain?" I inquired.

The man studied me for a few seconds. "Yes, that's right. Vice-Captain Erlost Vulle of the war blimp Olympus Peak at your service. The captain was overseeing the labor teams and paperwork until this morning."

"When do we lift off, Vice-Captain?" I asked.

Erlost smirked. "Around now, sir." Nothing happened immediately so I sat down at a spotter's station. Crew rushed to their posts and one spotter was tasked with helping man the bronze listening tubes that led into the far bowels of the ship. After much yelling to and from said tubes, the blimp lifted off. At some point Verndralla and Adder had taken up sitting on the floor to either side of me. Greta had made a brief foray onto the bridge to introduce herself to the command staff, and with what I assumed was a nod to me and a warning glance at the women, she made her way to peek in on the engine room, after which Greta would get to work in the armory. Vice-Captain Vulle made his way to my seat. "Will you be spotting for us today, sir?" he asked respectfully. The spotting station was no more than a glorified periscope and headset plugged into an audio pickup outside.

"No problem. I need to get the lay of the land, anyway. This will help us both out." I nodded.

Vulle explained, "Spots only report if they see something that could endanger the ship, aircraft, artillery, big fires. That sort of thing. You keeping an eye on the ground should help when we kick you all off."

Adder tried to rise to her feet, ready for a fight, but Vern pulled her back to ground level. "He means when we make planetfall."

A few of the nearby crew looked up at the unfamiliar term 'planetfall.' I pretended not to notice. "Right. I'll keep an eye out for a good point to airdrop," I said, managing to cover up the long-unused phrase with another that fit what we planned to do in a way the crew could visualize better.

With a jolt the blimp lifted off. We passed over the valley, then over cliffs and a volcano, then a desert. Small ruins dotted the landscape as we followed the natural border of cliffs and small mountains that separated Farfallen from Drenneth. Close to three hours later I noticed off in the distance a fortress atop a rocky hill barely within Drenneth's lands. The fort's high walls displayed many large tears large enough for many fully armored men or a few large demons to push though. "My order needs to land within the walls," I called, finally taking my eyes off the periscope and seeing a large senior arctech standing where the vice-captain had been.

"No flyers have been seen but your teams will need to jump out from higher up if you want to land there. I am not risking this tub to antiair fire from those things," the senior arctech grunted.

Trish whispered in my ear. "That's the captain."

We glided closer to the fort. Even now, chunks of its heavy stone buildings were melting and crumbling. The blimp raised its altitude slowly so that by the time we were directly over the base we were almost in the clouds. "Can you still make a safe jump from here?" the captain asked without taking his eyes off the instrument panel that his fingers never stopped dancing across.

"I need to ask my support crew that," I told him.

"The speaking tube for the armory is right there. It's labeled A-1." The captain pointed at a cluster of tubes.

I walked over and swiftly found the right tube. Nothing about how it was labeled looked any different from my days in the fleet when we fled from Earth. Not for the first time, I had the nagging feeling that despite not having to learn words other than formal and scientific jargon, this was not quite the same language as in my life 5,000 years before. I looked over at the captain still hunched over at his command console. He had the awareness to wave at me *Hurry up*. I opened the lip of tube A-1 and said in roughly the same volume as the neighboring communication officers, "Greta Errant, you there?"

Muffled cursing and a few muted clanging sounds emanated from the tube. Soon after, Greta answered. "For all that is sound and good, where the frack are we?" She sounded faint and echoing thanks to the primitive acoustics.

"Are you near an altimeter?" I asked.

"An altima what?" my wife asked.

"Altimeter. A tool that displays the blimp's current altitude," I answered.

"Why else would I be running the staff here ragged?" Greta fumed.

"You don't want me to answer that. Try to slow down a bit. I know you're working yourself even harder than them. Anyway, can the suits drop safely from our current height?"

"Barely, if the help knows what they're doing," Greta told me.

"Ok, we will jump from here. Get the gear ready. I need you to slow down and get the blimp's armory crew to pick up the slack," I said. There was no way I could hide the grin on my face. Greta's energy and drive were infectious.

"Why should they?" she asked.

"Because they are not dropping into a combat zone. You are," I said. It may have just been me, but I could have sworn the captain stifled a snicker.

"Get the muscle heads down here then. That includes you," my wife commanded.

I turned around. "The Errant Order is moving out to the armory. Notify the unit leaders. All units are to line up and report to support team leader Errant for final equipment checks."

Once all of the order members on the bridge had set off, I made my way to the armory. One of Greta's team leaders waved me deeper into the armory, circumventing the line. In a small alcove in the far back I found my armor and Greta. "Get in," she told me. After I donned my gear Greta took out an old and very charred handheld computer. After using some wire to link up my armor and her computer, Greta busied herself with the diagnostic work. "So where is Pan?" she asked.

"What?" I coughed.

"The AI in your head. It is not connected to the armor anymore," Greta told me.

"Oh that. Well..." Pan answered for me with my mouth.

"No more secrets," Greta said as she leaned in closer than before to unplug the wires.

"We are more connected now, and that may continue until the minds are fused," Pan answered. Greta still seemed to believe I was the one talking.

She sat down on a stool. "Tell me in a way someone from this time would understand."

"Do you know what a split personality is?" I asked.

"I know some." Greta sighed.

"It's like that now. When this fusing is done it is unlikely either side will be themselves. I am a cyborg by virtue of the monster's nanobots that Pan is hitching a ride on. In short, an AI inhabiting a more or less biological brain and consciousness is uncharted territory," I said.

"Well, Lord Evans, see that you win," Greta told me. Then she got up and swiftly began to pack up her tools. "Your gear is a masterpiece, as always."

Greta made to strategically withdraw with great gusto. I looked at my wife's back and asked in a serious tone, "So if we have a child, what should we do about him or her?"

Greta turned around swiftly. She was unnerved. "What do you mean?" Her face clouded thunderously.

"I mean if our condition is passed on to our children. They could easily be the only ones their age with these unnatural abilities we have," I told her.

Greta's face contorted, then softened. "So, no grand-children, you mean?"

"Our child could expect this trait to be stronger than either of ours. It is something we will need to test and consider if we ever have a kid," I grimaced.

Greta stared me down. "We will think about that after this battle, not before or during. Focus on living until we have the luxury of worrying about this." Then she smiled. "So, get out there, clean up, and come back alive."

"What happened to the chain of command?" I laughed.

"The moment you married me you agreed to share the responsibility for a few things," Greta told me firmly.

"Like what?" I asked, confused.

"Just let me be worried for you in peace. Now go." And with that, my wife pushed me out of the armory.

I left the armory with Adder and Trish, then met a few team leaders who had equipped themselves first in a rapidly filling hallway surrounded by locker rooms. We were led down the main passageway of the lower levels and down a loading ramp by some of the ship's navigators, most of whom did not have much to do now that the ship was stationary at high altitude. The level we were at was used for holding cargo. Airdrops could be done by jumping out of its loading doors which extended along a large portion on both sides. Extra artillery could be mounted there instead. "So, we drop from here?" Trish asked.

"Yes ma'am," the young lieutenant in charge of our guides said stiffly. Then with one look over at me, the boy froze up.

"The rest will be here soon," he managed to squeak. Immediately afterwards, the guides rushed out of the room.

Trish glanced over at me and rolled her eyes. "What?" I asked.

"Your expression looks like you are ready to slaughter a lot of people." Trish sighed.

"But demons are not people," I protested. Most of the troops around me became nervous.

"That's right!" Adder bellowed. "The enemy is right below us. So why should we not be mentally in combat mode?" She got a few small chuckles for her effort.

Soon after, the rest of the order arrived. Erlost Vulle led some crewmen to open the ports. He told me, "We are directly over the fort. When your order finishes disembarkation this ship is going right back to our hangar."

"Shock troops and lancers first, then the skirmishers will land in order by squad and secure a landing zone. The snipers will provide covering fire from here and the support team will monitor what they can. When a landing area has been cleared, the snipers and support will land. After that, we kill every demon we find. Stay with your squads. The commanders can go off on their own to fight but must remain in contact with their teams and me. As for reacting to and dealing with what we find, that will need to be on a case-by-case basis. Above all, stay aware of your surroundings and be able to react to sudden shifts along with your teammates. Keep your teammates alive and coordinate with your leaders. Keep track of how much time of immunity you have left and fall back to a cleared zone with your unit before that time is up. Guard teams will be set up as needed for cleared-out zones. Now let's search and destroy!"

With that flourish, I leapt from the blimp. The shock troops bailed out after me. We sped past the clouds and then activated our landing gear. Some like myself simply powered on their shields to full, others used small parachutes or glider wings. Each team landed on a midsized demon and proceeded to hack it apart. I used the impact of my landing to blow apart a cluster of roughly dog-shaped demons. Less than a minute later the lancers touched down in the same way. Verndralla was the sole exception; before she landed, she thrust out her arm. A torrent of energy darker than deep space consumed the top half of a midsized demon and a small pack of beetle-shaped things buzzing around it. She then landed atop the half-dead thing because she had carefully slowed down enough by blasting her landing zone apart. Soon after, the demons began to close ranks, and so did we. We fired crossbow bolts that tore out a few demons' cores. Anything big and lumbering was hit by high-yield sniper fire.

Before the lancers could complete their shield wall, Adder and her skirmishers landed and sprung forward in a pincer move, trying to thin out the rallying horde. Only then did I see the enemy commander. It was flanked by some very large and well-armored gorilla-shaped things. I tried to focus my helmet's optics on it, but instead my focus was suddenly on each pixel of my helmet's display. Ripping off my brain bucket, I refocused again on the most well-protected foe on the field. It was human-shaped, covered in a natural exoskeleton, and its tail followed like a spirited puppy along the ground. Other than its feminine features it looked just like the creature I had fought a few weeks before in the lake of blood. Vern saw it too, as my opposite number among our foes began to make a beeline for Verndralla.

Radioing Trish, I asked, "You see the cluster of brutes heading at the center of our lancers?"

"I do," Trish responded. The connection was fuzzy but not terrible.

"Focus fire on them but don't hit me," I told her. Without waiting for a reply, I rushed at one of the four hulking bodyguards.

Before the enemy could regroup, more than two hundred guns unleashed themselves on my small knot of foes. As soon as the sky opened up, our long-range support touched down. Both the sniper and support teams arrived atop the wall behind Vern's line of spears. By the time our fire support landed, most of their primary weapons were empty. One hundred of them took out their sidearms while the other hundred reloaded. During this process they switched off between overheating, jamming, and other mishaps at any one time as at least eighty of our reinforcements kept up the suppressive rain. Three-fourths of the enemy charged our line. Their waves were chaotic. Anything not dealt with quickly by the melee teams and anything too hard for them to hit was a priority target and so got filled full of holes.

On the ground all but one of the gorilla-like monsters was obliterated. The plates of hardened matter covering the brute had either fallen off or been so badly dented that any flesh-and-blood being would have suffered a lot of internal damage.

The hulking monstrosity blocked my path. The solid human-oid commander leered unscathed behind it. A rippling bubble of antimatter covered it. The path behind the enemy leader was a small trench of glass. Vern charged the boss by running around the cluster of bodies. Before she was even halfway to the thing, Greta radioed the entire order. "Watch your feet!" Her words were still echoing in my ears when the first demons burst from the sand around the defense line.

While dodging around and under the brute before me, I managed to radio, "Fight in your teams! Watch each other's backs!" Of course, given my lack of a helmet, the clashes of the melee around me came though more clearly than my words. To a soul, the Errant Order knew what I meant, and began to break off into smaller groups, attacking anything that got close and keeping the enemy off the backs of any clustered allies they could help. After weaving around a few attacks, I rolled under the huge demon gorilla's legs, cutting one off and mangling the other.

While pulling myself up and rapidly calculating the angle of my next attack, I spied the enemy commander duck under Vern's sword, crushing one of her vambraces and then tear-ing her whole right arm off. I could not help her until my own opponent had died. "So hungry," something deep in my mind yelled as my lips mumbled the same verse like a curse. Before I knew it, Pan had taken control again, but the con-nection seemed far closer now. If I so wished, seeing into the depths of the AI's stored memories would be effortless. *Don't look, dummy,* Pan's voice boomed within my mind, dripping with scorn. The intensity of that thought drove all others from what was left of my consciousness. Pan drove my body into the brute's chest. My body was driven to do anything it could to tear off a badly dented plate over where a normal thing's heart would be. At one point as I was swung around on my perch, I noted that Vern had blasted a chunk out of her foe's body. Its right arm lay twitching on the ground. My fingers found purchase just under the gorilla thing's plates. Pan ripped off the heart plate, forcing my body to exert far more might than I thought possible. In one smooth motion the time-stilled sword pulled out the brute's core. Some of the dark matter mix clung around it. Pan forced me to swallow the thing's core whole.

I knelt, my gag reflex overridden, helplessly witnessing Vern reverse her grip on Caesar-Rex with her one remaining arm, a feat requiring at least as much dexterity as strength. She somehow kept her feet firmly braced even with the new discrepancy in her center of balance. My vision started to swim as Vern decapitated the still-staggering enemy leader.

I nearly passed out. An overwhelming feeling of violation swept my body and mind. I felt like a highly intricate clock that was getting oil and mud ground into it by some ham-fisted child. I really wanted to vomit and my ears short-circuited. The battle that I knew was still around me sounded like someone using a tuba as a drum echoing from the far side of a deep canyon. "Relax, I am giving you back full control," Pan told me. Whether in my mind or voice, I was in far too much discomfort and disorientation to know.

Suddenly I felt better. My eyes refocused and my mind was clear. The only background noise I heard was from outside my body. For what seemed like a lifetime, Vern shook me with both hands. I got a quick look at her arms. "You look worse than I feel," I managed to say.

Vern swiftly dropped me into the mud. "He's fine," she radioed. Vern's new arm was what could only be called a spoil of war. In place of her human arm and its armor was the dark-clawed exoskeleton-covered arm of the demon's commander. "Thanks for showing me how to use monster parts," Vern told me before sprinting away to support her lancers.

I got to my feet. I do not know if it was just me but the demons seemed to be slightly more sluggish. Holding aloft my sword, I radioed, "Keep it up. They are faltering."

Just as I stopped talking the ground at my feet trembled. At any other time, this would have seemed ironic. Jumping many feet into the air thanks in large part to my suit's traits, I looked down to see a gaping maw easily wide enough to eat three full-grown heavily-armored men in one bite, raised slightly out of the ground.

"Leave the big one to the commanders. Lancer leader, hang back and command our defense," Greta commanded. Somehow Greta still disliked calling Verndralla by her nickname.

Trish stalled but Adder was suddenly at my side. "For the record, I second that," I told Trish over a private channel. Greta and Trish raced after Adder. I left them and the maw for the now mostly deserted center of the fort, leaving Vern and the rest of the order to finish off the less imposing targets. Adder dropped low-yield breaching charges as we ran, our feet barely hitting the ground. Trish lagged behind by a few paces.

A meandering ripple followed after us. "The bait's working, Pops!" Adder hooted.

"Or it is hunting the leaders," Trish sighed. After a few moments of silence she added, "That means us." Trish then kicked off a large rock, allowing her to temporarily take the lead.

"Buzz kill," Adder muttered before somersaulting next to Trish.

"You are acting like children! All that matters is we have that thing's attention and will kill it," I told them.

"We are all kids to you," Greta laughed. Her voice took a firmer but still gentle tone. "Don't worry, we will finish this."

Suddenly Adder spun like a top and leapt, her back suddenly inches from Greta's. Adder raised both her swords. The ground erupted as if in challenge. Adder kicked Greta away and slashed one blade down and one across in a low crouch. One massive frog-like leg went flying and inky matter-eating gore rained. "Blood type same or worse than us!" Adder yelled.

Greta eyed a few puddles of nearby gore, all of which was boring holes into the dirt. "That thing's blood will eat anything."

A huge fanged maw poked out of the dust. It was only a snout but that was more than enough. I tossed a few grenades packed to the brim with incendiary compounds and metal-based heat-boosting powder, all locked in highly pressurized orbs, down its gullet. The grenades were almost as good as what I had used in my old life but only because we had ignored how volatile and reckless the simplified design was.

No failsafe-obsessed technician made these. It was all folks with far more desperation than good sense; in other words, the smartest chemists we could temporarily contract out of a penal colony for the totally mad and deranged.

"What did I just say!" Greta howled.

The ground shook and fire erupted from cracks in the dust. "And it's dead. What a letdown," Adder sighed.

"Well, it came from a very old-looking basement," Trish commented from over one of the holes the thing's blood had made. "That blood gave us an entrance and everything."

I peered down the hole "Well we know where the old flight control sub base went."

"The what?" Greta asked, looking up at me quizzically.

"FANG. Flight Automation Network Guidance. Now help us kill these small fry!" Vern radioed us. Trish was the first to rush back to our defensive kill zone. The rest of us soon passed her and hurtled into the melee.

The lancers and skirmishers were doing very well keeping our blindly ravenous foes off balance. The shock troops plugged any gaps in the defensive perimeter which shifted like the ocean tide on a small desert island. The snipers hit any target that presented itself. All the while the support crew dodged though our own lines, checking on everything from ammo to when to switch out the troops in the main line, with the resting backup in the center. The final blow to the enemy at large was when Adder and I started to hack away at the enemy's rear lines with a blade in each hand. After some time and a lot of support fire from Trish and the snipers, the enemy began to flee. A few grenades helped thin their numbers well, although from what I saw the concussive force of the explosion dealt far more damage than the blasts themselves, which I readily made a note of.

"We camp now. Set up guards on the perimeter and around the holes that big ugly thing opened. Unit leaders, assign some of your more rested members as scouts. I want to know if the enemy is still around and if they left a trail. Keep risks to a minimum," I ordered after assessing the area. Walking over to Vern, who was among the wounded, I stood behind Greta, who was in the process of fitting patchwork armor over Vern's new arm. Without announcing my presence Vern spat out a gob of paste. "For the love of the moon, my one regret is all food tastes like crap now."

"Well, rations in this time are bound to be even worse than in mine," I sighed.

Vern glared up at me and tossed a baggie of dried fruits at me. "Only if you were obsessed with chocolate bars," she hissed at me.

"You know me too well," I countered sarcastically.

Greta muttered with great annoyance, "Being part demon now has admittedly made food dissolve far more rapidly than normal, but Miss Errant, integrating that arm into your body likely will exacerbate the effect." It took me a few seconds to notice Greta put a little extra emphasis on the title Miss.

Ace of Spades

The troops set up camp, then I organized them into four-guard shifts. They ate in shifts and rotated between guard duty and sleep because it was not quite dark yet and I wanted to give my troops time to process their first engagement as a monster killing unit. Everyone other than the scouts got a turn at guarding the rest of us. As far as anyone could tell, we had accomplished the first successful large-scale infantry assault against the so-called demons of this world, as well as the first airdrop assault in living memory, not counting the few who remembered the ancient times of my birth and before. During the first shift Trish set up antimatter energy scanners which, thanks to their shoddy stands, worked as makeshift seismic sensors too, as anything more than a stiff breeze would cause very obvious reactions. During the second (and longest) shift I sat near the haphazard dining area we had set up well within the perimeter. We all slept in our armor, a few collapsible barricades shielding us from the wind. Most of the troops, other than those with lots of combat experience, took off their helmets, and after wrapping them in anti-shock foam or other non-critical things from their field kits, used that mishmash as a pillow. As long as no large clumps of sleepers were noted, the troops were left to their allotted sleep times.

Near the end of my shift Adder walked over. She was in the third shift. "So Pop, what are the plans for those holes?" She pointed over her shoulder roughly at the revealed entrance to the bunker-like complex I had expected to find from the data Pan and I had been collecting.

"During breakfast I'll take a small team down to do some light recon," I told her.

Before Adder could comment further, the strong stench of blood, shit, and cheap antiseptic endemic to a slapped-together medical area in the middle of a war zone wafted over to us, along with the sound of plodding steps of a lightweight overworked medic in armor. "How many?" I asked.

The footsteps stopped. After a good half a minute of sputtering from the newcomer, which I spent stargazing, Greta's voice answered from behind. It was wispy and hoarse all at once. "Excuse me?" she asked wearily. At another time I felt certain she would have sounded firm, acidic, or flat-out incredulous, and at those times I would not have blamed her. I briefly noted I may have been too standoffish and turned to look at my very tired and blood-covered wife.

"How many did we lose?" I asked my lovely support team leader firmly.

Greta sighed and answered lifelessly. "Three dead, five critically wounded. I don't know if those five can make it even if we had a passable medical ward. A few others got hit here and there. All of those are in fighting shape. Looks like the bad wounds were dealt by congealed demon energy. For the smaller beasts it should be a very draining thing to pull off, but from the reports I got, not impossible in all cases."

"How new is that congealing ability?" I asked, pondering just what this could mean and how it might affect our tactics going forward.

"First I've heard of it," Adder muttered.

Greta sat on one of the once-full supply boxes her team had dragged from our ride. The boxes were for the moment pressed into service as chairs for the officers, medical staff, and some of our guard stations. Greta was clearly ignoring the blood covering her gear and the lingering smell of the ward. "It may be similar to the shells some of the demons have. In smaller and therefore lower-powered and ranked demons, it would take a lot of energy all at once to force their body to condense at a single point. Such a move should be fatal for the smaller ones. In my opinion we were deemed dangerous enough to force them to use a previously dormant gambit."

Early the next morning the camp was awoken by the sounds of clanging, burning smells and calls of "breakfast is ready" given by stern-faced and hollow-eyed support crew members. A dour debate swiftly broke out about what god-awful food we would be subjected to. A swift consensus formed that whatever our meal was, it could never be worse than normal infantry food. At the mess hall all but our guards and scouts came over. Large tubs of thick yellow meaty glop were served, smelling sour in a lemony kind of way. All and all it was quite good. The sounds of clanging and burning smells, however, were not from the food but from our repair teams who were madly trying to fix up the melted and shattered bits of our gear. Given how advanced and specialized all our main equipment was, fixing even a small gash was hell. At best, most tools did not work on patching our armor and at worst, the tools broke. Apparently, the material for repairing our gear was either made in the capital by Clare, or in a few cases, like my swords or the original bits of our armor, the parts would be from other relics. Adder had been the one to wake most of us up. In a fit of rage, she had begun welding closed a hair-thin cut in her armor with a laser pistol, after some dubious adjustments to the pistol's power core, which caused many of our engineers to go very, very pale trying to estimate the blast zone if the thing went critical. Adder was the first to fix a suit of the order's armor. After her work was done Adder scarfed down one and a half bowls of breakfast. The second half belonged to a technician she had shown her laser trick to. Given the tech's worsening complexion he had likely lost his appetite upon seeing Adder's complete disregard for such revered relics.

Before Adder could finish the second half of her meal, Greta stormed over. "Have you lost your mind?" she asked, slamming her hands on the table and leaning over to glare at Adder.

Adder looked up. She would have been the very icon of serenity if not for the icy mirth in her eyes and the now broken spoon in her clenched hands. "I will go out of this world the same way I came into it, a raving lunatic," Adder blandly informed her adoptive mother.

"You could have set off an explosive chain reaction. Do you really have any sense of self-preservation?" Greta asked, now visibly enraged and not giving a damn about the worried stares from the lower ranks.

"Don't fear death. Don't run from life," Adder said, forcing a strained smile.

Greta glared over at me and jabbed her finger in my direction. "Did you teach this nutcase that?"

"I had no hand in your fellow officer's misguided innovation," I managed to croak with some sternness.

"Fine then, but..." Greta began.

"I'll have her take point when I look at the underground ruins very soon," I cut in before Greta could start undermining the officer's authority. She had already done a number on our dignity but given how we all smelled like blood and crap in the middle of a war zone, dignity was the last thing on anyone's mind.

"A skilled leader controls their subordinates' world view," Verndralla sighed from a few seats over.

I grabbed what was left of my breakfast and walked over to Adder. "Your gear all set?" I asked kindly.

Adder put down her tools neatly and looked up at me. "You bet ya, Pops!" she beamed.

"Then get your things sorted out and make sure to keep your breakfast light. When that's done, meet me where that tunneler was rampaging."

"You are taking me too, right?" Trish asked, seemingly

annoyed at how little attention she was being paid. My first thought was no way she was a spy, even though the facts said otherwise. We had wiped all the other old allegiances totally out of the rank and file, but info was still getting out in a controlled manner. I had to console myself that at least I knew who Trish would be talking to. That, and if no spies talked, who knew what the puffed-up piles of lard back in their posh manors would do next.

I answered, "As long as your team can provide lookout detail for the camp. We will need to double the troops on standby until both the scouts from last night and I am back. I'll be taking Sir Jason Wulfard and Sir Brandon with me as well."

"I'll get Folly and Whiskers on it immediately. They are the best team leaders I have right now," Trish assured me.

Adder had armed herself at almost inhuman speed and stood a few steps behind me. "Oh, what are their full names?"

"Able Folly and Felix Whiskers," Trish told her, looking unclear about the point of the question. I turned to look at Vern to see she was holding her laugher in even better than I was, but not well enough for me to miss. After all, most of her memories were mine, and experience had a way of shaping a person.

"I'll get Clark Seewood to help as well if you need an all-around medical specialist," Greta offered.

"Ok, that works. I'll take Puppet along. Keep in mind this trip could last half a day. In the meantime, stay on guard and let no one outside the order enter the walls. When the scouts get back, test them for mimics, then get their reports," I commanded.

Soon after, I looked over Adder's shoulder as she shone a lamp deep into the old FANG outpost. Our entry point looked like it led into the least rubble-filled room, but that could mean it had less supporting its ceiling. We all knew this was a calculated risk but the bigger the room the more stuff we might find. "Well Pops, mind if I go in first?" Adder asked.

"Knock yourself out," I said. Adder froze along with everyone else. "That means yes," I sighed.

"Ok, I got to remember that one," Adder snickered, then she lunged down the steel cable we had tossed down. Moments later a light stabbed around the room. Adder radioed on our temporary private line. "Come on down."

I rechecked the winch we had bolted to the steel-plated ground then followed after my daughter. Adder and I took guard duty for the line. The rest assumed positions for the others as they funneled down. Puppet, Sir Brandon, Seewood, Trish, and Sir Wulfard came down one at a time, in that order. Trish was the only one who had not switched on her flashlight. Even then, the large control room we had landed in was almost too illuminated. Bones were scattered about. Torn-up ancient flight control stations littered the room. Many had been smashed. Wulfard noted, "It's almost like a mausoleum down here."

Brandon and Puppet looked out of a smaller side room. "It is a mausoleum. Lots of graves in here," Puppet radioed over.

Trish paled. Her hand rested on a large red button, then part of the panels lit up. I swiftly pushed her aside and cut the panel into four large chunks. "Nobody touch the consoles," I said.

"What was that for?" Trish asked. She had every right to be miffed.

"That was the button for a relay beacon. Those need to always remain off," I warned her.

"Why?" Adder asked.

"Because there are a few otherworldly things far more dangerous than a demon plague," I told her.

"I don't believe you," Trish countered.

"If I had not lived through the other two times humanity almost got wiped out, I'd agree with you. Now all of you, turn off your lights and stay motionless," I grumbled. Once obeyed, I took off my helmet and my vision changed to be a high-end scanner, due to Pan fully becoming part of my mind. I looked around the room, noting the small holes signifying something had burst from the floor, which was almost definitely demon birthing pillars. I whispered, "Sometimes I envy how clueless most of you are."

Puppet looked nervously between Trish and I. Sensing a break in the disagreement that was far above his pay grade, the spearman finally managed to share, "There is a very fancy box in here," without sighing or wincing too badly.

Marching over, I ordered, "Show me." Brandon and Puppet led me by a honeycomb of shallow graves. Most were empty but had a sense of having been occupied once. Bone dust and a few scattered shards filled in the rest of the ancient makeshift burial area. "This was a very nice assembly hall once," I recalled.

"Tell me more," Adder asked. Somehow, she had snuck up behind me.

Pointing over to a clump of rust-covered rubble, I indulged her. "During flight control graduation there was a juice dispenser over there. I enjoyed it. Your grandmother found the lemonade flavoring very distasteful." I smiled inwardly, recalling my oldest friend's sour face at the dour drink menu.

Adder cackled over the radio. I put her on mute then looked over at Puppet, who had stopped over the deepest hole around us, present location excluded. "Here sir," Puppet told me, pointing down at a big sealed security box, the kind used to secure hazardous materials in case they were jettisoned from a starship in battle.

Trish peered over my shoulder at the one word carved into the box. "What does it say?"

"Records," I read out loud. "Someone really wanted to make a statement," I added. Given how much effort carving into a box that dense would be, I felt almost as if I was making light of the effort involved. Plugging a cable from my suit into the charging port of the box, I waved everyone back, then slowly transferring power to the box, I hoped for the best.

With a deep click the box's hinges opened. I was nervous that using an emergency starter on such an old relic would blow up in my face, but when the box swung open, I was glad my fears had not taken shape in reality. After giving the box a once-over twice, I pulled the solitary item from the box. It was a small data pad with "Blueprints" stamped on it. Rapidly I handed the pad off to Adder. "For the Builder?" she asked.

"That's right. Give it to your mom and tell her to transmit

what she can. We will look around for a little longer," I said. Nodding, Adder scurried away. Trish managed to hide her curiosity well enough that none of the grunts around us noticed.

Not much was left in the ruin. The other rooms we searched had been corroded away beyond recognition. "This was a big hive," Trish observed at one point, looking around what I remembered had once been three different and packed rooms.

"The chow hall, pantry, and kitchen have been hollowed out as one room. The rest are like they were, not counting all the furnishings," I informed the team, my mind briefly wondering if anyone I knew so long ago had gotten out of this place alive when this world collapsed.

"You traveled a lot, old man," Trish huffed, clearly thinking that I was not sharing all I knew. She was right, given that Trish was a spy and the only one I tentatively allowed any info that could be dangerous or used against me. Only Greta and Clare were allowed all the data about me and the mission. Our guarded information was compartmentalized and given out on a need-to-know basis.

"In my day, getting to the other side of this planet took only a few hours," I smirked, hoping this would get Trish's mind off whatever else she was trying to glean.

She took the bait. "How?" Trish asked, visibly startled.

"High altitude shuttles." I shrugged like it did not mean anything. "We used the old colony ship landers as a taxi service once most of this world was set up."

"What happened to them?" Puppet inquired.

"The Builder would know better than I would," I told him, then began walking. "Anyway, there is nothing else left here. The demons ate the foundations from under this place." I noted that some rooms had small craters all along the walls. Given the building had been built underground, it was not surprising the demon's pillars had sprouted from the walls long ago. I could only imagine what the personnel stationed here must have felt. Somehow, I could only feel sympathy for them but even the faces of some old colleagues who had been working caused me no real sadness, just resignation. At that moment I knew beyond a shadow of a doubt that I had drastically changed from how I once had been.

Back at camp the scouts had still not returned. After a long discussion it was decided to wait until midday before considering the scouting teams KIA. I gave Trish permission to contact the capital, after Greta had finished using the only transmitter we had brought that was powerful enough to reach one of the relay points near the Builder's tower. Vern and Adder, on the other hand, both challenged me to a sparring match at nearly the same time. I managed to reshuffle the patrols so that around half their respective teams could watch. Most of those temporarily taking over guard duty were my shock troopers. Adder was first by virtue of asking me a few seconds before Vern. Adder and I both wore our full armor. Adder had borrowed two swords from her subordinates and I had snagged a chunk of finely aged rebar from under our feet. "You are going with that? Really?" Adder could not help but scoff.

"What, are you going to complain about a handicap? It's not like we could use our regular weapons," I shrugged.

"A fine slice still seems like it would heal better than a lot of broken bones," Adder complained like the spoiled brat she almost once was.

"Your armor is not so weak to be done in by this over-glorified chunk of scrap," I said, while inwardly apologizing to the builders and smelters who had handled it, and the metalworkers of the current age who could only drool over the quality of metallurgy from my time.

"Fine, then try me," Adder sighed. Upon getting her tentative approval, I bolted forward. Adder blocked the bar with both blades crossed above her as she ducked, kicking at me. She cut bits off the bar and I took a step back. "Ouch, my foot!" Adder grimaced. I then swung a kick at the back of Adder's left kneecap. She dropped one of her blades and regained her balance but by that time the rebar was already pressed against her neck. Her other blade was caught in the chokehold it rested against. "You win, Pops." Adder surrendered.

"Your kick overextended your balance. That's why one change to your center of gravity was enough to get you to lose it. Also, never blurt out a real weakness to your opponent. It can work as a feint. So, if you must show an enemy weakness, be ready to use their attacks at your weaknesses against them," I advised. Then I disarmed Adder of the blade she still held and tossed the rebar aside. "Verndralla, you're next," I firmly stated.

Adder took the other sword with her to the ring surrounding us. Only then did Vern step in, garbed in full armor and grasping the kind of spear common to her troops. This confirmed for me that that Vern and Adder were likely doing this more for their troops than for themselves. "You ready?" I asked.

"A wise man once said unless I really screw up it will be up to me where I die," Vern told me.

When she said that I got a headache. "Wow, sounds like a pretentious asshole," I sighed.

"But I am quoting you, sir," Vern told the crowd.

Somehow, I had a very good idea what she was getting at and really hoped I was wrong. "Well yeah, when I was ten! Now shut up and fight me!" I commanded. For the first time since waking up in this radically changed world I was extremely embarrassed. Which may have made me get a bit serious. Vern charged at me as I had at Adder. I twisted my body slightly to avoid the spear point. Pushing it aside with Adder's sword, then with my free hand, I caught the body of the spear and flipped Vern over my head and to the ground before even three seconds were up. My borrowed sword was at her throat. "I win," I told her gravely. "Good form, but try to have a few different attacks ready to transition to at any time. I know you are skilled enough to do that. Also, if you will be disarmed with your weapon, keep in mind your body is also a weapon, and your opponent has theirs to take or use against them. It all depends where the approach takes you."

After that I cleaned my gear near our long-range radio, then walked along the walls on the perimeter. At some point I felt that something important was running far in the distance. The only word that seemed to fit would be instinct.

My vision swam when I focused on the offending hill. The mound of rock and dust zoomed closer. Normally this would be unsurprising but only if I was wearing my helmet, which at the time I was not. On the hill I could see Lue the skirmisher hobbling toward the base. It looked like her armor had more than a few long gashes but blood was coming from all over. I radioed to my unit leaders. "Wounded incoming from the scout team. Send a medic team to the south wall. Snipers on high alert and on the walls. Guard teams, look alive. Everyone else on standby, in full gear." Then I jumped down and rushed over to the young trooper. Despite being the smallest in her unit, Adder had nothing but praise for Lue. At some point the girl had even become a squad leader. I think part of it was Lue resembled Adder in many ways. Luckily Adder's mild psychopathic nature (milder than when I met her but still there) was not one of those.

Very rapidly I was next to Lue, who before I could ask anything, mumbled one word, "Ambushed," then fainted into my arms.

I was halfway back to the walls with Lue on my back. Greta rushed over and took her. "We will take it from here," she told me with a complicated expression.

"Ok thanks. If possible, I'd like to know what wounded her." I nodded.

Greta sighed and looked at me, her face an unreadable mask, then she looked over Lue swiftly. "Probably man-made weapons. Now let me do my job."

"Ok, you are the best," I told her. I bolted though the gates while activating the order-wide emergency frequency.

"All hands, battle stations! Expect human hostiles. Do not fire unless I say so. Report any attacks or incoming persons to me directly."

Trish leaned over one of the walls above me. Our eyes met and she jumped down beside me. "You think it's an info leak?" she asked.

"It's not like our mission was an ironclad secret, but I can't rule that out. You haven't sent anything I don't know about, right?" I whispered.

"No. You have seen all the final drafts," Trish said. "Even if this puts me out of a job, it's not like I disagree with what you are trying to do."

"Ok. Quietly root out any other spies for me and kill them," I told her. Trish paled before I put up one hand to stall her incoming outburst. "Do that and I'll owe you one. If you want a blueprint or my life story, I'll give it to you." All her previous requests to send out such detailed data had so far been denied by me. Our training regimens, personnel overviews and projected combat capabilities had all been shared with the Demon Slayers. That we were immune to the demons' disintegration in a limited way had been hinted at in Trish's reports, but I chose to overlook those borderline problematic statements thus far in a show of good faith.

"Fine then," Trish agreed, steeling herself. "But it will be messy."

"Then let's hope the other ones can take a hint. If there is nothing else, I have a battle to oversee," I told her, all levity gone from my voice.

"I'll be at my unit's command post," Trish told me. Then she ran off to the south wall.

Later Lue had recovered enough to report that her boy-friend Carol and four other scouts she knew of had been killed. She had no info on the rest of them. The demons had been simple to track but were far too fast. Well-armed humans had attacked her team. They had crossbows, spears, swords, lots of daggers, some high-end plasma weapons, and maybe more. That's all we could get out of her. By then her pulse had spiked and she had to be sedated for her safety. The shock of losing Carol right in front of her had hit hard. Adder had not paid attention to anything but the skill, talent, morale, and teamwork of her squads. Which to be fair was to the letter of my orders. Half an hour after we had recovered Lue, I got reports that eight hundred armored and armed humanoids were approaching. I radioed over the command line, "Block all gates but the southern one. Adder and Vern, you are with me. Greta, you have command of the base while I am out. Trish, keep an eye out and support Greta with holding this base." Before I could get any flack, I switched over to the Errant Order wide frequency. "All troops, hold your ground and do not let anyone in until I finish reprimanding the fools that toyed with our comrades."

By the time I was done the base was in a furor and I was approaching the south gate. Adder and Vern were by my side. Cries of "You tell 'em!" and "Slap those morons for me!" rose up around me. The order I had built with my close friends and wife were behind me a hundred and ten percent. For an old refugee, orphan, gambler, sword-obsessed idiot and killer, nothing besides Greta could make me happier. They knew I was up to something but none of them knew the depth of my rage at this moment. Anyone who hurt my troops and lived to tell the tale was on my kill list. This was a rude awakening in some ways because I now knew that even if my focus had shifted from me, myself and I to a few friends like a pendulum throughout my life, the me now was for the first time living and fighting for a team, my subordinates were under my care, and hell would implode before I gave them up for dead. Anyone and anything who did in those under my care would meet them on the other side by my hand. I was still someone who would get my hands stained with blood, only this time it was because I wanted to. At some point my life had become something I lived solely for others without my knowing.

When I passed under the gate Trish asked, "Are you going to let us shoot anyone today?"

I was a few steps outside the gate when I turned around to wave up at my order. "Sit back and watch the fireworks but if any new practice dummies make it past the walls, vaporize them."

Then I waited. My two swords were stuck in the ground at my sides and my helmet was on but nothing could disguise my foul mood. A good hour later the targets of my ire appeared, all eight hundred of them. Even from far away I could see their bloated egos leaking out as if to boil the very air. They wore iron and hide patchwork armor like a uniform. The number of spikes adorning their gear seemed to display their rank or macho-ness or whatever. As the soon-to-be-dead men sauntered closer, I could tell they had a surprising number of plasma weapons and grenades. *Pan, you still swimming around in my brain?* I thought loudly. *Always* came my answer. *Could you hack into those plasma weapons for me and blow them up when I tell you to?* I swiftly asked within myself. *Not a chance, but you could. After all, we are one and the same now* I was told by something that was me and not me. *Fine, how?* I retorted, now feeling even more insane than usual. Suddenly a great many memories from the time Pan was not also me flooded our shared consciousness. The words "A truly insane man would think himself sane or not care at all" spilled from my lips before I knew it.

"Being the psychopath is my shtick," Adder pouted from two steps behind me.

"And we love you for it, Adder, when you are pointed at our foes," Vern sighed mockingly.

"That's not news. Now shut up. The prey is here." Adder retorted with bone-chilling certainty.

"This fort is now ours. Leave all your gear and your women," said a tall man covered with more spikes and iron plates than common sense would deem wise. His idiot horde had even less common sense. The way they sneered was asking to die badly.

"And you are?" I asked.

"Your worst nightmare," the pompous spike-covered jester mindlessly informed us while he ran his eyes across Adder and Vern.

"Well, this is awkward. That's my name too," I told him. He had enough time to almost finish his double take before all his horde's plasma guns detonated into impressive fireballs.

The grenades near those blasts went off within seconds. "Welcome to hell, gentlemen. Tell death I will need to reschedule my visit." I had just swiped up my swords when a bullet was fired at me by one of the charred remnants of these man-shaped iron porcupines. The round dissolved in antimatter many feet from my face. "I have the center. Adder, the right. Vern, the left. Kill them all." I sneered, still overcome with my rage. I had never been this mad but I did not care. The spokesman of the fools lunged at me with a sword. His teetering steps and disorientation made him worse than a child playing war but I did not intercept his blade; I let my until-now-unused repulsion shield do it for me. The man's arm and sword broke and were flung back before getting even one inch from my armor.

The wannabe warlord looked up at me and hoarsely stammered, "Monster."

"Oh, another thing we have in common," I hissed. "Have a safe trip and remember to never piss off the ferryman," I added savagely just as my sword met the man's neck. With that mini-melodrama played out, Adder and Vern were almost done mopping up on their ends. I turned and held up my blood-soaked swords to my troops on the wall. "Ok, you can cut down my share. Just don't waste too much ammo."

I was glad the troops followed the chain of command I had outlined by not firing until Trish yelled, "One round per bandit. Any one that adds more than one hole to one of those pin cushions pays for the extra out of their pay. Now mow them down! Also, don't hit our own lunatics."

Adder walked up to me covered in gore. Vern may have

passed as splatter-covered but Adder looked like she had jumped into a lake of red iron-based paint. "Feeling better now?" Adder asked me as she wiped her hands off on my shoulders.

"Yes, much better now, and you?" I asked, finally calm once the last spike-covered moron was queued up at the river Styx.

"I feel alive," Adder laughed. Her voice had taken on a manic tinge.

"Enough with the adrenaline. Go clean off your armor and dunk your head in a bucket of ice water. You look and smell terrible in red." Greta called down from the battlements.

Adder looked over at me. "What you heard from your mother," I shrugged.

"And you," Greta yelled, pointing at me. "What the blazes were you thinking?"

"Nothing. I was mad," I told her. Before this could get out of hand in front of the troops I added, "Greta, let the queen mother know we are done here and heading back. The rest of you, stop gawking and pack up!" Greta saluted, a small look of triumph appearing on her face. She turned around and jogged back to the center of camp.

Packing up took the rest of the day. Breaking down the tables, field hospital, and cooking spots took the longest. The field hospital was taken down second to last with the main mess area the last to be packed up, after some troops made an extra-large hot meal and a few snacks for the order. Our attackers had come on horseback and mountain bike. We found their mounts hidden in a small canyon near the base along with most of our scouts' gear and some of our scouts' dead bodies. At some point during the very long preliminary performance review and supply tallying process I was coordinating, a sharp static buzz filled my helmet. Azull's voice was choppy but readable. "Grandmother said you will need a ride back."

"That's right," I radioed back. "You know a good landing site?"

Azull crackled back. "Near the main pass to Farfallen there is an old mining station whose lift still works. Use that to get the top of the cliffs. It's a long walk but that's the best we can do."

"Right. Any chance you can look for a few of my troops? A few are still MIA after a bandit attack. Three bodies and some knickknacks in total are missing," I replied.

"Ok. If we find them, I will see them returned to you," Azull told me. After a brief silence she added, "I will see to it that no one else will be entrusted with them." She knew my concern over theft by a nation or powerful noble before I could work out how to allude to it without the risk of giving anyone more reason to hate me and my order.

13

Call or Fold

We loaded up the horses. Our foes each had a mount of some kind, so we had enough for the entire order. It was getting dark but we had to head out before more things showed up. Given the rocky terrain it was risky, but our trek would be safer than staying around. Even though the Errant Order had completed this battle, the end of our war still seemed far off. Still, I was glad that some light was finally showing at the end of this dark spiral.

Many water breaks and careful steps later, at noon the outriders crested yet another rock-strewn ridge and reported seeing the man-made pass to Farfallen. A large airship roared up from behind us, heading toward the cliff above. A sheltered camp was cut from the rock once used to house those who had built the pass. A huge sun-blasted crane topped with a massive battered circular saw held pride of place over the camp. In the fading light of day, dark crystals shown dully behind the long-discarded mining gear. Adder was the first to speak up, radioing all of us, "Keep an eye out. Some crystal pillars are close."

Vern drew her blade and yelled, "More than some. Big one incoming!" Switching to the emergency frequency, she called, "Air crew, brace for impact!" Before she could explain further, a massive demon burst from the rock next to the crane and surged toward our ride out of this ever-maddening hellhole.

"Words don't encompass that," Adder grumbled. She took a few steps forward before turning to me. "I am going to kick that third wheel in the face."

"Ok," I told her. Normally I would have added a few lines about being careful and whatnot but the half-melted rocks being hurled our way would make any platitudes shallow at best. "Oh, fuck it. All units clean up that mine. Charge!" I bellowed. The order uncoiled like a well-oiled spring and flew as if it was one massive blade into the center of the swarm.

"Watch for burrowers," Trish reminded us. After glancing at the battle line, she added over the radio, "Aircrew, we are coming to assist."

"Then assist!" Azull yelled back over the command line. Shouts on both ends formed a unique kind of static all its own overlapping with our voices.

"Don't die, Sis," Adder radioed back.

"If you can't kill me, then no way these could. Now focus and hurry up! I can't save this blimp myself," Azull replied back in a scolding tone. The next thing I knew, my part of the line had hit the demon swarm and I had likely cut apart quite a few.

Once I was within the swarm the once-chaotic battlefield

became clear to me. We faced some tricky enemies and our backs were against the wall. A mass of knee-high foes still rose out of the ground from inky pools. A titan whose haphazardly fanged maw was a good one third of its body loomed nearby, and half-formed humanoid shapes and head-sized beetles covered in a miasma darker than space rushed to cut apart our formation. Vern rushed ahead of me. As she passed, she whispered, "You need to live through this."

Shaking my head, I muttered more for my own benefit than anyone else's. "Even if I am killed here, I will get back up. I'd bet my life on it. Too many debts still need to be repaid." Whipping out my plasma pistol, I set to work clearing chunks out of the horde. Vern cut down many foes with each swing of her blade. I saw more than one of my men pulled under by the raging inky swells before us. Feeling true sorrow in my heart, I pushed it aside with a murmur of "I'll cut down your share." I whispered that each time I spied one of my troops disappearing beneath the dark snapping sea. The titan was trying to scale the cliff right behind the crane. Trish, Vern, and I let loose at the same moment on the crane, managing to topple it onto the titan's back. It was then that the beast seemed to notice us.

"Boy, I am glad demon blood does not stain!" Adder cackled as she pirouetted by me, cutting gleefully as she went. Thanks to her taking point, foes before me had thinned out greatly. We had an almost clear shot toward what was left of the crane.

"Vern, with me! Adder, watch our backs!" I yelled. We rushed at the crane that was being absorbed into the giant.

Vern and I cut though the thinned mob in our way. At the base of the crane, I pointed at the giant's chest. "Vern, you're up!" Her helmet inclined and shoulders rotated briefly. The next thing I knew she was halfway ahead of me.

Adder held the base of our springboard. Vern managed to slice five times, opening a huge gash in the giant monster's chest. A massive hand backhanded Vern off our platform, throwing her into the airship far above us. The plan in the back of my mind came into focus. When I reexamined it, I was startled by its insanity. "Here goes nothing," I whispered to myself. "All of you stay back. This one's mine!" I radioed. I sprinted, raising my time-stilled sword to the sky. I willed a dark inky void into existence a few inches from my armor. With no better ideas, I leapt into the giant's chest and plunged deeper and deeper. All was dark. Time slowed, then a light glimmered through the haze all around me. Without any trouble I entered its core. The miasma I had surrounded myself with began to eat away at the monster's core. When the last speck of light died in the monster, a brief second of nothingness passed, only to be suddenly replaced by overwhelming light and motion. I spun in midair and fell.

When I looked up, glowing purple eyes like that of a cat or a wolf gazed down at me. Thick fog surrounded us. The eyes belonged to a young woman in a dark coat. I felt that I had seen her before. Another girl gripping in heavy gloves a sword built vaguely like mine walked up from my right. "Was this really ok?" sword-holding girl sighed angrily.

"Where's the other hunter?" I asked, finally remembering

the purple eyes closely resembled those of a stranger who had popped up a few times so far.

"He is fine. How do you feel?" the man in question replied evenly. A spear was held in his hands right over my head.

"Like crap. What happened?" I asked, feeling so numb I could not move.

"We pulled you out," the man said cryptically. Then he turned to the two women. "So, what now?"

"Leave him. His fan girls will be here soon," the swordswoman huffed. Then I blacked out. When I woke up, Greta was standing where the purple-eyed girl had been and the mist was gone, replaced by many corpses and half-melted divots.

"How do you feel?" Greta asked. I could tell she was pissed with me. I felt that was justified after the stunt I had pulled.

Adder ran over. "Hey, look at this!" she hollered. She held Puppet's arm in a firm vice grip as she dragged him over, then playfully ripped off his helmet and laughed in amusement. "See. See? Crazy, right?" she asked. Puppet's eye color changed to a glowing yellow.

I stopped Greta before she could rush off to examine his new condition. "Hey, how many did we lose?"

"Right now, seventy or so dead. By tomorrow, maybe a hundred. Not many more than that," Greta told me before dragging Puppet away and calling over to her medics to check everyone's eyes.

"On the plus side, the princess is alive and nauseous," Adder smiled down at me. Then her face stiffened. "But you know that huge one still only counts as one, right?"

I laughed, then coughed hard after I puffed some dust away. After a deep clear breath I inquired, "You were keeping score?"

"Always," Adder nodded, then she skipped off.

I peered around the field. It was even more barren than before. Troopers were hunkered over all around. "At least one of you is still energetic," Azull said from nearby. She sat on a rusted trunk.

As much as I agreed with the princess, I chose to keep my snide remarks to myself. "How long will your report be?" I asked, changing the subject.

"What?" Azull queried.

"You have been reporting to the kingdom, right? The cleanup of that airship will be a huge pain. Even so, remember to keep to a regular sleep shedyul," I told her.

Azull got a little flustered before forcing her poker face back on. "You are a pain, you know that? Have you been spying on me?"

"Nope, but thanks for confirming things?" I snickered hoarsely.

Azull glared at me, then sighed. She whispered, "I do not know what I ever saw in you." After an awkward pause I pretended to not notice, she asked, "So why did you lose so many?"

"Our ranged attacks were too weak for the big one and we had no time to plan, but mostly the guns," I replied calmly.

"So, it's the kingdom's fault?" Azull probed, leering forward.

"No, the demons are evolving. They are stronger and

smarter than the older records show. Your thoughts?" I shot back.

Azull thought hard for a while before replying. "You could be right. I'll ask around. Now answer my question."

I sat up with great effort. Azull even helped steady me. Looking the princess in the eyes, I told her, "The demon's tactics are far more advanced now. We did not adapt fast enough."

Vern called over. "The royal we? Or us lazy schmucks?"

"Both," I said. Vern walked over to us and before she could say anything else I asked her, "So you took less damage than me?"

Azull shook her head. "Says the man who jumped into a demon's stomach." All the while she gazed up in annoyance at Vern.

Vern looked away. "The most efficient way to land safely may have involved ripping apart the airship."

Azull held her head in her hands. Even if her poker face was still holding strong, she was now as down to earth as a star in the sky. "You completely trashed three whole decks of the most costly ship in the kingdom just to slow down," the princess whispered.

"But I did save what was left of the crew," Vern smiled. I glanced sideways, desperately trying to signal Vern to shut up. She glanced my way and stopped talking.

"And I will return that favor by trying to not hold you accountable for ripping apart my command ship," Azull grumbled. Then she looked up at me. "So, what now?"

"Leave the wounded with you and try to track the monsters to their home base?" I said.

Adder ran over, saying "Take me with you, but leave Mom with the princess." Azull was caught off guard by her former blood-relative's words. However, in a speed befitting a royal, her poker face returned in short order.

Opening my first aid kit I took a large dose of pain killers and crammed them into my mouth. After pinching myself hard I stood up and told the three leaders by my side, "I'll take the shock troopers who can still fight. Verndralla, Adder, get half of your fighting units prepared. Princess, kindly relay to Trish and Greta that some trackers and whatever medics we can spare will be needed as well."

"To do what with, exactly?" Azull demanded.

"To hunt," Vern said coldly as if she was talking to an inattentive child.

"You can find them?" Azull asked. It was good question. So far, the main hive, assuming such a convenient thing even existed, had never been known to have been found.

"They have a command structure now, of that, I am sure. Therefore, we use that to track them," I said.

"They have us tied up. So, all we must do is pull on that rope until it unravels for us so we can sock them where it hurts," Adder paraphrased.

Azull shook her head tiredly. "I don't know who is smart and who is the weirdo anymore. Fine, I will handle the details." Then she shook my hand. "After all, it is a good plan. Don't die, ok?"

"With all the life forms he needs to live for, that would be best," Verndralla agreed meaningfully with no context.

It took the rest of the day to set up our new base camp, scrape together working war gear, and prepare what was left of the dead. Luckily most of the beer had lived through the airship crash so the dead were stuffed into barrels of the stuff to be shipped home. Keeping tabs on what part was who and identifying the dead was bad enough, but making sure our pursuit force was fully equipped without ripping the camp and dead airship bare was much more of a tightrope walk. In the end it was decided that we could freely hunt in any lands we passed so long as they were under Farfallen's control.

The night was filled with paperwork and reporting back to Clare. I got three hours of rest before first light. The pursuit force slipped out of camp with minimal fanfare. Only Greta, Azull, a few cooks, and the guards on duty saw us off. We left a good number of healthy troops behind. Greta made any with glowing yellow eyes stay back as well. She had found a few more of them but the cause was still unclear.

We had to leave the horses behind to transport the wounded. The motorcycles would run out of gas at some point and were not suited to stealth. So, my splitter force walked back into the kingdom of Farfallen. We tried to keep off the roads and spread out in a long line across the thickening forest. A new radio frequency had been co-opted for the pursuit force's use. Greta, Azull, Trish, and Clare had been given access to it as well. After half a day of walking we had yet to run into any demons. "Any new sightings?" I radioed over the new setting.

I got a whole lot of negatives until Clare's voice groggily answered back minutes after the last response. "Yes. On the road to your new home a small swarm was spotted. The swarm fled in roughly the direction of Verndralla's clearing."

"My what?" Vern asked.

"The spot where you blasted out a chunk of the kingdom's woods," Azull told her.

Rapidly fiddling with the map and adding some destination markings which I forwarded to the splinter force, I answered, "On our way." It was regrettable that not all the suits supported the systems necessary to show an interactive navigational map, so I had to settle for a stock image with each team member's arrival location marked down.

"So, if a town was built in Verndralla's clearing, what would the name be?" Adder asked. Her question should not be too distracting and could keep the team from being overly tense, so I did not reprimand her.

"Muck Wood," Able Folly said.

"Render Dell," Sir Brandon Wulfard provided.

"Dull Golder," I chimed in.

"Render Dell it is. I'll update the maps," Clare announced.

As dusk fell, I ordered all units to halt, group up in teams of four or five, eat, rest, and stay alert. At first light it was decided we would move again. If we were fast our trip would take just over two days. If we were lucky, we would run into an enemy unit before then. Even if we did not see our target enemy, a swarm of any size would leave an obvious trail in the woodland that we could track. Noon the next day we got lucky, sort of. One trooper's life signs flatlined suddenly, then another, and by then all units were running over. One man was faster than the rest of us. He was the third death, but he managed to send an image of the attacker. It was one of the humanoid exoskeleton-clad officers surrounded by a small horde of miasma-covered beetles.

"Lieutenants with me, we have the leader. The rest of you, take down the bugs," I radioed mid-sprint.

We were almost to the dead when a tree I was passing exploded from inside, spraying a hail of large splinters all over the place. Reflexively I conjured a sheet of antimatter that lapped up the tsunami of wood chips. I activated my suit's shield and waited for the pulped wood to settle. Before the surroundings fully cleared, a dull bubbling voice echoed around me in tune with hissing footsteps. "Father was right about you, Mr. Evans. You really are full of surprises."

The dark bulky exoskeleton of one of the demon's commanders loomed out of the fine mist of wood dust. Any particle that touched its frame disintegrated. Its body was very clean. It had a tail and a human shape like the other two I had seen but its upper body was far bulkier. It had more horns and its face was much more reptilian than human. Its exoskeleton was heavier and had no visible joints. Raising my sword and lowering my stance, I asked, "So what are you called?" not expecting an answer.

"The Big One," the enemy leader said.

I would have face-palmed if not for the whole dangerous enemy right in front of me. "Jim's naming sense was always terrible. No offence." I sighed.

The thing rolled its shoulders. A grating tone extended

from its head. I tensed up for a counterattack but was stopped when the monster held up a hand and spoke. "Before I kill you, I was told to pass on a message from Father, or Jim as you call him. He will meet you at an old city by the sea in the depths of an underpass across from where you secured your profession."

The next thing I knew, The Big One moved in a blur. I barely managed to roll under its claw-swipe. I kept rolling until I was where the monster had been. Leaping up, I stomped on the end of one of my dead trooper's swords. The Big One was already next to me by the time the blade rocketed off the ground and sliced into the monster's chest. The sword gave me a way around its carapace. It left a three-or-so-inch gash before the entire blade was eaten away by the antimatter swirling within my foe's exoskeleton. Before the thing could taunt or regenerate, I punched it in the face and shot it point blank in its wound with my plasma pistol over and over again until the charge wore out. The thing's claws went to choke me but Adder tried to lop off one of them with her sword. Adder's sword began hissing so she chose to save her sword and punch the thing in the head from behind. We would have punched it some more in the face but the pain from the first hit made us pause. Adder managed to stomp down hard on The Big One's tail and I grappled the monster. Only then did Vern show up with her blade, and after two slashes, decapitated the monster.

I pulled out my laser pistol from the warp pouch and focused on taking pot shots at the surrounding small fries. Adder took the other two dead troops' weapons and went to aid the rest of the order. Vern went to the other side of the disintegrating encirclement and began mowing down the left-over demons. It took two minutes for the fighting to stop and five minutes until we deemed the enemy dealt with. I managed to contact Azull and told her about the ambush in detail. Her only response was, "There are a lot of small swarms popping up all over. You go and handle the boss."

Before I could ask for an up-to-date map, Clare secretly sent me an image file showing where to go. "Got it. Take care of my wife and the order for me," I told Azull.

"I'll do what I can. Stay safe, Sir Evans," Azull replied before cutting the link.

The given place for my meeting with Jim James was in a city abandoned since before the demons came. It was where Clare's family had lived when the refugee ships landed on this world so long ago. The city had been one of the first areas the dark matter appeared from. I could still remember the frantic reports soon after the spines appeared, that we had to give up on any living being that was too close to those formations.

My whole life had been a roller coaster. I was trapped in the stasis field that changed my destiny. Earth died out, we left, we almost died out again. Then a few years after, we had to seal ourselves off from the rest of the refugee fleets and there-fore humanity due to a terrifying plague. Our new world was trashed. Losing almost everyone close and the whole world was a burden nearly all of us suffered. Waking up after so many thousands of years makes that feeling of loss sting more, not less. After all, to but one of those around me, this was all lost, ancient history.

I knew where the old coastal city was. It was a few days on horseback from Verdant Valley Eight, my new home. My goal was the highway tunnel across from the army recruiting station I had gone to a lifetime and a half ago. "I'll lead the way. First stop is the home of the Errant Order. This is the final push for the demons and Farfallen," I radioed my force.

We walked for almost two days, running across many small hordes of demons. Beetles, hazy humanoid forms that could solidify themselves to an extent, and lizard- and gorilla-like things no bigger than a horse made up the bulk of these encounters. When the gates of my land's border checkpoint came into view, Vern was walking next to me. She connected to an old relay tower nearby. Only Verndralla, Adder, Clare, Greta, and myself had been added into the closed transmission. "Hey leader, if you had a kid, what would you name it?"

It was an odd question but not unexpected. "Don."

"What if you had a daughter?" Adder asked.

"Dawn. Same sound, different spelling," I told her.

"And twins?" Verndralla asked.

"Lue or Luann?" I told them. "Why?" I felt compelled to ask.

"So you can focus," Clare answered.

"She means so she can focus," Adder sighed.

Then we were at the gates. On our trip many had become tired and many more sported wounds. We were also running low on the immunization boost to keep the troops from being dematerialized. In the end I had to leave the bulk of the force in my territory. Adder, Vern, five elites, and ten of the more fit troopers were all I chose to bring on what could turn out to be a suicide run or a fool's errand. Either way, I owed this world and the ones I had gotten close to, as well as all of those I had outlived, to try to put right the past. I know that sounds grandiose but my only feelings were remorse, rage, and hope. Justice or love had very little play here. The eighteen including myself rode off with all the gear we could borrow from our fellows and take from the village storehouses. We were muddy, dirty, and tired. Not one of us felt like heroes. We were just desperate folks trying to set things right. Our goal kept us going, nothing else.

We ran into a few more small swarms on the way. Over the next few days, I observed fewer mobs of demons. One night we found ourselves camping in a small clearing. Brambles and a few large rocks formed a ring around us. If needed, the team and I could decimate the land around us. I had just relayed a written report about the enemy presence lessening as we neared their base when one of the sentries cried out, "Mimic!"

A voice called out even louder before the guard's words had finished. "I surrender."

"Search the perimeter!" I ordered. The troopers woke up and crept around our camp while I went to see what was going on. Adder walked with me.

The mimic looked like an older version of my old friend turned nemesis, Jim. "Who are you?" I asked.

The Jim James look-alike tilted its head at an odd angle. "You've never seen the mimics' default appearance?" Adder asked.

I ignored Adder's jab. "Ok, so why surrender?" I tried.

"The god of demons wishes to inform you that your

kingdom will be overrun soon, so hurry up and fight him," the mimic told me robotically before its arm became a sword which stabbed through its own core. A brief flicker of light later, all that was left of our intruder was a small divot in the ground.

"Your friend must hate you," Adder sighed.

"I can't tell if he is giving you a fighting chance or mocking you," Clark Seewood said from atop a nearby rock.

No signs of more foes appeared that night but we still shifted camp half a mile onto a rock-covered outcrop. A little before first light we packed up camp, silently resuming our trek. The last of the horses collapsed around noon. A few had died from demons. Most had been overcome with exhaustion and thus were used to supplement our rations. That night we came to a ridge overlooking the ocean. A shattered city lay below us. Rust and salt-covered steel were all that greeted us. A few mobs of demon bugs crisscrossed the open land leading to my last goal. "I have lived to fight ever since Earth was lost. After this, I hope I can take a break from breaking heads."

Adder looked quizzically at me. Even with her helmet on I could tell that much from the slight tilt of her head. "But you fight for life," she said, then after a pause, "Oh, I get it."

I ignored her and addressed the team. Luckily, we had not lost anyone yet but they could not last for many more battles given how grueling our pace had been. "All right, when we get to the tunnel, Vern and I will go in. Adder, you take command and defend the tunnel. If I am not back after twenty minutes, flee."

Adder's mood soured. "Is that an order, sir?"

"Yes. You have more experience leading. Vern is more resistant to the demons." I put my hand on Adder's shoulder. "You can do this. I need you to do this."

Adder brushed off my hand. "Fine. I trust you, Pops."

I turned to Vern. "You will stay back when we find the big boss. If I am not done in twenty-five minutes, you will flee as well."

Vern took a deep breath. "Ok."

"Now let's try to avoid the demon's patrols as much as we can. Everyone follow me," I commanded.

14

Jacks of Clubs and Hearts

We moved in sync. Rocks and shrubbery became our hidey holes. It took time to notice the demons had set patrol routes, which was not something these monsters had done before. That left me, Verndralla, and Adder as the folks with experience infiltrating a stronghold this size. For me and by extension Vern, that experience was mostly through holographic simulations where one could feel like they were dying. The quality of training I had was far better than what this world could offer now. No one fell behind me. Our trek was far faster than if we had tried to fight our way through. Honestly, given how tired everyone was, we could only last two or three small-scale battles at most, which was amazing but still not enough for this hellhole. No communication towers were up within range. Even if they were, radios were out of the question. With Jim as my enemy, there was a good chance any call for support would be found out. Even if we did get a message through and some unit was available, it could take days for them to arrive. When a fight could be over in seconds, even an hour was too long.

It was nerve-racking but my team was well trained. Those that lived through this would have an invaluable experience. I hoped no one would lose their minds by the end of this. I had seen more colony ships lose themselves to PTSD when the Earth fell than I can recall. Biting into my lip, I kept myself in the here and now. My blood was bland and not metallic in the least. The taste only served to remind me how much I had changed.

We arrived at the city outskirts. Pillars of corroded iron were all around. We slithered under a pillar that was more salt than iron and snuck into a hole that had once been the basement of a small restaurant. Ankle-deep fetid seawater clung to our boots. I took a chance and projected the most up-to-date map we had, one that was hundreds of years old. Much had collapsed since then, making the map almost useless. Now that we were here, distance was the only thing we could calculate with a reasonable margin of error. I pointed to our destination on the map. "This is where we need to go," I told the team. Then I pointed out to the city. "If we go three miles that way, we should get there."

Vern shook her head and pointed a little off from where I had. "Two miles that way, if we account for how the shoreline has changed from your memories."

I thought for a few seconds. "True, a lot has been washed out. I would not be surprised if this place was hit by a tsunami and a few earthquakes. We will go in that direction first. If we find nothing, then we keep going with my prediction."

Adder looked around the room. "It's unlikely we will be able to go in a straight line all the way. We will need to keep an eye out for likely roundabouts." Then she popped a small camera out of our hole and looked around.

It took me a few seconds. "She meant detours, right?" I asked Vern.

"No, roundabouts. Detours is what was said in your time. They mean the same thing," Verndralla told me.

We crept out of our hole and scampered around, what little was left of the foundations all around us zigzagging to and fro. At times when the general area seemed even more devoid of life than normal, I had someone go a few buildings ahead and take a peek around.

We spent hours and a few close calls like this. Our minds were frayed more than our bodies. I was worried that one or two of the troops might snap like a rusty hinge and doom us all. Thankfully at one of the nerve-racking scouting trips I received an image sent over via laser transmission. It showed a seemingly bombed-out and half-decayed and heavily pitted building built like a squat, shifty-looking shop. One roadway away was an underpass that looked like a gaping lamprey's maw with dark crystal teeth. Knee-deep dark water leaked from it like so much spittle. I forwarded the image over to Verndralla with a side note saying *Look familiar?* because she had many of my old memories that were, for better or worse, clearer than mine due to how recently she had been given them and how wonky my old memory unit had become. All I got in response to my question was a grinning emoji sporting a thumbs-up. I had to wonder who had programmed emoticons into her suit's systems.

I gathered the team around me in a ruined water truck's container. "One street over is our objective. Adder, you and the grunts are up. Thanks for all your help." Adder seemed to puff up a bit. "I mean all of you, thanks. I mean it. If this goes like we think, the demons will all die here. Let's go." The team got their swagger back. With my task done, Vern and I took point.

We leapt out of the more or less half-melted container and rushed out. Our scouts had determined the area was clear for now. Somehow, the closer we got to this point the fewer demons we found. We bounded past the old recruitment spot where my life had begun again after years of fleeing Earth. My fifth home was in a very sorry state. Before I could even finish that thought, I was past the lips of the underpass-turned-cave. *Look out for the teeth*, I texted Adder.

We got your back, Dad, Adder texted back.

Vern ran by my side into the abyss. "This may be a bad time, but you know Greta may have a bun in the oven?"

I choked. "What, whose?"

"Yours, stupid," Vern told me in a very annoyed tone.

"I am an idiot," I sighed.

"Only with women and their feelings," Vern snickered. Then she stopped running and told me, "After this is over, I'll get your wife to set you straight."

I kept running while grimacing. "Sure, no pressure. So cliché," I had to mutter to myself.

I darted around a few heaps of rubble until I came to a

huge dark blob. "Took you long enough," the blob croaked in a watery voice that reminded me of one of my oldest friends.

"Jim, I hardly recognized you. Try to look more demon god-ish," I mocked without hate and only a little resentment.

"Tell me about it. A dragon or serpent eating its tail would fit me way better, but NO, I had to be the one true blob of evil. My luck is bullshit even five thousand years in." Jim the blob rippled. The sloshing conveyed words. Maybe it was due to the demon building blocks in my blood, but Jim's feelings were transmitted clearly.

I took off my helmet and tossed it aside. "So why help me get here?" I queried.

"Because even if the me now hates you, the me before being this would give you a chance to kill this thing I have become." The blob seemed to deflate slightly in more ways than one.

"Is that what you want?" I asked, not that it mattered a lot, but my conscience and curiosity demanded I ask regardless.

"It was. I even tried a few times. Whole lot of nothing that did. It took a while, but I can accept what that botched experiment did to me," Jim told me.

"I saw a few records. What were you trying to achieve exactly?" I asked.

"Wipe out the monsters or gain control over them. We failed the self-destruct plan and had not counted on such a complex hive mind. By the way, I am the demon's central pro-cessor. Without me, all units will be lost. The nanobots that control them may just commit mass suicide without me," Jim answered back.

"Well, here I come," I told him. Then I plunged one finger into the goop that was once my friend. Part of my armor dissolved.

Well, this sucks. Pan, catalogue all my memories and transfer them with part of yourself to my helmet's systems. If this kills me, let your next master see them. Chuck swiftly commanded me. That order broke off some of his sense of self as well. A bundle of confusion and worry was left to stew in the memories of Chuck Evans as we watched his body plunge into the blob.

Our master must have used himself as an antibody to purge Jim from the world. Master Evan's body had evolved to have some similarities to the demon's but he was still mostly human. His differences allowed him to wipe the demons off the face of our adopted world but that was not enough to save him. A puddle of smoking goo and the time-stilled sword were all that were left of Jim James and our master. *If you have a descendent, we will serve them first,* the sliver that was both the AI named Pan and part of its master vowed.

It took many years spent in the vault of our master's manor in Verdant Valley Eight to fully catalog and narrate the story of his fight. In time, we hoped his daughter Dawn Errant would get a hold of this record of her father. However, that is a story not yet written...

Evan A. Cushing lives in Salem, Massachusetts.